THE MARAUDER BETRAYALS

NOVEL

CHRIS O'GRADY

ISBN   Softcover   978-1-950580-16-3

Printed in the United States of America.

To order additional copies of this book, contact:
Bookwhip
1-855-339-3589
https://www.bookwhip.com

CHAPTER ONE

Roper came alert when the two men parked their car across the road, just short of the Chesapeake Motel.

The second he spotted them, he sensed they were his clients.

For a few minutes, they just sat there.

Roper watched them through the windshield of his rented car, from where he was parked in a strip mall shopping center, across from the motel.

Presently, the two men got out of their car and climbed the ramp into the parking area inside the horseshoe-shaped motel. They went past the manager's office without even glancing in and, sure enough, went across to Room Seven, where Roper had put the actor.

Roper signalled Jeff Lasalle's beeper. The rich actor-voice sounded in Roper's ear-piece.

"I see them."

"Be careful, Jeff," cautioned Roper.

Lasalle chuckled.

"I'll be careful. Roper, we've rehearsed all this. I'm getting good at it."

"Ahuh. But try not to sound so actory, okay?"

"Shuah," Jeff replied. "I'm fvom Bvooklyn."

Roper grinned.

"Don't overdo it, either."

Putting the cell phone down, Roper adjusted his camera's telephoto lens, murmuring, "Just turn your heads a little, guys."

Almost as if they'd heard him, first one, then the other man turned and looked back at the manager's office. Roper clicked away and got good full-face and partials of both of them. When he took the eyepiece away from his eye, he saw the manager standing outside his office, watching the two of them.

As the door of Room Seven opened, both faced the other way. The completely disguised actor admitted them.

The manager was facing the other way, but Roper took a picture of his back anyway, for luck.

Placing the camera on the car seat beside him, Roper stared through the windshield, but he wasn't seeing anything. He was listening to the two bugs planted inside the room, one worn by Lasalle, the other stuck underneath the desk chair.

He ought to be able to follow what was said in there well enough.

Idly, he memorized the license plate of their car across the street.

"My name's Reynolds," one of them was saying. "This is Mr. Adams. I take you're Dispatcher."

"Right. Sit down, gentlemen."

Roper grimaced. Jeff sounded too friendly.

"We won't be here that long," Reynolds said.

"Shall we get to the business at hand?" another voice asked, Adams.

"Certainly. You want something done, and you've already wired the first twenty five thousand offshore.

"That's a lot of up-front money," Reynolds complained.

"You want quality work, it costs."

Roper smiled. The actor had delivered that line just right. He was really was getting good at this, although Roper hadn't used him too often. Never overdo anything, or anyone.

"All right. Here."

"What's this?"

"New I. D. for you. Application forms for passport, driver's license, the second twenty five G, and other things you'll need."

Silence for a few beats. Then Reynolds went on: "Get passport and license photos taken of yourself and mail them in that envelope. We'll have them laminated and return them to you at this motel by mail. When you get them, call us at that number. We'll be ready by then with further instructions."

"Okay. And the remaining hundred thousand?"

"When the job's done."

"And the job…what kind of work is involved?"

There was a long pause, during which Roper shook his head, thinking, *The damn fool pushed it just a bit too far.*

"The kind of work your ad in HOUSE AND GUN magazine said you were good at," Adams said coldly.

"Fair enough," Jeff said, recovering nicely. "All right, gentlemen. Get pictures taken, send them to the address on that envelope, then call you for the next step."

"You got it."

Roper had the camera up and ready when the door of the actor's room opened. When the two men emerged, there was a ringing sound in Roper's earpiece.

"Phone," came Lasalle's voice. "You men expecting a call?"

"Take it and we'll find out."

"Hello? – Yes, this is Room Seven. – Oh, no, everything's fine. Just a business meeting. – Thanks, anyway, sir."

"Who was that?" Reynolds asked.

"The motel manager. He wanted to know if everything was all right. He saw the two of you come in…"

One of them grunted. They turned in the doorway and Roper got the camera going again, taking single shots of each of them as they came back across the parking area inside the horseshoe. When they passed the manager's office, one of them glanced toward it.

Roper blinked. He could have sworn the man nodded imperceptibly toward the manager's office.

When they came sloping down the entrance driveway to the street, the manager stepped into sight and stood outside his office, watching them go.

Roper took a couple of rapid-fire shots of the manager, too, a tall job with wide shoulders. Then the man went back inside his office, and Roper picked up his cell phone, watching as Reynolds and Adams got into their car and pulled away from the curb.

Tapping a number in, he read their plate again as they drove off. When the voice came on at the other end, he said, "Marge? Your men in place?"

"All set to go."

Roper told her their license plate numbers and letters.

"Got it," Marge said. "Hold on a second, Mr. Dickson."

Roper waited while she went away. Then she was back.

"One of my team just reported in. They're on target. I gave him the plate number you just gave me. He confirmed."

"Okay, Find out where they go. Keep your people as close as you can without tipping them they're being tailed."

"Will do."

Marge hung up and Roper switched off the cell phone, and then just sat and waited.

CHAPTER TWO

Tansy Burns yelped: "Walter, I'll never make it."

Walter Noble checked the wall clock. "You've got almost twenty minutes. Your crew's already there, Tans…"

Groaning, she raced out of Noble's office and down the corridor toward the elevators, snarling as she went: "It'll take me twenty minutes just to reach the Rayburn building…"

Catching a cab, she used her cell phone to call ahead.

"Billy? Tansy here. What floor is Melford holding his briefing on? – Third? I'll never get there in time."

"You'll do fine," the cameraman assured her. "These Congressional types are always late for things like this."

"Not Mister Uptight Melford." She switched off the phone, tossed it into her packed tote bag and prayed for no traffic at all.

Her prayer was answered. Hurrying across the vast sidewalk toward the entrance to the Sam Rayburn Building, she checked the time. Only eighteen minutes. Why was that boss of hers always right? And why weren't these sidewalks like New York ones, nice and narrow? Six strides and you're inside your building, in New York. Down here…

Forcing herself to slow down, Tansy eased toward the third floor room where they held press conferences, 'they' in this case being average run-of-the-mill Representatives about to make announcements not too many people were all that interested in. Except for herself and her sound-and-mike crew and other newsies like them: they had to be interested. It was their job.

Slipping inside, she relaxed. She was in time. The Honorable Congressman from Whateverstate was just stepping behind the podium and putting down his handful of speech-papers.

Slithering like an upright, snake, Tansy got through the half-filled audience and joined Billy and the mike-meister, Jerry, just as Melford began speaking.

CHAPTER THREE

Working the way he chose to work, always keeping himself at a distance from the operation so he could move in any direction in any given situation, Roper had limited means of generating access to new jobs in his line of work. One such means was ads placed in publications like HOUSE AND GUN, adroitly worded so they indicated to possible clients the sort of service he provided. Signing it with a name like DISPATCHER helped clinch things.

Getting the potential client to wire twenty five thousand dollars to one of his off-shore numbered accounts, that was the tough part. Luckily, it was the part that came right at the beginning. If Roper managed to do a good enough job convincing a client to come up with that much money as a down payment, then he was willing to follow through and explore the rest of the project. It helped that he assured the clients that they would get their initial payment back, less incidental expenses, if Roper decided anywhere along the line not to take on the assignment. Returning the money insured that none of them would be coming after him to get it back. It also left the door open for possible future jobs they might need him for, provided he could accept the work on his own terms.

Those terms included the stipulation that complete control remained in his own hands. He wouldn't even accept a job unless that one thing was understood, right at the start.

Apparently this time he had convinced whoever it was he first spoke to, after receiving their carefully worded response to his ad. When he told the voice to stay at the same phone, the voice had agreed, allowing Roper to hang up after forty seconds, get to another payphone, and call back...for another forty seconds.

Three or four of those, and the voice at the other end had said grimly: "You sure are careful, Dispatcher. I've never carried on a phone conversation in forty second bursts before."

"I stay in business by being careful," Roper had replied. "This forty seconds is up. Get back to you again in a minute or two."

But that had done the trick. The weary voice at the other end of the last payphone said, "All right, Dispatcher, you sound as if you know what you're doing. I'll take a chance and wire the first payment."

When Roper assured him that all but basic expenses which might be laid out would be refunded if he didn't take the job, that was what finally sold the voice. The money reached the off-shore account, was immediately dispersed to five other accounts, and was withdrawn from those by close of business the next day. Roper had it in hand stateside and into a safe deposit box by noon of the third day, his own private escrow account. If he had to return any or all of it, the money was there, available to be returned. If he took the job, the money then became available for his on-going costs, which were sometimes considerable, the way Roper worked.

Now he sat in the rented car waiting for Marge to call back and let him know where Reynolds and Adams had gone, after they left the actor in the Chesapeake Motel across the street.

A cab pulled into the horseshoe area and stopped in front of Room Seven. Jeff Lasalle emerged carrying the attache case he had brought there a few hours earlier.

Carefully locking the door of his room, he had the driver stop at the office so he could turn the room key over to the manager until he returned. That allowed them to clean in there. Then the taxi dipped down the exit driveway, turned toward the city and was gone.

Roper watched it go and just stayed where he was. He knew the actor would return to New York, where he would mail to Roper's pre-arranged Post Office Box both microphones he had used in the room for the visit, wire fifteen of the twenty five thousand he had just been handed, and get on with his life doing go-sees for parts in TV or theater or movies or commercials, anything he could get.

Thinking about the actor, Roper shook his head. The man was a magician with makeup. That was his true calling, but he kept following the other dream, the nearly impossible one: he wanted to act.

Smiling, Roper settled himself more comfortably behind the wheel until the cell phone rang on the passenger seat beside him.

"Yes, Marge. You got them? – Good." He scribbled in a notebook on the seat beside him. "Fourth floor. Watkins Construction." He read the complete address back to her, and when she confirmed, he said, "Thanks, Marge. Bill me the usual way, okay?"

"Right, Mr. Dickson. You be good, now, yuh heah?"

"I'll surely try, darlin'."

They hung up chuckling and Roper drove on out of there.

He could have had Marge handle the bugging and phone tapping in the Watkins fourth floor offices, but he liked to keep different segments of the work spread around, not ever having too much of it done by any one person or outfit. In fact, he might even do the bugging himself on this project. There was no big hurry. Everyone had to wait until the lamination work was done with Lasalle's pictures, for the driver's license and passport, all of which Lasalle had presumable mailed in already.

Shaking his head as he drove downtown, Roper laughed.

What a crew Reynolds and Adams were. All the wasted time! When the fake license and passport were mailed back to the temporarily absent tenant of Room Seven in the Chesapeake Motel, maybe his two clients would be ready to get started on whatever the assignment turned out to be. It would depend, then, on whether Roper did the bugging work and the job itself on his own, or hired someone else to do all that.

Always leave your options open.

CHAPTER FOUR

Congressman Melford didn't start as Tansy expected, with his usual assertion that it was time to rein in Pentagon spending. Instead, he launched into a seemingly interminable explanation of why his sub-committee would recommend increasing the budget of the Immigration and Naturalization service.

"We must reduce the numbers of illegal immigrants crossing our borders," he cried out, after all the boring statistics had almost put everyone to sleep. "There are two ways to accomplish this: One, try to get illegal-alien-friendly states like New York to quit getting under-paid farm laborers for the lobbyists for upstate farmers'. None of those laborers are protected by law, incidentally. And two, we must beef up the numbers of guards interdicting border crossings, both Canadian and Mexican crossings, of course."

Then, before anyone could get in a question, he began on the Pentagon. Everyone settled down and listened closely here. Unlike his opening topic, this was important. The half-filled conference knew too well that the Military-Industrial Complex was still alive and trim and doing splendidly, considering that there really wasn't all that much of a foreign enemy on the planet the nation had to "defend" itself against anymore, except for the terrorist threat, naturally.

This was the kind of story ordinary taxpayers could understand. That other immigration business only bothered working people, whose jobs were always being taken by all those "give me your tired, your boors, your huddled ass-holes yearning to breed free." American taxpayers seldom trouble themselves about working people being ground down by farmer lobbies that control state legislatures.

When question-time came around, Network people got the Congressman's nod first, as usual. Tansy waited, her nerves stretched to the snapping point.

When Melford began gathering up his papers on the lectern, she quivered, almost breaking in on the last words of his reply to the current questioner. When he stopped, however, she instantly called out her own question. She was just in time. He had begun to turn away. Facing forward again, he gave her his answer, while Billy kept the camera on him and Jerry made certain he picked up Melford's reply with his extended pole mike.

Then it was over. The dark-haired Representative was gone, and everyone was packing up and drifting on out.

Billy grinned at Tansy admiringly.

"Just got it in there," he muttered, inching along beside her.

"It's an ulcer-maker," she admitted ruefully. "Jerry, did you get his response?"

Jerry nodded. "No problem."

Tansy sighed with relief. "Another day's pay safely tucked away."

"Now let's see if they run it on tonight's newscast," Bill pointed out.

"Why wouldn't they?" Tansy laughed. "Unless there's an assassination or something big enough to bump it."

"Don't even whisper a thing like that," Bill cautioned.

CHAPTER FIVE

Three men were in the car that discreetly and expertly followed Jeff Lasalle's cab downtown. They saw him get out near a photo place specializing in passport photos, go inside, come out fifteen minutes later, and drop a white letter-sized envelope into the first mailbox he passed on his way to the nearby railroad station. He hurried the last block, but once inside the station, he glanced at the clock and the timetable above the information desk, and then he relaxed.

Two of the men in the car followed Jeff inside the depot. The third parked nearby and stayed behind the wheel. He tried to make a cell phone call, but got no answer and gave up.

One of the inside men returned and spoke to the driver, who tapped in the same number he had tried to reach earlier. This time he got a response.

"Subject is catching a train to New York," he told Reynolds.

The other one told him: "It leaves in ten minutes."

The driver repeated the information, and waited while Reynolds decided what to do. When he told the driver, the man listened, said, "Okay," and hung up.

"He wants both of you to go along up to New York with that guy. A car will be waiting up there to meet you. I'm to go back to the office."

"Right," the other one said, straightening and turning away. Over his shoulder, he said, "Call back and tell Reynolds about the photo shop he went into, and the letter he mailed when he came back out."

"Yes, you're right," the driver said. "I forgot."

While the other man went back inside the station, the driver tapped in the same number again, and passed along the added information.

Inside the Watkins Construction Company office, Reynolds said, "Thanks," and hung up. To Adams at the desk across the room, he said, "The big Dispatcher apparently followed instructions. So far, at least. Stopped at a photo shop and mailed an envelope on his way to the train station."

Adams nodded, but didn't reply.

Reynolds studied the expression on his face a moment before asking: "What?"

Adams glanced at him and shrugged.

"Probably nothing."

"Maybe it isn't nothing," Reynolds said. "Spit it out. What's bugging you?"

"It's just that he doesn't seem the type."

"Dispatcher?"

"Yeah. There's something too soft about him."

Reynolds nodded and thought it over.

"Still, we've both known nice quiet types who could turn in a nano-second into real hard cases."

"True," Adams admitted. "But this one…" He shook his head in doubt. "You said it yourself, awhile ago."

"I did?" Reynolds grinned. "What did I say?"

"Not so much what but the way you said it," Adams explained. "When you called him 'the *big* Dispatcher'."

"I was kidding."

"I know, but you were saying what I've been thinking," Adams insisted. "You were mocking a guy like that coming on like a hitter."

Reynolds nodded.

"Understood. We'll see. I just want to make sure we find out where he goes to ground, and especially where he stashes that twenty five thousand we handed over to him. If he turns out to be some kind of dud, we might not be able to recover the twenty five G we wired offshore, but I'd like to at least be able to get this bundle of cash back."

"They'll keep tabs on him," Adams assured him.

"They'd better. The sound people call yet? With the results of the voice-comparison tests?"

"Tollman's motel phone call, and our earlier ones?" Adams pawed through his IN box and shook his head. "Not yet. They ought to have them done by evening."

CHAPTER SIX

Norma Melford stood beside the desk in her husband's outer office, watching him out in the corridor, smiling and chatting up some home-state folks visiting the Capital.

A smile touched her lips. She flicked a glance at his political adviser, Roger Brent. As always, Brent stood near Tim Melford, and a little behind him.

"Rather like a courtier at Versailles," she thought, "in the time of Louis Fourteenth."

Then her husband worked his usual magic with voters and got rid of them without letting them realize they were being gotten rid of. When she saw that accomplished, she turned and went past Helen Johnson's desk and on to the inner office. A moment later, the two men joined her.

"How'd it go?" she asked, studying her husband's face.

"Pretty well," he said, giving her a quick bear-hug before going behind his desk and slinging his briefcase onto the floor beside the leather-cushioned swivel chair.

But she could see that he was still all charged up, so the news conference must have gone better than he'd expected.

"That well, huh?" she murmured.

Near the other corner of the desk, Roger Brent glanced at her, his eyes smiling, but his face inscrutable, as always.

Her husband chuckled.

"Can't fool you, can I, dumpling?"

"Not often."

Grinning, he sat, reached for her with his right hand while his left began sifting through the paperwork Helen Johnson had carefully laid out for his easy access.

Norma gazed down at the top of her husband's head, while he kissed the palm of her hand, never stopping his quick run through the paperwork in front of him.

"We've got that reception tonight," she reminded him.

Melford nodded.

"Brent's got it under control."

She smiled across at the adviser.

"Brent's always got everything under control."

"The day I haven't," Brent smiled, "is the day you won't need me anymore."

"That'll be the day," Melford laughed. "I couldn't get through a week without both of you."

"You couldn't get through a day without us," Norma corrected him.

"Not even an hour," Brent added.

"Right, right," Tim Melford agreed good-naturedly. "Give yourselves a raise. Now, if I could only find a copy of that amendment to the Bill I'm going to present on the House floor…it was next to the oversight committee's report on Langley."

"They're both right here, under this other crap," Brent said, going around behind the desk and finding the needed document.

Turning toward the door, Norma said, "See you at six."

"Six it is, dumpling," Tim replied absently, his glance running down the amendment.

"That means a real six," she emphasized. "Not one of your 'Honey, I got tied up in committee…'"

"I'll see he gets there," Brent called after her.

Smiling mechanically at Miss Johnson, Norma nodded. She knew Brent would do just that. He always came through.

* * *

Just about then, in the Watkins office, Adams slid a report onto Reynolds' desk.

"Sound check," he said. "The voice comparison. The original Dispatcher you spoke to, and the one Tollman phoned, while we were in the hotel with him."

Reynolds examined the report and grimaced.

"They're two different voices."

Adams nodded.

After thinking about it a moment, Reynolds came to a decision.

"Okay, now that we know, we'll have to keep trying to make contact with the jobber. The original one I spoke to on the phone. Best chance is phones. If he doesn't know we're onto him, he may get careless and stay on the phone long enough for the call to be traced. Put a tap on the phone in that Chesapeake Motel room. Hook it up to the tracer unit. Maybe we can put one in wherever he lives in New York, too."

Noticing the skeptical look in Adams' eyes, Reynolds shrugged.

"It's all we've got. Right now, anyway."

CHAPTER SEVEN

"That's the early evening news," Tansy said to the camera. "Now stay tuned for Renn Parkhurst's first interview…"

She watched her own face on the monitor replaced by the handsome visage of her colleague on the second half-hour of their news-and-commentary show. As she had many times, Tansy thought: "God, how I wish I were that beautiful!"

Smiling at her thought, she left the studio. In her office, she prepared to leave, but called home first.

"It's me, honey."

"You're looking good on-camera, Tansy," her husband said. "You're getting a relaxed look."

"Not too relaxed, I hope," she laughed. "How'd the lobbying go today, Paul?"

Now he was the one who laughed.

"You don't want to know."

He was right. She didn't.

"I'm starting home. How are the kids behaving?"

"They seem okay, Sarah's tooth is about to pop."

"Be there in a little while. Don't hold supper for me, if it's nearly ready."

"Okay, we'll start without you."

"I'm headed for New York afterward, on the evening flight."

"That talk show appearance?"

"Yes. I'll stay overnight."

"Gonna give your friend up there another go?"

She laughed, huskily.

"Yes. Sooner or later, he's bound to come through for me. See you soon."

Hanging up, she scooped up her tote bag, flicked the light switch and was off for Arlington.

CHAPTER EIGHT

The first of Hal Walker's usual two beers stood beside his chair, on an end table. Whenever he could, he kept it down to one beer a night.

The second guest of the late night TV talk show was coming on, Tansy Burns, of the cable evening news show.

Webster Henderson greeted her with a smile, a handshake, and a big hug.

Tansy was a pretty little thing. She was one of Webster's favorite people in the world. He said so, while she was seating herself in the chair beside his desk.

Hal took a swig of his beer while the banter proceeded.

Early on, Tansy coughed softly, raising her hand to cover her mouth.

When Hal noticed the cough, he nodded. Was that one of the signals? Was Tansy-baby still one of his many-membered fan club? He wondered whatever had happened to that nice famous marriage of hers? Maybe nothing.

He shrugged. Maybe it wasn't a signal. Everyone coughed, once in awhile. He had learned long years ago not to let his imagination get itself into an uproar every time one of them coughed on these talk shows, or sent out one of the other time-worn signals.

The jollity continued. Henderson's studio audience laughed at the badinage between the two of them, as did Hal. Tansy was an experienced presence on camera. Her own cable show had sharpened her skills, so she held her own against Webster's quick wit.

Then it was time for a commercial break. While the camera was full on her, Tansy licked her lips. Hal raised his glance to her eyes, and, sure enough, she was peering straight into the camera, with a direct serious expression on her face. The shot faded on her, and a commercial came on.

"Okay, sweetie-babe," Hal muttered, getting up. "Two signals, or maybe-signals. Welcome back to the wunnerful fun-and-guessing-games club."

Circling the chair he had been sitting on, he went out to the hall closet. The door was always kept wide open, back against the wall. A calendar was tacked to the outward-facing inner side of the closet door, one of those calendars with a square for each day of the month, each square an inch-and-a-half across by an inch-and-a-quarter down.

"Let's see," he murmured, taking out a nylon-tipped pen.

The upper left corner of each square was for TV "signals", while the upper right corner was for items that showed up in newspaper gossip columns. Across the bottom was where he entered the initials of whatever gal he may have run into that day in her inevitable disguise.

In the upper left corner of today's square, Hal printed TB, and then a question-mark. Since he could never really be sure it was one of "his" signals, in order to keep some slender grip on his own sanity, he always added a question-mark. It was like keeping meticulous records, almost as if he still lived in a sensible prosaic world, just like most people did.

He returned to his seat. The commercial break was ending. They came back onscreen, and Tansy's segment resumed.

Carefully, Hal watched Tansy's lips, in case there was any more lip-smacking, or another cough. Clinchers.

There weren't. The interview ended, Webster Henderson rose, clapping his hands, then held his right hand out to present his guest: "Tansy Burns, ladies and gentlemen," he called out, above the sound of the applause.

As the two of them faded onscreen into another commercial, Hal grinned, nodding at the smiling face of the demure-looking young woman.

"All right, Tansy," he grinned wryly. "Now all I have to do is recognize you behind whatever disguise you'll undoubtedly be wearing when you show up...*if* you show up...and then the only thing I'll have to do after that is try to learn how to pick you up, nice and skillful, just like it says in the construction-workers' morons' manual, the way all you cunt like it handled. Nice and roma-a-antic."

He laughed.

"That's all it takes. Now, let's see: how would I handle it if I, too, was a moron, just like the rules require...?"

CHAPTER NINE

It was fairly late when Jeff Lasalle got back from the acting group he worked with.

At least now he could afford an apartment on West Forty Second street, thanks to the occasional job Roper threw his way. Traveling didn't take him nearly as long as it used to, when he had to roost out in Queens.

From habit, he hit the answering machine, and then went about his business until he heard the voice of his agent, Larry Walter.

"Bingo, Jeff-boy! That go-see paid off. Didn't I tell you? They want you to start on PASSION'S PLAYTHINGS in two weeks. Be in my office first thing Monday morning. You'll start getting scripts by mid-week. Didn't I tell you? I felt it in my bones. You got the stuff, Jeff, I always knew it!"

All Jeff could do was replay the message over and over, hunched in front of the answering machine, listening to it. When it finally sank in that he hadn't imagined getting the call, he went on with the rest of his evening, but it was still as if he were sleep-walking his way through a magical dream.

Removing the extremely heavy make he'd worn to meet Roper's clients, he gave his face an extra going-over to get any residue out of the pores of his facial skin.

He had to wash his thick wavy blond hair to put some life back into it, after all those hours wearing the airtight wig.

Roper had wanted a complete disguise, as usual.

"It's for your own protection," he had told Jeff several times.

So Jeff went along.

It made sense, too. He didn't want any of the people who thought they were hiring him to whack somebody coming after him, later. Maybe Roper could handle that sort of dude, but Jeff knew he himself sure as hell couldn't.

Whatever Roper advised him to do on these jobs, he did.

Then it hit him. If this soap opera deal worked out, this might be the last time he would be doing a job for Roper.

That thought gave him an additional lift. In fact, he was ambitious enough to fix himself a complete supper, TV frozen dinner and everything.

"Hell!" he excused himself, as he sat down to eat. "It's the perfect night to celebrate. Get one job, lose another. Typical actor's way."

In the middle of the meal, however, he thought of the downside.

"What if I can't cut the mustard? Soap operas shoot twenty or thirty pages a day!"

After worrying about that for awhile, he shrugged, stopped fretting, and went on eating. He knew he could do it, no matter how many pages he had to memorize each day. He was ready. He'd been ready for years.

CHAPTER TEN

Hal walker rode his bicycle three blocks to the check-cashing place, where he always paid his phone bill.

A woman was coming out of the check-cashing place. He walked his bike across the sidewalk toward her. Beyond her, he could see no other customers inside the place, only the girl in back, behind the plexiglass protector that extended from counter-level up to the ceiling.

The woman's eyes met Hal's. He half-smiled. She did, too. She looked familiar. One of his TV gals?

Starting to wheel his bike past her, he looked at her again.

Once more, their eyes met. Far back in Hal's mind, the remembrance came: a woman doesn't lock glances with a guy unless she wants to. With women, in matters of that nature, there are no accidents.

"Hi," he said.

Her eyes crinkled.

"Hi."

"Is your name…Tansy?"

For some reason the name of the gal on the TV news show popped into his head.

"No."

She shook her head, but her eyes were still warm.

This was the moment when Hal usually took their standard No as his excuse to duck out and be on his way…but something about her eyes and face, and the way she stood there, waiting, changed his years-long habit.

"My name's Hal. What's yours?"

"Martha."

"You staying around here someplace?"

She nodded, pointing vaguely along the street.

"Could I come see you? Do you have your own place?"

"Right now?"

He grinned.

"Sure. Why not? I could borrow a cup of tea and chase you around the coffee table…."

She laughed.

"I haven't got a coffee table."

"No problem. We'll improvise. We draw an X chalk mark on the floor, and that'll be the coffee table. I can chase you around that."

"All right."

It was that simple. All the times he had avoided getting to this point and beyond, and it turned out to be so astonishingly easy!

They drifted along the sidewalk.

Somehow they were talking. No problem there, either.

Then she turned into a big apartment building's front courtyard, and he was lifting the bike up some steps into a vestibule, while she unlocked the door inside it that admitted them to a lobby. Up in an elevator, then along a third floor corridor.

"Okay to bring the bike inside?"

She nodded, unlocking the apartment door.

"There's plenty of room."

"You're sure, now? I can always lock it to the stairway railing out here…"

"No need. There's lots of room. See?"

She swung the door open to reveal a wide foyer. Over on the left was an empty stretch of wall long enough to lean the bike against.

In the kitchen, she started water boiling.

"You don't really have to make tea," he grinned. "I was just kidding, back there."

"It's all right, Hal," she assured him. "My grandmother used to get highly insulted if she visited anyone and wasn't offered a nice hot cup of tea. It's hospitality."

The rest of it went unbelievably well, too. When she passed near him in the narrow kitchen, he put his hand on her arm above the elbow and caressed it. Next time she came near where he sat at the dinette table, she put a hand on his shoulder and pressed her thighs against him. He found his lips kissing her breasts through her white blouse. Her arms folded gently around his head. His arm circled her waist. He didn't try to rush things. He wasn't sure he would be able to manage anything, this early in the encounter, anyway, so why come on like gang-busters?

"Do you like to kiss me like that?" she asked.

"Yes. Your breasts are nice and soft.'

She smiled and nodded, gazing down at him a long moment. Then she seemed to make up her mind about something. Reaching out, she turned the gas off under the almost-boiling water.

"Come into the other room," she murmured, taking his hand and pulling him gently to his feet. "We'll be more comfortable in there."

They were, too.

Hal watched it all unfold, amazed at how easily Martha managed things for both of them. Their clothes dropped off with no embarrassment except a giggle on her part and a grin on his. In bed, even the love-making part he was never sure of went off without a hitch: one interval was just hugging and kissing and caressing, and the next moment he was sliding inside her, and they were making love.

They spent several hours together, but around four in the afternoon, Martha murmured: "You'd better be going now."

"Sure."

He began to get dressed.

"Think we can get together again sometime?"

"Would you like to?" She lay there in bed, watching him, smiling gently.

"I sure would."

"All right, let me have your phone number. I'll call you."

He did that and left, pushing the bike around in a tight u-turn in the foyer and out the front door. In the public corridor, he glanced back at her standing there, peering at him around the edge of the door.

"Thank you," he said. "That was a nice…cup of tea."

She laughed.

"I'm glad you liked it, Hal."

"See you, Martha."

She nodded.

"See you. I'll call."

Down in the street again, Hal pedalled his bike back to the check-cashing place and paid his phone bill with cash. Then he went to the supermarket a block away, bought a few things, and got the afternoon newspaper in the candy store across the street, all the chores he would ordinarily have taken care of earlier in the afternoon.

Somewhere in the midst of all of it, Hal's mind finally allowed itself to register what he had perceived sometime in the middle of the afternoon, while he was lying beside the young woman: she really was Tansy Burns, the TV semi-news show gal.

Usually his brain didn't work at all, with any of these women he was supposed to pick up on his "tours" during the day, but apparently being that physically close to this one had loosened his mind enough to allow it to actually work a bit, resulting in his finally figuring out with whom he had spent part of the afternoon.

Fortunately, she hadn't been wearing all that much of a disguise, either. That helped.

Okay, maybe the ice-jam in the river of his life had broken at last: he had finally doped out who one of them was, before he crawled back into the cave those detective agency street trash had driven him into, all those years ago, with their bothering and harassing routines.

"Finally!" he murmured, with a refreshing sense of relief.

CHAPTER ELEVEN

Emma Sorle sat in Mrs. Rodriguez's kitchen, stirring her fifth or sixth cup of tea, trying to dissolve the sugar cubes she had dropped into it.

You'd think the woman could afford to buy granulated sugar, Emma was thinking again.

She glanced at the clock.

Almost four.

Beside her, Peter was fidgeting worse than ever.

"Can't we go home soon?" he asked plaintively. It must be the twentieth time he had asked the same question.

"Pretty soon, Peter. Look at the magazine some more."

Apologetically, she glanced across the kitchen at Mrs. Rodriguez, who smiled understandingly, round-raced and placid. She had kids of her own. Fortunately, they were out playing. Emma wished she could send her own three out to play, too, but this apartment they were waiting in was only a block and a half from where they lived. The two girls might play right down in front, but she didn't trust

Peter to not race home in an effort to find out what was going on there. She had promised as part of the agreement to keep herself and the kids away until Mrs. Rodriguez got the all-clear phone call, even if it took the entire afternoon.

"I already looked at the damn magazine," Peter said sullenly. "Don't say damn," Emma chided him mechanically, glancing once more at the clock.

Peter noticed her glance. "We've been here an awful long time, Mom," he protested reasonably. "What are we waiting for?"

"Not much longer," she replied, smiling down encouragingly, running her fingers through his straight black hair.

He pulled his head impatiently away from her caressing hand.

"You've been telling me 'not much longer' all afternoon," he grumbled.

"You want me to give them some more cookies?" Mrs. Rodriguez asked from over by the stove.

Emma shook her head.

"I'm afraid it might spoil their appetites for supper," she explained.

She glanced into the next room where both the younger girls were playing with paper cut-out dolls she'd had the foresight to bring along for them. She wished she had thought to bring something that might have kept Peter occupied through this interminable afternoon. But even if she had, it probably wouldn't have worked. Peter was one of the restless ones. He kept wanting to know why, about everything. And this was simply one of those things Emma knew she couldn't possibly explain why about, in even the vaguest way…not that Peter would have accepted anything but the most precise explanation. Better to not even try explaining it to him at all.

Almost four o'clock. Another few minutes maybe.

Emma sipped more tea. She was heartily sick of tea. It was nice of this woman to keep offering refills, but…

She wondered how much money Mrs. Rodriguez was getting to provide a place for herself and her three kids to stay while…while whatever was happening in her own apartment…happened.

There was no way of asking. Everything about this sort of thing seemed to entail asking no questions. You simply went along, did whatever you agreed to do, waited until the phone call came, and then just went back home and acted as if nothing had happened.

Only Peter's impatience and his perpetual questions made things needlessly difficult. Peter was one of those who had not yet learned how to just go along, without making any waves by asking a lot of questions.

Emma was almost surprised when the phone finally rang.

Mrs. Rodriguez answered it, listened, murmured something, hung up, and smiled across at Emma.

Sighing, Emma rose from her chair at the kitchen table.

"Thank you very much, Mrs. Rodriguez," she smiled. "Come along, girls. Say thank you to Mrs. Rodriguez. You, too, Peter."

The two girls thanked Mrs. Rodriguez with pretty smiles. Peter did, too, quite pleasantly. Now that they were leaving, he felt a lot better.

All the way home, he wanted to ask his mother why they had been sitting in that dopey apartment all afternoon, but he knew it was no use. He had already asked her half a dozen times, and the last time, she acted just annoyed enough so he knew she wasn't going to change her mind, and he'd better quit asking.

The first thing Emma did when she unlocked the door of their third floor apartment was go into the bedroom where she and her husband slept, and strip the sheets from their bed.

Peter peered in through the open doorway, watching her.

"Mom, why are you changing the sheets in the middle of the week?" he asked.

"I think they need changing," Emma replied, rolling the top and bottom sheets up into a bundle with both pillowcases, and taking it all out to the bathroom, where she stuffed them into an almost-full hamper.

"But you never take the sheets off the beds until Saturday!" he went on, puzzled.

Emma took a deep breath, held it a long moment, then made herself reply patiently to her son.

"Peter, you've been wanting to go out and play all afternoon. Why don't you go out now?"

He looked disgusted. Again he wasn't going to get an answer to a question.

"It's too late," he muttered. "The other kids are practically ready to go home for supper, by now."

"Well, go out for a little while, anyway," she suggested. "It'll do you good. You've been very patient, Peter, all afternoon. I want to thank you for being as patient as you've been."

He looked up shyly from beneath his eyebrows. He was pleased at the unexpected compliment, and wished he deserved it.

"All right," he smiled. "Maybe some of them'll still be up the block."

Turning, he ran for the front door, unlocked the spring lock, and almost ran into a stout woman right outside in the corridor.

"Oh, sorry," he said hurriedly, ducking around her and racing toward the stairs, just this side of the window overlooking the courtyard.

"That's all right, sonny," the woman said cheerfully.

Grabbing the upright post at the end of the railing, he spun around, holding onto it, and started plunging down the steps to the floor below. The last thing he saw was the stout woman bent over, sliding something white under the door of his apartment.

He remembered seeing her somewhere in the building, but she wasn't from this floor.

Wonder what she's doing, slipping an envelope under our door? He thought she was probably selling something.

He shook his head, glad when he burst out the front door of the apartment building.

Sometimes Peter just had to get away from grownups. Mostly they weren't too bad, but sometimes they really got on his nerves.

He went racing up the block, trying to see if any of the other kids were up there, playing, or had they begun drifting on home already? It *was* pretty late…

Emma heard the slight sh-h-h-ing sound out by the front door of the apartment. Going into the hallway, she saw the white envelope on the floor, just inside the public corridor door.

Picking it up, she pulled the flap out and counted the money it held. Nodding, she sighed with relief.

Thank God it was over! Now she at least had enough money to get through the rest of the week. And it wasn't as if she had done anything wrong herself.

Back in the kitchen, Emma put the money with the rest of the household funds, and then went on preparing supper.

Once she stopped her work, wondering if she ought to tell her husband. She shook her head, deciding not to. Not unless Peter blurted it out.

She smiled, knowing that Peter was certain to mention it. So she would simply wait until he did, if he did, and then she'd tell her husband. He'd understand. He usually did.

CHAPTER TWELVE

Late Monday afternoon, after seeing Larry Walter, his agent, Jeff Lasalle used a payphone to call the Chesapeake Motel in Maryland. He had already called the previous Thursday, and again Saturday.

"Any mail arrive for Room Seven?" he asked the motel manager.

After a moment, the voice said, "One letter."

Jeff sighed.

"Okay, I'll be down that way in a day or so. I'll pick it up then."

"We can forward it, sir," the voice said. "It's a standard service…"

"No, that's all right. I'm due down there anyway."

Hanging up, he checked his time. Under forty seconds.

Roper told him to always try to keep even payphone calls under forty seconds. For once, he'd managed it.

Turning off West 42nd Street, he headed toward the old unused church where his Acting Group worked out in a basement area.

He would have to catch Amtrak down to D. C. tomorrow, to get that letter. It would contain the fake passport and driver's license they'd made up with the photographs he'd sent them. Once he picked them up and sent them along to Roper, he was out of it. He hoped.

Jeff wished he was clear of this job right now, so he could concentrate on that soap opera gig he'd gotten. But he knew he had to do this one last part of it. Roper wasn't the sort of guy you wanted to mess with.

Jeff took the blue stone steps two at a time down into the church basement, wondering if Roper really did these hit jobs he seemed to set up, now and then? Or did he get someone else to do that, too…the way he'd had Jeff himself handling this preliminary part of things.

As he turned into the half-crowded auditorium, he was thinking: "I'll probably never know the answer to that question."

And he sure as hell didn't want to know the answer to it, either.

Later, on his way home, he used another payphone to make a local call, let the phone ring four times at the other end, and hung up. The four-ring call would reach Roper, and he'd be in touch when he could.

Jeff was barely finished cleaning up his supper dishes when his phone rang. He recognized the almost-whispering voice.

"Your appointment's been changed to three."

"Okay," Jeff replied. "I thought it was ten. Good you called."

He hung up and went out, walking swiftly along 42nd and turning up Ninth Avenue to the phone he and Roper knew as phone number Three. There, he checked his watch. Still a couple of minutes till the ten minutes were up, so Jeff stood there with the receiver at his ear, as if he was on the phone to someone already. But he kept a finger holding the cradle-bar down, so he'd get Roper's call when it came.

A young woman approached along the sidewalk and stood waiting for him to finish with the phone. Jeff had to talk occasionally into the dead instrument a few times, so she'd think he was really using it. She kept waiting. When the phone rang, his finger released the cradle-bar instantly, but she heard it, gave him a dirty look, and stalked off to find another phone.

"How's it going?" Roper asked, still in the whispery voice.

"The motel down there is holding a letter for me."

"That'll be the passport and driver's license."

"I was thinking of going down for it first thing tomorrow…"

"Better go tonight," Roper interrupted. "We can get this job on the road that much sooner."

"Okay," Jeff agreed. "I'm on my way."

Hanging up, he shook his head, and went back to his apartment, where he spent over an hour putting on a facial disguise similar to the one he had worn the last time he was seen in the Chesapeake Motel.

"Wouldn't want to show up looking like someone else," he murmured to himself, as he completed the final touches and left the apartment.

Glancing back inside, he wondered when he would be able to spend any real time in this new place of his. Perhaps when he got going on that soap.

When Jeff's train left Penn Station on its run down to the capitol, one of the men shadowing him put in a call to Reynolds, who instructed him: "Send in the technical guys. I want that apartment of Mister Jeff Lasalle completely bugged and taped before he gets back to New York. And get a video camera in there, somewhere. We may want some tape of him, too."

CHAPTER THIRTEEN

"Hi!"

Hal took a second look, and only then recognized her.

"Martha?"

She nodded, smiling.

He swung off his bicycle and pushed it up onto the sidewalk and over to where she stood waiting.

"I still haven't gotten any better at this," he apologized.

"At what?"

"Recognizing people. I thought when you and I got together last time, I had passed some kind of milestone in…all this. But ever since then, it's exactly the same with all the other gals I…who walk past. I can sometimes guess who each one might be, or sense it might be one of them, vaguely, but the locking-in of my brain on exactly who each of them is, while I'm right there looking at her, still doesn't happen until I get back to my place, which is usually not till a half hour later."

"I'd like to see your place, sometime," she said.

"Huh?" Her spoken wish was so far from what Hal had been trying to explain that, for a moment, he was nonplussed by it. Shrugging off what he had been saying, he touched her hand.

"Come on up, anytime." He told her the address. "You're always welcome, Martha."

"Maybe I will," she said. "I'm glad I ran into you, Hal. I'm going to be down in Atlantic City, later this week. I was wondering… would you like to meet me down there?"

"I'd love to," he said quickly. It was such a relief to be back on what he had thought was his newly-discovered run of accomplishment in this weird semi-occupation he had been dragooned into, all those years ago, that he didn't want to screw things up with this one gal he had finally managed to successfully make contact with. If she asked him to jump off a high roof with her, he would probably agree without hesitation.

"Good!" She smiled. "I was hoping you would."

She looked up and down the street.

"Let's go have a cup of tea or something in that Burger King. We can plan the best way to get you down there…"

Inside the hamburger joint, around the corner where the tables and booths were located, they nursed cups of hot tea, which they had brewed for themselves with hot water gotten at the coffee and tea stand, while Martha explained how he was to get to South Jersey.

"Here's a roundtrip bus ticket," she said, taking an envelope from her shoulder-slung tote bag. "It's one of those gambling excursion busses. I took the liberty of getting it, hoping you'd be able to go. I also made hotel reservations for you. Just get there after noon on Thursday,, and they should have everything ready for you. Here's some money, too, for incidental expenses. There's always something at those places: cabs, tips. But that should be enough to get you through the weekend. Although we won't be spending the whole weekend, of course. I'll be going back to Washington Sunday morning…unless I get another assignment sending me somewhere else."

She watched him when she'd finished speaking. Hal just nodded and took the stuff she handed him.

"How does that sound?" she asked, finally.

"Sounds great!" Hal grinned. "I'm glad we ran into each other, too."

She laughed.

"Hal, I waited inside one of those pizza stores, near the corner there, for over fifteen minutes. That's how we ran into each other."

"There are no accidents in this business," he observed. "Sorry I was so late. Some afternoons are just…too bloody much. I had to work at that downtown messengering job this morning."

"It's all right. I didn't mind waiting."

"Can we…go to your apartment now?" he asked. "I could practise kissing your sweet face some more…"

Smiling, she reached out and covered his hand with one of hers.

"Hal, I wish we could, but…" She shook her head regretfully. "I've got so much on my plate between now and Thursday! We'll practise kissing when we get together in Atlantic City."

Hal's discouragement was obvious, and she noticed. Her eyes softened. She squeezed his hand sympathetically.

"It'll be all right," she assured him "We'll have a nice time. Just call that number when you get down there, after you've checked into your hotel room. Leave your room number, and I'll be in touch with you, first chance I get."

Hal nodded, studying the folder containing the bus ticket, the money, and the other information she had included in it.

"Okay, Hal?"

"Yeah."

"You'll be there, won't you? You're not just saying yes and then go and forget…?"

He shook his head.

"Martha, how could I forget someone as lovely as you?"

She smiled and nodded.

"All right, then. I'll see you Thursday. Gotta go now. No, you stay. Finish your tea."

Rising, she slung her tote bag from her shoulder, touched his face with her fingertips, and studied him for a moment, peering down into his eyes. Then she turned and walked up front, went around the corner toward the street doors, and was gone.

When Hal got outside shortly afterward, she was nowhere to be seen.

Maybe she'd had a car waiting to pick her up, he thought.

He unlocked his bike. He still had his regular store-going to do, so he rode the three blocks down the main drag beneath the El tracks and waited for the traffic light to change at the busy cross street.

Coming toward him from the other side of the street was a big girl with a heart-shaped face. Watching her as she, too, waited for the traffic light to change, Hal thought she looked a lot like the model Ronnie Jarrett.

While he studied her, their glances met, and she smiled at him.

Astonished, Hal smiled back reflexively, but when the light changed, he rode his bike past her to the opposite corner, up onto the sidewalk, and got off it in front of the newspaper store.

As he locked the cable securing his bike to a building upright, he looked back and watched the young woman getting farther and farther away, as she continued walking back the way he had just come.

Hal could hardly believe his eyes. Could that really have been Ronnie Jarrett? Was he supposed to pick her up, too? Both her and Martha/Tansy on the same afternoon?

Hal shook his head, took one last look at the distant woman, and went inside the store for the paper.

One girl an afternoon was plenty! More than plenty!

CHAPTER FOURTEEN

Roper could hear Reynolds put the phone down in their Watkins Construction Company office. The bug Roper had put in there picked up even the sound of putting a phone back in its cradle. The tape had already played the phone conversation Reynolds had just wound up.

Now the tape had Reynolds saying: "The technical guys in New York decided they'd better not put any cameras inside Dispatcher's apartment. Too obvious. Anyway, they don't need to: there are already security cameras installed out in the public corridors. One of them on his floor gives a clear shot of this Lasalle's apartment door. That's the name he goes under, Jeff Lasalle. He's an actor."

Another voice said: "That should be enough. It's happening tomorrow, so there's no need for a big production, where the guy lives."

That sounded like the one called Adams, decided Roper.

What was happening tomorrow?

Reynolds again: "Better this way. We just want to know if Lasalle gets any visitors at H-hour, so we can adjust if we have to."

Barely audibly, Adams muttered: "Less crap to clear out before the cops get there."

Roper turned up the sound. He would have to do some fine-tuning with those bugs he'd installed at their Watkins office.

"Let's call it quits for the day," Reynolds suggested. "We can't do anything more now. Anyway, it's all happening up there. You taking your own car up to New York tomorrow?"

Adams chuckled.

"Hell, no. Plane's good enough for me. Has Tollman been briefed?"

Reynolds laughed.

"Till it's coming out his ears."

That was all, but Roper went on listening, in case the tape activated again when anyone spoke further.

The office he had rented was two floors below Watkins Construction's. All he'd had to do was drop a couple of wires down the outside of the building for the two floors, making them look like the other stuff dangling out there. He was lucky it wasn't one of those newer buildings, where TV antennas and cables were all inside in shafts.

When it was obvious the two men were gone for the day, Roper just left the bugs and phone taps on Voice-activated-record.

He hadn't yet developed a pattern that would have told him when they'd usually be in that office of theirs, two flights above his.

The bad news was that they had bracketed Lasalle. How the hell had they followed the guy?

Roper shrugged, impatient with himself. If might be his own fault. Maybe he should've had Marge tail the actor from that motel just to see if anyone else was following him.

From the sound of those two on the tape just now, they had a fair-sized organization. Look at all the things they were able to do: tapping the actor's phones, deciding they didn't need to install a video camera inside Jeff's apartment because the security camera out in the public corridor would serve them well enough.

Which meant they could get access to its tapes.

Roper strolled over to the window and stared down at the street. Who were these guys? Cops? Private dicks? Roper didn't want to get mixed up with either of those outfits: both had too much manpower.

Shrugging, he turned away from the window and got ready to split.

First thing he had to do was contact Jeff Lasalle and let him know they had followed him from the Chesapeake Motel and knew where he lived. He would have to arrange for the actor to get clear of them, if Jeff wanted to give it a try.

Going down in the elevator, Roper knew that was the big difficulty. Suppose Lasalle didn't want to disappear? He was dug in up there, following his actor's dream. How could he just disappear and go on with his acting?

Roper shrugged and stopped worrying about it. He paid guys like Lasalle pretty big bucks to do what they did for him. This was one of the risks. He could help the man disappear for a few days, but that was pretty much it. The job didn't have any lifetime witness protection guarantees built into it.

Thinking that, Roper chuckled.

But out on the street, he stopped at a payphone a few blocks away and put in a call to the actor's apartment, up there in New York on West 42nd Street.

The least he could do was warn Jeff as soon as possible.

He got nothing but the first four rings, then the answering machine kicked in. When the voice part stopped, Roper said: "Fifteen," and hung up.

He'd have to try again later.

*　*　*

Jeff Lasalle didn't get around to checking his answering machine until late that night, too late to implement what that one word Fifteen told him to do.

He spent a sleepless night, wondering and worrying what was up. Fifteen was a warning signal. It was supposed to trigger specific evasive tactics on his part. It meant great danger, so great that Roper would meet him at the pre-arranged place and spell it out for him.

But knowing all that didn't make it any easier for Jeff to get through the night and half the following day, wondering what had gone wrong.

Just in case, before he left, Jeff stuffed basics into the ample pockets of the casual jacket he picked to wear, things he would need if instant flight was necessary: toothpaste and brush, shaving gear, his own passport, some cash in a money belt.

Should he try to get some more money out of the bank? If he had to go on the run, that twenty nine thousand would come in real handy. He'd have to ask Roper about that.

Wear two sets of underwear, two shirts, with a tie on the underneath shirt's collar. Let's see, what else? Extra socks? Okay, one pair, but no more. If he needed more stuff like that, he could buy it on the journey.

By late morning, Jeff was a wreck. No sleep, a breakfast he could hardly get down, and lunch not much better. Still more than an hour till he could go to the meeting place and find out what was so important Roper would actually break his own cover to meet with him.

Then the doorbell rang.

CHAPTER FIFTEEN

One of the regular drops on Hal Walker's midtown messenger job was delivering scripts to soap opera people, every Wednesday. At least it was as regular as anything gets in a messenger job.

He dropped the usual three big envelopes at the appropriate apartments in the usual building on West Fifty Eighth Street, just short of Seventh Avenue.

It must be a good building for actors to live in, he was thinking, with three of them on this one soap opera all bunched together in the same building.

Unfortunately, the fourth envelope was a new one added to the collection he had to deliver. No convenience about this one: it was located way down on Forty second Street and over by Ninth Avenue, maybe even Tenth.

Okay, it was a nice day for a walk, and once Hal made this final drop of the day, he could head on home and get ready to meet Tansy 'Martha' Burns down in Atlantic City the next day.

The drop turned out to be one of the over-cautious sort: he didn't want to open his apartment door.

"Can you slide it under the door?" he called, without opening up at all.

Hal chuckled.

"Mister Lasalle, it's a script of some kind. Too thick to fit under the door."

"Oh."

A pause. Then: "Oh, yeah, that's right. They were going to send it today. I forgot all about it."

Trying to sound cheerful, Hal went on assuring him it was all right.

"I just dropped off three more, up on Fifty Eighth Street," he said. "You live kind of out of the way, over here."

The door opened an inch or two, on a chain. The tall young man with wavy blond hair who peered out at Hal seemed nervous. Since he was obviously not going to take the chain off the door and open it any wider, Hal upended the script and slid it through the narrow opening, holding the delivery ticket firmly against it with his thumb.

"Sign the ticket, okay? And put the time on there, too, if you've got a watch handy."

The young man nodded, took the ballpoint pen Hal slipped through to him, and scribbled on the ticket.

"There you go," he said, handing the ticket and pen back. "Wait, let me get you something…"

He went off, returning a moment later, and handing a dollar through the opening.

"Thanks," Hal grinned, turning away. "Good luck with the show."

The actor laughed.

"Thanks, I'll need it," he said, closing the apartment door.

Hal stood under one of the two security cameras positioned above the elevator door, one pointed in each direction along the carpeted corridor. It was a nice building. Acting in soaps must pay pretty well, for the blond guy back there to be able to afford a place like this. He seemed young to have a job on one of them. Still, that's who were on most soap operas, young, good-looking people, as well as the regular old war-horses of both sexes, who had been on them for years, sometimes even decades.

Hal wondered which soap the scripts he delivered were for. They never said on the outside of the envelopes, just the name of the production company…which meant absolutely nothing to Hal.

Inside his apartment, Jeff sat staring down at the script he had just opened with shaking hands.

He couldn't help thinking that this should be one of the happiest days of his life, getting a crack at acting on an established soap opera like PASSION'S PLAYTHINGS. Hundreds of thousands of other actors would do anything for a break like this, and here he sat, wondering if he should buckle down and try memorizing his sides, or stuff everything he could carry in his pockets, get that twenty nine G out of the bank and run for his life.

He sat staring out the window at the Hell's Kitchen rooftops in the middle distance off to the west

Why was the timing of some things so damn rotten? And when was Roper going to get back to him. He'd already made two more of those four-ring phone calls from payphones.

Sighing dispiritedly, he went on waiting until Roper finally got around to calling him and filling him in on what it was that had gone wrong.

CHAPTER SIXTEEN

Nothing could have been more normal: at 1:24 PM, a Member of the House of Representatives and his small entourage left their taxis in front of a middle level hotel in the mid-Sixties on the Upper East Side of Manhattan. Congressman Tim Melford was a speaker at a fund-raising dinner scheduled in the hotel for later that evening.

A few local reporters were in attendance, one with a TV camera crew. The Congressman stopped to answer a reporter's question under the overhead canopy, halfway between the curb and the hotel's revolving entrance door. The reporter was a short man. Melford bent, leaning forward to hear better, and a couple of shots rang out. Both bullets struck Roger Brent, but afterward the police decided that there was little doubt the shots had been intended for Melford himself. He had bent down so suddenly that the shooter missed him entirely and killed his adviser by mistake.

There were so few bystanders nearby that it was impossible not to identify the shooter, a tall big-shouldered young man with a reddish sunburned-looking face under a baseball cap. He had stopped his bicycle to watch and take in the scene, pushing his bike up onto the sidewalk, out near the curb end of the canopy. Raising a camera, he had pointed it at the Congressman. No one gave him or the camera a second thought, until the camera suddenly spit two gunshots at the small group of arrivals.

Dropping his gun/camera into the wire basket attached to his bike's handlebars, the bicyclist took off like a flash. Near the corner, a big man yelled as the bicyclist approached him.

"Stop that man!" someone hollered.

No one did. He was going too fast. The big pedestrian tried to intercept the bike, but when he stepped in front of it and tried to grab the handlebars with both hands, it swerved and eluded his grasp, but not before one of his reaching hands came close to the cyclist. All his hand got was the baseball cap, though. Then the blond-haired man on the bike turned the corner and was gone.

The big man lumbered to the corner after him, waving the cap and yelling. When he, too, had disappeared from sight around the corner, everyone beneath the canopy at the hotel entrance stared at one another and down at the man bleeding on the sidewalk, as if they couldn't believe it had really happened, right there in front of them.

CHAPTER SEVENTEEN

When at last Roper called at half-past one, he told Lasalle, "The meeting's on the second, not on the fifteenth."

Instead of responding with the usual coded reply, Jeff asked: "Is this about that shipment I sent you from down South?"

He could sense Roper's irritation at the other end, but Jeff had to know. The hell with code procedures.

After a moment, Roper said in his peculiar whispering voice: "You mean the one due on the fifteenth?"

There was that fifteen again! Danger!

Jesus, what could've gone wrong?

"I got that shipment okay," Roper continued. "It's another load that's causing the problem."

Click

Sweating, Jeff shrugged on the jacket loaded with all the stuff he had jammed into the pockets, and carefully locked all his apartment windows, after which he checked everything else, in case he was going to be gone a long while. Then he started out.

Since Roper's call had come at 1:30, he knew he had a half hour to rendezvous, which was only fifteen minutes away at his regular walking pace: he had checked it several times, in case he ever needed to get there in an emergency.

As he waited for a cross-street traffic light to change, he realized he had never really believed there would be an emergency. Now look!

No one was inside the church when he entered it at two o'clock.

He knelt in the last pew to make sure no one came in right behind him, and to check on anyone else already there.

No one was, and no one followed him in. When he was certain of that, Jeff rose and went over to the confessional at the right rear corner of the old church. Inside, he crossed himself and said, "Bless me, Father, for I have sinned..."

"You and General Napier, two unregenerate Sinders," muttered Roper, after sliding back the little door in the priest's central section of the confessional booth.

"What? Who's General Napier?"

Jeff was confused.

"Never mind," Roper chuckled. "You were tailed from the Washington area the other day. They know where you live. Something's going down, today, so you've gotta disappear..."

* * *

There was a communications glitch. Reynolds couldn't stay in touch with the rest of the team for over ten minutes after H-hour.

"I never knew it to fail," he snarled. "Right when we want no interruptions whatever, that's exactly when everything fucks up. Happens every time!"

Adams chuckled.

"Try them again," he suggested.

Reynolds did. This time he got through.

"Did it go over?" he asked Stoddard.

"Yes. He's down. Sorry we couldn't get through to you, Chief..."

"That's all right," Reynolds said abruptly. "Things happen. How's Tollman doing?"

"He got clear away. No problem there. Subject went down like a stone. When Tollman was splitting the scene, his back-up grabbed the cap off his head, so no one could miss seeing the wavy blond wig he had on."

"Beautiful! That was important. Keep us posted."

Switching off the two-way, he told Adams: "It all went off as planned."

"Of course," Adams said. "Tollman's a pro."

The two-way buzzed.

After listening a moment, Reynolds snapped: "Are you on him? – Okay. Don't lose him. We'll be there in two shakes."

Adams watched, listening.

"Anything?" he asked, when Reynolds signed off.

"That bastard Lasalle just left his apartment," Reynolds growled. "Right when we just want him to stay put for another couple of hours, he has to start wandering around." Shaking his head in disgust, he said: "Head up Tenth Avenue."

Adams put the car into motion.

"Don't get so riled up, man," he murmured. "Just so we still have the guy bracketed, we're all right."

* * *

Jeff felt as if he'd been kicked in the stomach.

"Disappear? Where can I disappear to?"

Roper gave him an address across the river in West New York.

"Just go down to the Port Authority bus terminal and catch a bus over to Jersey. This safe house is right across the river. When you go north along Kennedy Boulevard on the Palisades over there, get off the bus at Liberty Street and go to the address I just gave you. Go in and straight through and out the back door, climb a wooden stairway into a building that faces the next street up, Clifton. Apartment three. I've left the door unlocked. There are keys to the place in there, on the kitchen table, and plenty of food. You can lie low there a few days, and I'll try to find out what's going on with those people."

"But I start an acting job next Monday," Jeff whispered, trying to listen, to remember everything Roper was telling him.

"Okay," Roper said encouragingly. "With luck, that might be long enough. Stay holed up over there till Monday. Maybe by then, whatever those people are trying to pull off will have blown over…"

"What are they pulling off?" Jeff cried, alarmed. "Does it involve me?"

My God! he thought. What have I gotten involved in here?

"I think it does involve you. Are you okay with money?"

"I've got a few hundred on me, but I can get that dough out of the bank I stashed it in last week…or most of it. Did you get the fifteen thousand I wired you?"

"Yes, that's okay. But keep away from your bank. If they know where you live, they know where you put that money."

"Oh!" Jeff hadn't thought of that. "That's right."

"I've put ten thousand cash in an envelope under the kneeling board in the pew right outside this booth. There's a gun beside it, just in case…"

"I don't want a gun," Jeff said hurriedly.

Roper peered at him through the wire screen separating them.

"In a country with two hundred million handguns and counting, everyone needs a gun."

"No," Jeff insisted. "No guns."

He could see Roper shrug in the dimness beyond the screen.

"Okay, it's your choice," Roper growled. "Get going. Good luck. I'll try to find out what those people are up to. If I do, I'll let you know. Just dig in over there in Jersey for a few days."

Jeff stepped out of the confessional, let the cloth draped over the doorway fall back into place, and knelt down in the pew directly in front of him. Praying, he first made sure there was still no one else in the church. Then he carefully reached under the board he knelt on and found a thick envelope. Beside it, he felt another, harder package, but he only picked up the envelope.

Glancing at the money inside it, he slipped it under his jacket before rising and leaving the church.

Roper gave it five minutes before he emerged from the confessional, backing out as if he had been cleaning the center section. No one was there to take in the act he was putting on, so he knelt where Jeff had, fished on the floor, found only the gun down there, retrieved it and left the church at the other end, the official end behind the altar where the priests came and went.

CHAPTER EIGHTEEN

"He's leaving the church," Caldwell's voice squawked from the radio Reynolds held.

"Yes, I see him," he replied.

Their car was parked facing eastward on the side street, across the avenue from the corner church. Dispatcher came down the church steps and started south on the avenue. Partway along the block, he turned and stared across at their car, back in the side street shadows.

"He spotted us," Adams muttered.

Reynolds turned and faced Adams.

"Don't look in his direction again. Say something to me. We're arguing."

They put on an act, as if they were two men discussing something in the front seat of a parked car. Reynolds held up a newspaper, resting it on the steering wheel in front of Adams, pointing at it, as if he was proving something with written documentation.

"Okay, he's started moving again," Adams murmured.

Reynolds kept up the act, though. It was just as well he did, because halfway down the block to the next cross-street, the wavy-haired young man turned and looked back at them over his shoulder. All he saw was the same two men arguing in a parked car.

"He's out of sight," Adams finally said. "Should we…move from here yet?"

Reynolds shook his head.

"Better not. We're out of it, for the time being anyway…"

Into the two-way, he said: "We thought subject made us for a second, there, but he decided we weren't watching him and kept going south. You'll have to take up the slack."

"Roger," Caldwell replied.

"Do you still have him in sight?"

"Yes. Five of us, and two local police."

"If anything happens, make sure you get to him first, not the cops…understood?"

"Understood."

"Keep us posted. We'll stay where we are a few more minutes, to let him get over spotting us."

They sat there, listening whenever the radio gave brief progress reports.

When the subject was almost down to Forty Second Street, Reynolds said into the radio: "Okay, we're rejoining you. Where's he at now, exactly?"

"Just turning east along Forty Second."

Adams started the car and drove onto the avenue, turning southward.

They were at Forty Sixth and Ninth when Caldwell's voice suddenly squawked: "He's crossing Forty Second. Seems to be headed toward that bank, the one he put the…"

"I know the one," Reynolds growled. "Careful what you say on these things."

"Uh, yeah, Chief."

"If he looks as if he's going into the bank, stop him out on the sidewalk."

"Stop him? You mean…?"

"I mean just as per plan: stop him. You've got the package. Deliver it anyway you have to."

Putting the radio down, Reynolds said: "Damned if I'm gonna let local law impound that twenty five thousand of ours Dispatcher put into that bank."

"You're right," Adams agreed. "The more dough we can keep from throwing around, the easier time old man Graham will have getting the company's budget approved."

Shooting the car forward, he a beat traffic light, trying to reach Forty Second before anything went down.

"Hurry, George," said Reynolds. "I want us to be there. Otherwise, they'll fuck things up, sure as apples."

Adams drove as fast as he dared, but when he turned screeching eastward onto Forty Second, they could both see by the crowd gathering in front of the mid-block bank that it was over.

As they jolted to a halt, Reynolds saw one of his men, Stoddard, straighten beside the downed blond-haired man lying on his back on the sidewalk.

Stoddard held a handgun by the barrel, and he glanced toward Reynolds in the car.

Reynolds returned Stoddard's nod and turned toward Adams, who smiled for the first time that day.

"All right," Reynolds breathed. "That's taken car of. The murder weapon was found on him.

But just as they began to get out of the car, a plain-clothes cop went charging across the sidewalk, grabbed the gun from Stoddard's hand and shoved him against the wall of the bank beside the front entrance.

"You think I never saw a gun planted before?" he yelled. "Who the hell are you guys? Officer, keep everyone away from that man." He pointed down at Jeff Lasalle, bleeding on the sidewalk from gunshot wounds.

The two uniformed police officers did what the detective ordered them to do.

Reynolds took in the scene and decided not to even bother trying to talk to the detective.

With a glance, he instructed his five men to go along with it, not to make any waves. To Adams, he said: "You stay near this trouble-maker and keep me posted. I'll contact Blanchard and get him started pulling wires. Find out who that plainclothes bastard is that's fucking things up for us."

"I'll be a pleasure," Adams grinned, getting out of the car and coming around to the sidewalk side, where he leaned in as Reynolds slid over and got behind the steering wheel. "Do they still send them out to Staten Island?"

"More like Red Hook, these days," Reynolds said grimly. "Or East New York, to stem the drug trade."

Adams chuckled.

"Like Hans Brinker holding a finger in the dike during a tsunami…"

"That wasn't Hans Brinker," Reynolds shouted, as he swung the car away from the curb.

"Who was it, then?" Adams yelled after him.

Reynolds called something over his shoulder in reply, but all Adams could see was a glimpse of him shaking his head, presumably meaning he didn't know.

Shrugging, Adams turned to deal with the disaster in front of the bank.

CHAPTER NINETEEN

"You're certain you're all right?" Norma Melford asked her husband.

She held the phone pressed to her ear, staring down at their rear garden from the projecting window-surrounded balcony. "No one would blame you for skipping the banquet this evening, Tim."

"No, I'm fine," Melford assured her. "I just wonder if it's in…oh, bad taste, to go on as if nothing had happened."

Norma felt numb, holding the phone so tightly just to hold onto something, even if it was only a telephone.

"Poor Roger!" she said softly.

"Yes. Talk about losing your right arm! I don't know what I'm going to do without him."

She stared down at the garden inside the twelve-foot high brick wall surrounding the back end and part of the street side of their corner lot.

How long had it been since she had done any gardening? She couldn't remember.

"He was always alone," she murmured.

"Yes, poor guy," Tim agreed. "Still, I think he preferred it that way, ever since that girl Linda Stevens died, back in Coal Springs…"

"Odd!" she said. "I never made the connection…I mean, between his lack of interest in women and Linda dying in that car accident they were in. They were engaged, weren't they?"

"I think they were," he said, vaguely.

"I recall once thinking perhaps Roger might be gay, but that thought didn't last long. The check of his habits and life-style you ordered would have shown that up, wouldn't it?"

"Definitely. Whatever it was Roger might have lacked, it certainly left him with the ability to focus on his work. I've never known anyone who had such mental stamina as Roger Brent. Hon, I really meant it when I said I don't know what I'm going to do without the guy."

"I'll help you keep things organized, sweetheart. It seems like the end of the world right now, the shock of his killing, and all you must be going through up there in New York. But in a week or two, we'll be able to get ourselves back on track again. It will be almost as if he'd never been considered irreplaceable."

"I suppose so," he husband said, but he didn't sound his usual positive self.

Norma sat straighter.

"Tim, I've changed my mind. I'm coming up. You can't be expected to get through something as awful as this by yourself. I'll catch the evening shuttle."

"You're sure you want to, Hon? I hated to ask you."

"Yes, I'm sure. You just go ahead with everything, and all of a sudden I'll be there beside you. We'll get through the dinner together."

"Perhaps you're right, Norma. It would look a little better if we were both here. Not quite like I was going on with the speech and the rest of it, as if Roger was just another…I don't know…statistic?"

"See you there, my dear. Get a little nap, even if it's only fifteen or twenty minutes."

"You're right, Hon. I'll do that."

Hanging up, she rose, relieved to have something to do besides stare gloomily out at the untended back garden and think about the sudden unexpected murder of Roger Brent, up there in the streets of New York.

CHAPTER TWENTY

Like most other people, Roper first heard about it on that evenings' five o'clock news.

The pictures roved back and forth, covering the sidewalk scene of the slaying, behind the reporter on the spot, who was calling in the coverage on camera.

"As you know," the man was saying, "we have no pictures of the actual incident in front of the bank, here on West Forty Second Street, but piecing together our report from various eye-witnesses, we can only find praise for the quick work of the Federal and Local law enforcement officers in tracing and very nearly succeeding in apprehending the alleged perpetrator of this afternoon's terrible attempt on the life of Congressman Melford, which resulted in the tragic death of his chief advisor, Roger Brent, across town…"

Roper's lips curled slightly in a sardonic smirk as he peered past the talking newsman at EMS people in the background carrying the dead actor off on a gurney.

"Why the hell didn't you steer clear of that stupid bank, man?" he murmured.

Getting up, he strode into the kitchen to freshen his cup of coffee, muttering irritably: "What do you think I gave you that ten G for? So you wouldn't have to go near your God damn bank, that's what for!"

But by the time he got back to the TV again, he had forced himself to calm down.

You can do just so much for people, and then you have to let it go. If Lasalle had to make a try for the money he'd stuck in his bank safe deposit box a week ago, and they blew him away while he was doing it, that was his choice.

Except for the ten thousand!

Roper couldn't help feeling a twitch at that loss. It cut down his take from the initial fifty thousand less the ten G the actor had kept as his cut, to only forty thousand. Now he had to force himself to not regret handing over today's additional ten grand to the actor, which left him with only thirty thousand.

It was just too bad the poor bastard hadn't cut his losses and hauled his ass over to West New York or Weehawken or whatever it was, and holed up there for the next four or five days. Then this Congressman's assassination, which Reynolds and his buddy Adams had set up, might blow over, or at least they might've had to find themselves another fall guy for it instead of Lasalle.

That must have been the way they had planned it all along: hire Roper as their Dispatcher, then whack the Dispatcher and "find" the murder weapon on his body. The only thing that spoiled their plan was that they'd killed the wrong Dispatcher.

Which meant that it wouldn't have blown over in a couple of days.

Thinking of that gave Roper pause.

Maybe they would have gotten Jeff eventually, no matter how long he hid out in the Jersey safe house. They had arranged their hit entirely too carefully to just walk away from the designated substitute for whoever did that fucked-up shooting, over on the East Side. Even if the actor had gone over and disappeared in Weehawken until next Monday, they would still have been looking for him to reappear.

Which meant Lasalle's life was effectively over, anyway. But at least he might have spent the rest of it alive in the pen instead of dead in a hole in the ground.

When Roper worked all that out in his head, he didn't feel so bad about Lasalle catching their bullets.

Once they dogged the actor's steps to where he lived, he was done for. Which meant it had been out of Roper's hands. It was no longer his responsibility. He had hired the actor and paid him extremely well to be a stalking-horse in this business enterprise of his. Ten thousand dollars was damn good earnings for a then-out-of-work actor to pull in, posing as a shooter in the opening stage of negotiations, setting up a job. It went without saying that a pay envelope that good carried with it some of the risks such an endeavour entailed.

That afternoon, Jeff Lasalle had found out the hard way exactly how great the risk had been all along, every time Roper had used him to get a job off the ground.

Now the TV news coverage was branching out, telling about the NYPD Detective Crayton, who had braced what Roper assumed were Reynolds's men, after they blew away the actor there on the sidewalk in front of the bank, before he could enter the place.

Carefully, Roper watched the footage showing Crayton's angry face, and he couldn't help smiling at the news reporter's voice-over narration of the way the detective had kept the Feds away from the victim in the first few minutes after Jeff went down. Roper wished they had gotten footage of the actual scene as it happened, the furious plainclothes cop holding two or three Feds at bay, maybe even making them spread it against the wall of the bank, while he made them prove who they were.

"The Special Agent in charge denied Detective Crayton's accusation that one of his subordinates had planted the weapon on the dead man," the newsman was saying. "Eventually, Detective Crayton admitted that he might have been hasty when he interfered with their handling of the situation…but he refused to do so for us on camera."

Hearing that, Roper chuckled. Crayton smelled something.

Roper made a note of that name, Crayton. From the Midtown South Precinct? He could always find out.

Maybe a time would come when Roper could find a use for a cop like that Crayton: too dumb not to be honest, or too honest to play dumb?

Right now, though, Roper had to figure out where he himself stood in this maze of double-crossing Reynolds and Adams had dumped on him.

Obviously, they had arranged all this to knock off that Congressman, and only an accident had prevented them from accomplishing that.

Still, there was something a bit out of kilter about that, too. Roper couldn't recall previous Members of Congress being targets for hitters. Why this Melford guy?

He would have to make a note of that, too: find out what legislation the Honorable Representative was trying to get passed.

Finally, the TV news switched to another story.

Roper turned the set off. He could always get more details on it in the next day's newspapers.

Pacing up and down, he thought about it.

He already had bugs and phone taps set up in Reynolds' dummy construction company, down in the D. C. area. That was a plus. Which left some digging to be done into the target their shooter had missed, Rep. Melford.

As for the extra ten thousand dollars he had given the actor as getaway money, Roper would simply have to write off the money loss and forget it. Those things happen. They were unavoidable.

As nearly as he could see, Roper was pretty much in the clear. Given the careful way he started off with clients on jobs like this, the only one at risk was his bird-dog, in this case, Jeff Lasalle. With Jeff's elimination, maybe Reynolds and his grunting buddy Adams thought they'd gotten the same hitter they had hired, case closed, on to the next one.

But Roper sensed he was missing something.

Somewhere along the line there might be a connection to him. He tried to trace back, going over every step he had taken, but he couldn't come up with whatever it was that bothered him.

Finally, shrugging, he let it go for the time being. If it were important, it would come to him, eventually. Until then, he would have to begin his

investigation into the past personal life of the Honorable Tim Melford.

CHAPTER TWENTY ONE

Hal Walker got off the bus almost in front of his destination hotel in Atlantic City, shortly after four o'clock on Thursday afternoon.

When he registered, he was almost surprised to find that there was actually a reservation in his name. He was afraid to ask how much his room would cost per day, in case the money Martha/Tansy had given him along with the round-trip bus ticket wouldn't be enough to cover it.

Upstairs in his fourth floor room, the first thing he did was make the call to Martha. A woman answered. He told her his name.

"Walker?" She sounded as if she didn't know anything about him, or that he was supposed to call. Hal's hand became slick with sweat holding the phone.

"I was supposed to leave my room number," he added lamely, not sure whether he should use the name Martha, and unwilling to use the name Tansy Burns. Technically, she wasn't Tansy Burns until and unless she told him she was, so…

"Oh, yes, Mr. Walker," she said. "Here it is. Sorry. We're a little rushed here."

"Sure," he said, relieved. "I was just supposed to leave my room number."

"All right, Mr. Walker, I've got it. I'll pass it along."

Uncertain whether he should go have supper somewhere, Hal got his things distributed and stretched out on the bed to wait.

Around half past five, the phone rang.

"Hal? This is Tans…Martha, I mean." She began to giggle.

Hal laughed, too.

"I let the cat out of the bag," she said. "Or the bag out of the cat… Anyway, you made it safely. Have you eaten yet?"

"No. I was afraid I'd miss your call."

"Ah, you poor man. Go have supper. I'll have a ticket left for you at the desk, downstairs, for the first lecture tonight. I never eat before the first interview. Nerves, stomach, lots of reasons. But maybe we can have a late supper. I can usually keep something down, once I've gotten that first question-and-answer session out of the way."

"Great."

"Oh, there will also be a key to a room adjoining one of the rooms we're using, myself and my people."

"Ah."

She chuckled. "The all-purpose 'Ah!' Hairdresser, costumes, makeup, voice coach…you wouldn't believe. Anyway, the key is to a room registered to one of my people, but they are doubling up, so you and I can have someplace to ourselves, without having to go back and forth in the public corridors of this place."

"Makes sense."

"After the first session tonight, use that key and wait there for me, all right?"

"Will do. Uh, good luck with the session. I hope it goes okay."

"Thank you. See you afterward."

Down in the casino, Hal found out what time the two political meetings were to be held. He also bought a few five-dollar chips, in case anyone asked him what he was doing there: he'd be able to show them the chips.

After eating a light supper, he went back up to his room. An envelope had been slipped under the door. It contained a room key as well as a ticket to the first conference that evening. Hal left a request for a call to wake him half an hour before it, in case he dozed off. Then he lay down.

The phone woke him at the time he'd asked for. Washing and shaving, he went downstairs and was inside the main lounge ten minutes early. The place was already crowded. Buying a drink, he tried to find a seat, but all the tables were taken. He was stuck with standing room only, in back.

Perhaps you were supposed to get there earlier than ten minutes to secure a seat.

The session was surprisingly interesting. Hal enjoyed it very much. He was surprised at how professional Tansy Burns was, putting over her questions…and she looked beautiful in the blue gown she had worn. The rest of the audience thought so, too. They gave extended and even wild applause after each of her exchanges with the administration's people and the other newsies like herself.

Hal was beginning to realize he had known very little about Tansy Burns's professional career, outside of that evening show of hers, which he'd been watching on and off for several years.

After the session let out, Hal didn't have a clue what he should do next. He loitered in the thinning crowd for a few minutes, and then he went up to the fifth floor and let himself into the new room with the key Tansy had sent him with the ticket to the question-and-answer session.

Turning on the TV set, he skipped channels, trying to find something worth watching.

About fifteen minutes into a movie there was a tapping sound on the door connecting his room with the one next to it. Turning the knob, he found it was locked when he tried to open it.

From the other side, Tansy said, "Oh, I forgot to unlock it."

She did and the door swung wide. She stood there in a soft pink peignoir, arms upraised on each side, posing.

"Ta-da!" she laughed. "How do I look?"

"You look terrific."

"I wanted to look special," she said, reaching out and taking his hand. "After that house-wifey outfit I was wearing the first time we…got together, I wanted to look absolutely ravishing."

"You do. I'm absolutely ravished."

She pulled him through the doorway.

"Come in, come in."

In the next room, she closed the door behind him, thought of something, opened it again, and went into his room and over to the corridor door. In a moment, she was back, closing and locking the connecting door.

"Just making certain you locked the outside door to your room. Now, look at my surprise.

She led him by the hand to a table set up in the middle of the suite's sitting room.

"Dinner for two," she announced proudly. "Or at least late supper for two. I hope you're still hungry."

"As a matter of fact, I am, a little," Hal assured her. "I made sure I didn't eat too much supper. You mentioned that we might be having a late snack…"

"Good. I'm glad. I want us to have a lovely first evening together, and there is nothing that can start things off better than something good to eat."

She gazed up into his eyes, then came close against him.

Hal slid his arms around her, and her lips were on his, holding in a long soft kiss, during which her mouth was constantly in motion against his. Her tongue slipped between his lips, and their tongues mingled with one another.

Hal could feel her softness all the way down to his knees. The wrap she wore was smooth against his palms. He caressed her as if the material was an aid to exploration rather than any kind of hindrance separating them in any way.

When their lips parted, she smiled up at him. Her eyes were moist.

She stood in his arms a long moment, then kissed him once more, softly, quickly, afterward murmuring: "All right. Now, let's have our first supper together."

CHAPTER TWENTY TWO

Earl Gordon looked up and grinned.

"Mr. Graham," he said.

The older man smiled down at him.

"What brings you to Atlantic City, Gordon?"

"Same kaffee-klatch as you. That was a good speech you gave tonight."

Earl waved to the empty barstool beside him.

"Sit. I'll buy you a drink."

Graham glanced around the bar.

"Why don't we sit at a table over there," he suggested. "We can watch the poor gamblers down in the big room."

"A depressing sight," Gordon said. But he picked up his drink and rose. "However, it that's what entertains you…"

Graham ordered a drink from the bartender and pointed across the room before following Gordon over there. They sat by the plate-glass wall overlooking the field-wide casino's main room, beginning to fill up with players, even this late in the evening.

"You're with the DOI now, aren't you?" Graham asked.

Gordon nodded.

"Why'd you leave the Company, Earl?" the older man asked, watching him curiously.

For a moment, Gordon hesitated, then said: "It's gotten too big."

Graham grunted.

"Can't argue with you there," he admitted.

"Mine eyes done seed de truff of thoings," Gordon chanted. "Hamilton won after all."

"Hamilton?" Graham eyed him with amusement. "When did our conversation acquire a Hamilton?"

"Alexander Hamilton," Gordon explained. "Burr may have killed him in that duel, but old Ham-baby won the war."

"Which war was that, Earl?"

"De war ob de rich and big bidness agin de rest ob us folks."

"Ah, that war! Well, the rich and big business usually do win, all through history."

"But not so adroitly, so masterfully!" Gordon pointed out. "They got it both ways. They not only fobbed off that Constitution of theirs to make it look as if this was a Republic instead of what it really is, an Oligarchy, but all that detail has fooled everyone for over two hundred years, now."

"Fooled everyone but you, of course," Graham observed dryly.

"Right," Gordon agreed, nodding ponderously. "And it didn't fool me only because I've had one or two more of these than I probably should have." He held up his drink. "Lucky I'm doing all this babbling into ears as discreet as yours."

"I've always been known as someone any man can trust with his innermost secrets," Graham said sincerely. Then, into the sleeve of his dinner jacket, he murmured: "Are you getting all this, Soundtrack?"

Gordon laughed.

The bartender brought Graham his drink. He signed for it and took a sip, observing the younger man before saying: "You sound as if you've just made an original discovery, Earl. It's always been right out in the open, who really runs things. What do you think campaign contributions mean except bought Congressmen and Senators? Why the sudden shock?"

"I am begging to difference with you, mein freud-liar," Earl intoned, meticulously mouthing each word. "It took half a lifetime before it became obvious to me who owns and operates that racket of a government of ours. And I'm a fast learner. The average guy out there hasn't got a prayer of ever finding it out."

"On the contrary," Graham disagreed. "Perhaps you really are only one more of the simple folk at heart, just another of those ordinary people down there." He gestured through the plate-glass at the people gambling in the vast room below the bar they were in. "They are the ones who need to believe in all that detailed instruction about voting and who does this job and who that, and who succeeds whom. They've got to believe all of it makes sense and everything is nice and safe for them. The Constitution and all those laws you deride so cavalierly have provided that comfort for them."

After thinking about that for a moment, Gordon nodded judiciously.

"Could well be," he admitted. Then he brightened. "Do you know that the only two political statements made in this country in the entire last century having any real meaning were made by former Governor George Wallace of Alabama, and David Rockefeller?"

"Strange companions in politics, wouldn't you say?" Graham murmured dubiously.

"Wallace was speaking about the Democrat and Republican Parties," Gordon elaborated. "He said there isn't a dime's worth of difference between the two of them."

He stared owlishly into the older man's face, searching for his reaction.

"In other words," he went on, trying to clarify, "all that crap about elections only means we're either voting for tweedle-dee or tweedle-dum."

Earl nodded profoundly several times.

"And what did the estimable Mr. Rockefeller say?" Graham asked.

Earl had to think a minute before he could come up with that answer.

"Oh, yeah. He's supposed to have been remonstrating with his brother Nelson, asking why he kept running for all these political offices, adding: 'We've already got the real power. Why bother with the window-dressing and grandstanding, like Governorships, or even the Presidency?'"

Gordon peered craftily into Graham's face, his own wearing a cunning expression.

"Kinda makes you think, don't it? Out of the mouths of babes, right?"

"Those two make an even stranger pair of babes than they would have made companions in politics," Graham observed dryly. Rising, he asked: "Do you have a room here in the hotel, Earl?"

"Of course," Gordon said, fumbling in his pocket and bringing forth a room key.

"I'll see you to your room, if I may?"

Gordon laughed.

"Think I'm snockered, do you?"

"It's not that," Graham assured him, as they started out. "But I believe Pat Buchanan and Rush Limbaugh attended some of the sessions here today. I wouldn't want to pick up tomorrow's Washington Post and find myself reading about a man found nailed to the wall of an Atlantic City casino with a crown of thorns wrapped around his whizzer."

Gordon burst out laughing.

At the door of the bar, he took Graham's coat sleeve between two fingers, raised it and peered into it.

"Just checking." He shrugged. "No mike in that sleeve."

"A man can't be too careful," Graham said with approval.

CHAPTER TWENTY THREE

The meal was perfect, and all through it, Tansy was a delight.

Hal wished it could have gone on longer, but when she rose and led him by the hand from the suite into his room, she sat him down on the edge of the bed, returned to the connecting door to make sure it was locked, checked the corridor door again, too, and returned to stand in front of him.

"Just making sure no one comes walking in on us," she smiled.

She opened the robe. It fell around her feet with a soft rustling sound.

Her breasts were soft on his lips, the way he remembered them from the other time, in the little apartment they had gone to…but this time they felt even sweeter on his mouth.

It was almost dawn when Tansy aroused him from sleep, whispering in his ear: "Time for me to go."

Nodding, Hal stumbled out of bed, groping for his clothes.

"Don't bother dressing, silly," she giggled. "I'm just two rooms away from here. You can go back to sleep."

"Okay," he said docilely, sliding under the covers again.

She kissed him, murmured, "Have a safe trip home," and then she was gone.

He heard the connecting door close softly behind her, its lock clicking almost inaudibly when she turned the key.

Hal shook his head. He was beginning to realize that knowing Tansy Burns was going to be a lot more complicated than any simple wham-bam-thank-you-ma'am kind of deal. Apparently it was going to be one long endless courtship.

Settling under the covers and starting to doze off, he was right about it. Women knew best in these matters,]. He would just relax and roll with it.

As he drifted off into sleep, he hoped he remembered to get his stuff from the other room before he caught the bus back to New York.

In her room, beyond the sitting room separating their rooms, Tansy was on the phone early to the Nanny in Arlington, making certain the kids were all right. When she was sure they were, she told Nanny not to waken her husband.

She replaced the receiver.

There was no need to talk to Paul. He knew and approved of what she was doing, but there was no need to push it. Life played its little tricks on people, and all one could do was deal with them.

CHAPTER TWENTY FOUR

"What?" Reynolds asked.

Adams was still deep in thought when he looked across the office at his partner. He shrugged.

"I was wondering… Why'd he go into that church?"

"The actor? Lasalle?" Reynolds shrugged. "Maybe he had a premonition or something."

"Or an appointment. Those phone calls we got on tape, the ones he got from the other guy. Fifteen. And the earlier one: that business about changing an appointment to three, and Lasalle thought it was ten. Sounded like a code."

After thinking about it, Reynolds nodded.

"Could be. The ten might have been a time element. They said in the report that Lasalle reached a specific phone near where he lived, but he didn't use it right away. When he did, it was about ten minutes after he took the coded call in his apartment."

Adams nodded.

"And that particular phone might've been the one he and the other guy agreed in advance was phone number three."

"So…maybe the number fifteen meant to meet in the church, is that what you're thinking?"

"The thought occurred to me."

Reynolds sighed.

"Meaning we should have sent someone into the church after him."

"Yeah." Adams watched him. "Still, nobody can make all the right choices all the time."

"I was concentrating so hard on staying with the program," Reynolds said plaintively. "Top priority was to not lose contact with Lasalle. I wasn't even thinking about the other guy, the one we first spoke with on the phone."

"Anyway, if the actor did meet the real Dispatcher in the church, and he turned over that envelope with the ten grand to Lasalle, it shows how careful he is: no prints on any of the bills, or on the envelope. Except for Lasalle's, of course."

"Yes," Reynolds agreed. "Whoever he is, the bastard's careful. No feedback yet from the voice prints?"

"They don't come up with any record on either of them, not Lasalle, and not the other guy, either."

Reynolds looked unhappy.

"Too bad," he grunted.

"Have you come to a decision on how we should deal with the real Dispatcher?"

Reynolds swung his chair around and gazed out the window that had Watkins Construction Company on it in reverse, in gold paint. Presently, a smile stretched his face.

"Why don't we act as if nothing at all happened?"

He turned and watched Adams's reaction.

"Hell," he went on, "we paid him to do a job for us. We fixed up those phony papers for him, driver's license, passport, the rest of the stuff. Now all we have to do is get in touch with him and give him an assignment. When he shows up to carry it out, we grab him. That way we've got us a professional hitter we can use or put away any time we want to."

"If he shows up," Adams pointed out.

"Okay," Reynolds conceded. "*If* he shows up, we nab him. And if he won't get taken easily…" he grinned significantly. "Hey, all we can do is try, right?"

Adams chuckled.

"I reckon."

CHAPTER TWENTY FIVE

From the evening of the two killings on the streets of New York, Roper had taped every TV newscast that ran footage on them. He also bought and scoured every newspaper that covered either story, or both.

Again and again, he studied the TV footage and took notes from the print stories, paying particular attention to the shooting of the congressman's aide, Roger Brent.

Regrettably, there was only one video record of that hit, and as luck would have it, the local station's cameraman had been focused on Melford when the two shots rang out, not on the shooter. That would have been asking too much of any cameraman, that kind of luck.

He had swung around and caught the swift departure of the bicyclist, and of the passerby grabbing for him as he raced by, only succeeding in snatching away the cap he wore, revealing the wavy blond hair for a moment, before the shooter whipped around the nearby corner on his wheels and was gone out of range of the news camera.

But that single video sequence was enough for Roper. It clinched things for him, as he ran the copy he had pieced together from snippets he'd gotten from this newscast and that.

He listened more than watched, as Melford bent forward to hear whatever the short newsman had been asking him. In the background, a look of shock appeared on his aide's face when the shots were fired. The aide fell instantly, looking as if he had been pushed straight down toward the sidewalk by a giant invisible hand.

"Twice," Roper murmured, satisfied with his final examination. "A complete surprise, his target bends over, yet he squeezes off two shots. And the wrong target goes down."

Except it might not have been the wrong target!

Nodding, Roper switched the set off and filed the various copies he had made of the newspaper stories, grinning once or twice as he read some of them: "…'unmistakable signs of a professional assassination'…"

Poring over another paper, he read some of the excerpts in that one aloud: "'No doubt in the minds of veteran police officers handling the case…the work of a seasoned pro…'"

Roper shook his head, dismissing the newspaper stories, but storing them carefully.

"All the signs!" he muttered. "Some seasoned pro."

Standing to one side of the picture window, he stared off at the distant panorama of New York's skyscrapers across the river.

"When his target suddenly ducks down, the seasoned pro fires twice into the wrong target. Twice!"

He shook his head again, decisively.

"All right," he muttered, turning away from the window. "Time to get to work. Let us now appraise famous men."

CHAPTER TWENTY SIX

Hal was surprised at how relaxed it felt to be home from the weekend with Tansy Burns in Atlantic City, or the couple of days, anyway.

His years of living a life of humdrum sameness every day had become habit, and any disruption of the routine dullness, such as a day away, anywhere, tended to throw him off a bit. It usually took him several days to settle back into his schedule again.

The nightly talk shows were the same as ever.

Maggie Moore was telling about the movie she was so excited to be working on in London…in a taped segment on Entertainment Tonight.

Flora Rhine took a turn along Route Sixty Six with Kyra Weller, in Lifestyles, extolling the thrill of seeing varying cultures along the famous historic highway.

Dany Hunt had a segment about her childhood, on Inside Edition.

On one of the Late Night talk shows, Laura Gillian discussed the subtleties of degrees of infidelity. The host was most sympathetic. No detectable conclusions were drawn on the subject, however.

On one of the other, even later, Late Night shows, THE HOSTESS, Phyllis Omega got off a cute little zinger to open the show, something about forty five minutes for her husband to deal with a screw in a mundane household task. Obviously a man not great around the house with tools.

It turned out to be a two-beer night for Hal, and on the whole, a most enjoyable time was spent before his several black-and-white TV sets.

Hal couldn't spot any of the gals sending signals of any kind.

When the last latest talk show finally concluded and it was time to shut the remaining set off and turn in, Hal washed his empty beer glass.

On the whole, a relaxing, entertaining evening. It was good to be back at the old information-stand. It might not be much of an information-highway compared with ones other people could afford, but it was the only one he had.

However, as he lay in bed trying to sleep, he kept remembering the recap stories about the killing of the actor he had delivered a script to.

Hal could swear he had made that drop at just around the time Jeff Lasalle was supposed to have been off assassinating some political wheeler-dealer across town, in front of an Upper East Side hotel.

Rolling over on his side, he decided to rummage around in the basement tomorrow morning for some leftover newspapers from Thursday and Friday. That was the only way he could get the story straight. You could never get detail about news stories on TV news shows. With them, everything had to be bright and quick and to the point, then on to the next story, to the next olds, which most of their stuff was. All they did was eternally recap previously told stories, and then tell the viewer/listener there was nothing new on it, but maybe tomorrow there would be…

As Hal turned over yet again, he murmured sleepily: "They should call it the five o'clock olds, or the eleven o'clock olds, not the five o'clock news. Nothing is news under the sun…"

Chuckling at that last, he finally began to doze off.

CHAPTER TWENTY SEVEN

Laurie Buchan leaned into the doorway of Earl Gordon's office. "Better not let Farris catch you daydreaming like that," she cautioned.

Earl swung his gaze away from the façade of the building across the street from the Department of Information's offices.

"Just recovering from an overdose of 'Sorry, but that's classified.'"

She leaned against the doorframe, nodding in sympathy.

"I believe I've heard that myself, once or twice. What does he have you working on?"

"Just collating data on that shooting last week…up in New York."

"Which shooting in New York?" she grinned. "There are so many…"

Earl grinned dutifully.

"The Congressman's aide."

Laurie nodded.

"Oh, yes, Roger Brent. Why would that arouse the Classified routine?"

Helplessly, he spread his hands.

"You know the Feebles. When in doubt, color it Classified."

Her eyes were thoughtful.

"I haven't been assigned to that case," she said, "but just as a TV news buff, I recall thinking something, the evening it happened…"

She stopped.

"Thinking what?" Earl prompted.

"Just a thought that crossed my mind," she went on. "I wondered about the Feds doing such quick work, for them, tracking down the actor who did the shooting…"

"Yes," he agreed. "Usually when it comes to street-smarts, FBI guys have a tough time finding the J. Edgar Hoover Building without guide dogs." He tapped the thick file open on the desk in front of him. "Their involvement seems tenuous, though…at least from the time-frame I get from the material. Their people don't show up until after the shooter was found and got himself wasted, there on the Forty Second street sidewalk…

Laurie was listening intently, but she suddenly checked her watch and jumped almost a foot backward.

"Earl, I'm due in Farris's office a minute ago, but if you like, I'll take a look through that file, when you've finished with it. Jot down the things that bother you, okay?"

"Sure. But that's an awful lot of extra work for you, Laurie."

She grinned, turned and disappeared, calling: "You've whetted my curiosity."

Grinning, Earl again dug into the mass of material he had worked up on the two shootings. He was thinking that it had been a long time since he was interested enough in anything here at DOI to want to ask for an extra helping of it to get dumped in his lap, the way Laurie was doing.

She must be newer here in Washington than he'd realized.

"She'll get over it," he thought, amused.

Once again, he wondered how much he had shot off his mouth to Graham the other night, asking himself once again when he was going to learn to keep his big mouth shut.

Earl was still glad he had eased out of the Company and gotten a slot over here at the Department of Information. At least here you tried to find things out, not just try to keep anyone else from finding out about you.

CHAPTER TWENTY EIGHT

Roper tried to get Marge to put a phone tap in Congressman Melford's Georgetown home, but she wouldn't.

When he asked, she told him: "Mr. Dickson, there are a few things I really can't do. And I think that's one of them."

"All right, Marge," he soothed her. "I should never have asked you."

"No hard feelings, but…you know. I do have a license to protect."

"Not at all, Marge. I'll have another little task for you in a few days, the kind you can do."

She laughed.

"Okay, Mr. Dickson."

Roper thought about trying to find a specialist in the DC area, decided not to, then gave some thought to sending in someone he had used before to do the necessary chore.

He finally decided to do it himself.

He picked up Marge's report, which contained, among other things, the home addresses and phone numbers of those two Watkins Construction specimens, Reynolds and Adams. One lived southeast of the capitol, the other northwest, almost as far as Wheaton, Maryland.

Then he remembered something and called Marge back.

"Forgot one thing," he said. "Find out where the other people live who go in and out of Watkins Construction. Just names, addresses, home phone numbers. Oh, and keep a log on each of those associates. I want to know which of them is most tight with Reynolds and Adams, if any are."

"Got it. How long should the log run?" Marge asked.

"Make it two weeks. Then we'll see."

"I'll get right on it, Mr. Dickson."

CHAPTER TWENTY NINE

"You're sure it's all right?" Hal asked nervously, glancing around the hotel café at the other breakfasters.

"Am I sure what's all right?" Tansy asked.

"Us being seen together like this," he explained. "In public, I mean."

Smiling, she reached across the table and squeezed his hand reassuringly.

"Don't worry, Hal. I'm getting my crew accustomed to seeing you. And the other people we run into. I've been needing a personal assistant for some time, now, and I've finally found one. That's all. No big deal."

"Okay, Tansy. Should I come to this funeral service with you?"

Finishing her coffee, she shook her head.

"No need. You don't even have to go out to the cemetery. We'll ease into this personal assistant thing slowly. Give people time to get used to it."

Putting down the empty coffee cup, she rose.

"Gotta go, Hal. Take care of the bill, will you?" She started to turn away, then turned back, delving into her enormous tote bag.

"Here," he said, sliding a plastic credit card across to him. "That's the credit card I keep forgetting to give you."

Then she was gone.

*　*　*

After the ceremony, in the cemetery outside Tucson, Tansy maneuvered as best she could beside the grave, but each time she was about to ease alongside Norma Melford for a few words, yet another mourner would engage the Congressman's wife in conversation, and Tansy would have to draw back and give them privacy.

But when one man remained with Mrs. Melford longer than Tansy thought he should have, she signalled Jerry to lower his mike pole. She wanted to find out what was so important for the anxious-looking man to take this long with his commiserations.

In her earpiece, she managed to catch snatches of their talk.

"...send you a list of the inventory of Mr. Brent's personal possessions...if any of it looks business-related...of course, I'll keep in touch with you, no question."

"I appreciate that, Mr. Merritt," Norma Melford murmured.

"Probate should be in a week or two..."

"How long have you and Mr. Brent been friends?" she asked idly.

A curious expression on Merritt's face accompanied his next words: "Actually, I only saw Roger Brent once," he said, "and that was over twenty years ago, just before he went off to college..."

*　*　*

In downtown Tucson's Municipal building, the young man was telling the clerk: "Human interest material. Hometown boy, that sort of thing. His funeral's today."

"Is that a fact?" the clerk asked, typing data into her computer.

"I understand he's originally from around here..."

"Yes, here's a Roger Brent. There isn't very much on him, I'm afraid."

"All I need is date of birth, where he grew up. I thought a little detail couldn't hurt the obit they'll write at the paper…"

He copied the birth date she gave him, then had to ask: "What was the name of that town again?"

The woman smiled.

"Gold Run. It isn't really a town."

Jotting that in his notebook, he asked: "Where's Gold Run, outside Tucson? A suburb?"

She laughed.

"Lord no. It's just a… I don't know, maybe only a signpost. Gold Run was one of those boomtowns, except as near as I can recollect, its boom ended almost as soon as it started."

He looked puzzled.

"The vein ran out," she explained. "They barely got the usual tents set up for the first saloons and gambling hells than the mining engineers found there wasn't any deeper vein. That was farther south. So they all packed up and headed there. That's why Tombstone got all the notoriety instead of Gold Run."

"But…if Gold Run doesn't exist, how could Roger Brent have it listed on his birth certificate?"

"Oh, thirty or forty years ago, I guess a few families still lived there, but now I'm not even sure they still put it on road maps."

She watched as he put away his notebook and turned to leave.

"Sorry I couldn't be more help."

"No, no," he called over his shoulder. "You've done fine, ma'am."

At the nearest payphone, he made a long distance call.

"Marge? Not much on Roger Brent here in Tucson. All I could get was date and place of birth. – Okay, I'll check school records next."

*　*　*

Later, back in the hotel after supper, in bed with Hal in his room adjoining hers, Tansy murmured: "I'm not sure which of us was more surprised, Mrs. Melford or me."

"Why surprised?" Hal asked, more to be saying something than for any other reason.

"Well, you'd think that if a man is your attorney for most of your adult life, you'd have a little more in the way of contact than just the one visit, back when you were a teenager."

They made love once more, and then it was time for her to leave for the local affiliate station.

"Meet you on the plane," she told him, when she was dressed and ready to slip back into her own room.

"You're not coming back here first?"

Hal was dressing hurriedly, although he had no idea why he was hurrying.

"No need," she said, standing beside him and running her fingers through his hair. "Just take along that one big bag I'll leave by the door in my room, and the tickets…you've got the tickets, haven't you?"

He nodded, pointing to the envelopes on the bedside table.

"Good. Then just meet me at the departure gate between eight-thirty and nine. That gives you…an hour and a half."

She peered down at him while he laced his shoes. When he straightened, she put her arms around him, grinned, and kissed him.

"Getting used to this? Being my personal assistant, I mean?"

Hal grinned and nodded.

"Getting there."

"Okay, see you at the airport."

CHAPTER THIRTY

"Altogether," Reynolds said into the payphone, "I don't think we came out of it too bad, money-wise."

At the other end of the line, Blanchard said: "How do you figure that, Mike? We hand over fifty thousand dollars in two packages to this Dispatcher, but I don't see any of it coming back to the Company. Mr. Watch-That-Bottom-Line Graham doesn't like that kind of numbers crunching."

"I know it doesn't look great on the surface," Reynolds admitted. "I thought that Lasalle bastard would stash the twenty five G we handed him, either in his bank account or in that safe deposit box he had there. Instead, he turns around and wires fifteen of it offshore, to the same account number we wired the initial twenty five thousand to."

"That leaves us only ten thousand," Blanchard said coldly.

"Let me finish, Chief," protested Reynolds. "Lasalle had twenty thousand in his account, and ten thousand in cash on him when he died. I guess he had to keep the twenty thou in the account so it would be enough to cover amounts he wired offshore, like the fifteen G he sent last week. He kept a thousand for himself and put the remaining nine thousand into his safe deposit box…"

"All that still leaves us sucking air like guppies," Blanchard interrupted. "Those local cops up in New York will impound the safety deposit box's nine thousand for months. And as for the twenty G in the account, no telling how long it will take us to get our hands on that."

"But it comes to a total of thirty nine thousand dollars," Reynolds pointed out. "That includes the ten thousand in cash he was carrying. Granted, it isn't the full fifty thousand we laid out, but hell, Chief, cost of doing business…"

Reluctantly, Blanchard had to agree.

"Yeah, you're right, Mike," he admitted. "It could be worse. Now let's see how long it takes us to establish prior claim to that thirty nine thousand."

"The legal sharpsters can't ask for a more valid claim than a sting operation to apprehend a potential assassin," Reynolds pointed out. "We couldn't prevent the hit, but we at least nailed the hitter a couple of hours later. We could've come out of this whole thing a lot worse, Chief."

He could hear Blanchard chuckle at the other end of the line.

"I suppose you're right, Mike. Send me a breakdown of your figures. I'll get our people busy filing claims for that money before the NYPD's evidence office manages to make it all disappear."

Relieved, Reynolds laughed.

"Now, Chief," he protested unctuously, "is that any way to talk about New York's Finest?"

That got a chuckle out of Blanchard, too.

Hanging up, Reynolds felt as if a load had fallen off his back. Even though Blanchard had ended the conversation by repeating his request to have the numbers on his desk by five o'clock the next evening, Reynolds was glad to have gotten through the session in reasonably good shape.

CHAPTER THIRTY ONE

Norma Melford never had a shortage of things to talk about, whenever she called her daughter Jessy at Radcliffe. She was in the middle of describing her most recent encounter with the redoubtable Senator Thaddeus G. Westbrook.

"He gave me his usual fatherly hug, but also, as usual, that baseball glove-sized hand of his went sliding down my back just the teeniest bit lower than it ought to have done…"

They were both giggling, and then there was a scratching sound in Norma's ear. The line went dead.

"Hello?…Hello, Jessy?"

Norma, listened, impatiently put the phone back in its cradle, and got her cell phone out to call her daughter's sorority house.

"Jess?… Glad you waited. – No, it was at this end. The line just squawked and went dead. Where were we? Oh, yes, Thaddeus of the wandering hand…"

Later, she sat up waiting for Tim to get home. She didn't think about the phone problem until she heard him coming in the front door, downstairs. Then she picked up the phone, heard a reassuring dial tone, and nodded, returning it and going down to see if her husband had eaten anything for supper.

CHAPTER THIRTY TWO

When Hal Walker got back from making a drop, the dispatcher took the signed ticket from him, checked it, and then pointed toward a corner of the little office.

"Guy to see you."

Hal glanced over. A man in a rumpled suit stood and approached him.

"Mr. Walker? Like to ask you a few questions."

Hal blinked. *What did I do?*

"Okay," he said quietly. "How can I help you?"

"Not here. Let's get coffee across the street, there."

In a booth inside the coffee shop, Hal waited, watching the man nervously.

Sliding a picture across the table between their two cups of coffee, the man asked: "Recognize this man?"

It was the actor, wavy-blond hair, good-looking face, nice smile.

I knew it, Hal thought. *There's been a screw-up.*

"Yes. He's the one who got shot a couple of hours after I delivered a script to him last week."

The man sighed and nodded.

"You're positive that's the man you delivered the script to?"

He's a detective, Hal realized. They're following up on it. Took them long enough to catch on they shot the wrong dude.

"That's him."

The detective slid another page across to him. In its center was a copy of the time sheet for the delivery.

"And you're sure that's the time you made the delivery?"

"Positive."

Oddly, the man seemed depressed rather than glad at Hal's information. After thinking a moment, he asked another question: "Is the time here in your handwriting?"

"No. I had this Mr. Lasalle write the time down on the ticket."

The detective's eyes widened. He sat straighter.

"You didn't write the time in yourself? Is that usual?"

Uncertainly, Hal said: "Well-l-l, no. I don't have a watch, so I had to ask the drop to write the time down himself. See, he wouldn't take the chain off his door…"

Suddenly, the detective smiled broadly. Retrieving the photos, he asked almost absently: "Do you always have the drop write in the time of delivery, Hal?"

"Not usually," he replied, feeling a little stupid, for some reason. "Just since I lost my watch. I've been trying to find another ninety-nine cent one…"

It sounded so dumb, when he said it out loud, so by way of explanation, he added: "I keep losing expensive ones."

The detective slid out of the booth and stood there, looking down at Hal benevolently.

"But ordinarily you'd be the one to write in the time of delivery, right, Hal?"

"Yeah, sure."

"How about today? Are you writing down the time yourself again?"

Hal hesitated, wondering why he felt irritated at the tone of the question.

"No. I still haven't gotten another watch. I'll get one today, though, on the way home…even if I have to get an expensive ten dollar one."

"All right, Mr. Walker. I just wanted to check with you on a couple of things. Just routine. Everyone who had any contact with Mr. Lasalle around the time of his alleged…activities…later that day. You understand."

"Oh, sure. Glad I could help."

"Don't talk about this to anyone else, all right?"

He patted Hal's shoulder.

"Stay and finish your coffee, Hal. No need for both of us to leave a full cup of coffee."

"I better not," Hal replied, nodding toward the front of the coffee shop at the messenger place across the street. "The dispatcher can see me."

Grinning, the detective called over his shoulder as he left: "Okay, Mr. Walker. Thanks for your cooperation."

Hal took one final sip of his still-scalding coffee, as he watched the plainclothesman go out to the sidewalk and turn out of sight. Then he left the place, too, crossed the street, and went back to work.

CHAPTER THIRTY THREE

Every so often, Tansy Burns developed a story she could work on at home. Sometimes the kids were home from school when she did, but usually she picked times when they were not.

Today, after she had gotten both of them off with Paul, and the housekeeper was busy cleaning up the breakfast mess, Tansy went into her former "den", locked the door behind her, entered the wall-wide walk-in closet, pushed aside the clothes hanging on the rack, and shut the sliding door behind her.

At the right hand end, inside the closet, she pushed against the hinged panel. It swung back, and she stepped into the unknown part of the closet, holding onto the iron handle on the hidden side, so the panel wouldn't bang loudly when it shut behind her.

The door-panel had two bolts on the inside, one at shoulder height and the other knee-high. She had never used either.

Using the same key she had used to lock the den door inside the big apartment, she unlocked the heavy wooden door which led into a duplicate unknown part of the twin wall-wide walk-in closet she'd had built on the other side of the separating wall, when she bought the adjoining apartment from the departing original owner of the thirteen-apartment building.

Pulling open the panel-door with its iron handle, she entered the second closet. No clothes hung on its rack, except for one old business suit and skirt she had hung there. Somewhere, Tansy had heard that all you needed to establish occupancy anywhere was to hang one coat or a suit, or even just a jacket, inside a closet in an apartment, a hotel or motel room, wherever.

Sliding open the door of the almost-empty second closet, she stepped into the adjoining apartment and closed the closet door behind her.

A feeling of peace settled upon her.

Taking her time, she set up her material in the computer alcove. She even took the added time to make herself a cup of tea in the well-stocked kitchenette, before settling down to her morning's work.

It hadn't started out to be any kind of "secret" hideaway apartment. When she and Paul had moved into the building, she hadn't even been aware that the elderly landlord-owner in the small adjoining apartment had built a private stairway leading down from his apartment into the only garage-space the building contained, in a sealed-off section of the basement, directly beneath his apartment. When she learned of it, the knowledge had been only mildly interesting. "Lucky guy!" she had thought. He didn't have to go out in all kinds of weather to reach his car, whenever he wanted to go for a drive anywhere.

However, after Tansy clicked at Amalgamated Cable News, and especially after she got the new contract around the time Mr. Hoskins decided he wanted a small place all his own, because this building was too much for him at his age, then the adjoining apartment became a thing of increasing interest to Tansy.

Even then, it took awhile. She would attempt to get some work done at home in the den, while the kids were home, but it was never long before one or both of them were scratching at the door, wanting to get in and see what Mommy was doing. Being a parent, Tansy dealt with it as best she could, until one day she found herself staring at the empty wall across the room, with the suddenly-on-the-market efficiency apartment on its other side.

Once the idea had time to lodge in her head and get past her solid sensible mind-set about things like buying apartments, the deal went swiftly, and then the adjoining flat was hers.

First, she had a hole broken through the common wall near the inner corner of her den, and a solid wooden door installed.

The little landing at the top of the carpeted stairs which led down to the single garage space was open, but in case her kids ever got into the other apartment, Tansy didn't want either of them taking a tumble down those stairs, even if it was a carpeted stairway. So she had the entire head of the stairwell walled in, with a door accessing the landing. The lock in this door took the same key she needed for the door leading from the hidden end of her den-closet into the identical hidden space in the closet on this side of the wall. She didn't want more than one key for all this artful dodging of hers. Bad enough she was indulging herself in the extra apartment, without making a pain in the neck out of it with three or four keys required for all the doors involved.

As for the two wall-to-wall-appearing closets on each side of the common wall, that idea came to her shortly after the door had been installed near the inner corner of the two rooms. She had waited until the kids were away for a few days before having both closets put in, hoping the workmen didn't think she was too strange, because of the two hidden sections beyond the hinged swinging end-doors giving access to the regular door connecting the two closets.

Oddly, the youngsters never made a thing of *where did the missing door go?* Both had been quite young at the time, so Tansy assumed that had been the reason for their lack of curiosity.

Anyway, now she had her secret workplace with two locked doors between her and the children, and only Paul had another copy of the key that opened all three doors, plus the lock to the regular front door of the small apartment, whose lock she had finally gotten around to changing so that it, too, matched the locks of both doors, top and bottom, of the garage stairway, as well as that of the hidden closet's door.

When all of it had finally been taken care of, she had to modernize the outside entrance door of the garage below. The old wooden swinging double doors had required her to get out of her car to unlock and open them. That would no longer do. Now it had to be an overhead door electronically opened and closed, one that swung up and down at the click of a remote. When that was taken care of, the work was finally complete.

Today, she put in a good morning's work. When at last she had her material organized the way she wanted it for that evening's broadcast, she wandered through the tiny apartment, checking the automatic on-and-off lighting system she'd recently had installed. An apartment which was always dark was a certain invitation to burglars even if it was curtained and venetian-blinded to a fare-thee-well.

Tansy ran a finger along a window-sill. No dust. Good. The cleaning woman who came in once week was doing a fine job. When she checked the fridge, she was satisfied. Well-enough-stocked, she thought. Everything but milk. That she had to bring in herself, whenever she came in here.

Smiling, she moaned aloud: "God, the hardships of life! I have to bring along my own milk!"

Time to get back next door and have a bite of lunch. She would phone Paul and see if he was going to try to get home for a midday snack.

It wasn't until she was about to re-enter the nearly-empty closet that Tansy was suddenly struck with the thought: Why, this would be a perfect place for Hal to stay for a few days, every now and then.

She stood thinking about it, then regretfully shook her head, smiling ruefully.

Possible, she thought, but not really wise. Too close to home.

Sighing, she entered the closet, pulling the sliding door shut behind her.

Too bad! It would be so sweet to have Hal right here, next door. Whenever she wanted to, she could slip in here and play with him. Just like in those hotels…

CHAPTER THIRTY FOUR

When Roper figured a sweep was about due in the Watkins office, he went in at night and removed the bugs and phone taps he'd installed. A few days later, he put them back in place.

He had no way of knowing if Reynolds and Adams had the place swept in the interval, but he stuck to a pattern in these things. Over time, the pattern's odds usually paid off. The extra work he put in was worth the effort.

After the reinstallation, the first tape he retrieved contained some interesting material.

Adams' voice chuckled: "This ought to cheer you up."

"What is it?" Reynolds asked.

"Copy of the Precinct report, up in New York. That guy…"

"What guy? Damn it, man, I'm up to here with it, lately. I don't need any guessing games…"

"The messenger who delivered a soap opera script to that actor at the same minute, damn near, that Tollman was attending to that little matter for us, across town."

Reynolds chuckled.

"I love your cautious phraseology. 'Attending to that little matter.' George, we just had this place checked for bugs and taps. Relax! Lemme see that report."

Listening to the tape of their conversation, Roper grinned. The odds had paid off for him once again.

"Oh, my gawd!" Reynolds crowed. "He had the actor write in the time of delivery on the ticket. Great! There's our out, if it ever comes to a close examination: Jeff Lasalle was setting up an additional little something to help establish an alibi for himself, in case *he* ever needed one."

"At least it's a step in the right direction for us," Adams admitted soberly. "Don't forget that video tape out in the corridor. The time of delivery on that confirms the time written on the messenger's ticket."

"No problem," Reynolds insisted. "This gives us exactly what we need: doubt. Give me one second of doubt to drive into an inquiry and you can take a week of every kind of evidence there is… including the times and dates recorded on that corridor video tape. How many times have we found those things weren't even adjusted for daylight savings time changes, just as one for instance?"

"True enough, but all this gives us is an edge," Adams cautioned.

"I'll settle for an edge anytime," Reynolds responded complacently. "You're right, though, George. This does cheer me up. I need something like that report every so often. Here, make copies of it for our files. One for our friend at the front office, too, of course."

There wasn't much more on the tape, but Roper was satisfied to hear the business about a messenger delivering a script to Jeff Lasalle exactly when…who did they say, Tollman?…exactly when Tollman was 'attending to the little matter across town.'

Roper sat there in the second office he had rented in the Watkins Construction Company building, not the one two floors below

Reynolds and Adams and their scheming. This office was a place for Roper to retreat to. The other one was where the bug and phone tap information was gathered. He tried never to spend more time there than it took to retrieve the recordings and replace them with fresh tapes.

Okay, now he knew about some messenger involved in the deal. What he needed was a copy of that Precinct report Adams had turned over to Reynolds.

Which way to get it? Have Marge find out what messenger service the guy worked for and bracket him that way? Or just ease once more into Watkins one fine night and browse in their files?

Decisions, decisions!

CHAPTER THIRTY FIVE

J ust about the time Roper in the capitol was finding out about the mysterious script delivery, Tansy Burns was hearing about it for the first time, too, up in New York.

She turned her head on the pillow and stared at Hal's profile, outlined against the drawn window-shade in his bedroom. Her mind was racing, trying to process all the ramifications and possibilities of what he had just told her.

Softly, she murmured: "Hal, why are you telling me this now? Why did you wait so long? It's been more than a week…"

He shrugged carelessly.

"It's no big deal, Tans. There are probably lots of follow-up witnesses to that sort of crime. Every doorman, every elevator operator, whoever installs the video tapes in the corridor cameras outside that actor's apartment…I forget his name. Jeff Something…."

"Lasalle," she said absently. "Yes, that corridor video camera, too." She squeezed his arm excitedly. "I'm glad you reminded me of that. Hal, tell me about it."

"About what? This plainclothes man was waiting there at the messenger place when I came back from a drop, and he and I went over and had coffee in the coffee shop across the street. And…he asked his questions. No big thing, Tansy."

"Wait!" Sliding from under the covers, she scampered naked across the room to where she had hung her laden tote bag on the bedroom doorknob. Back under the sheets beside him, she held the recorder out toward him. "Now…what kind of questions? But first, what was his name?"

"Lasalle. You just told me his name."

"No, I mean the detective. What was *his* name?"

"Oh." Hal stared at the ceiling. "You know, Tans, I don't believe he ever mentioned his name."

Dumbfounded, she stared at him.

Forcing herself to speak gently, she said: "Sweetheart, you answered all kinds of questions put to you by a man you never saw before, and you never even asked his name? Did he show you his shield? No? Ohmigod, I don't believe this!"

Shamefaced, Hal offered a mild protest.

"Tansy, I'm not an experienced newsie, like yourself. A guy says he has some questions to ask me about a delivery I made to an actor who was supposed to be killing someone fifteen or twenty blocks away across town at around the same time, I just answer. I don't give anyone a hard time. After all I've been put through for the last six or seven years, what with the working-over that detective agency of yours gave me with their street-peoples' bothering, there isn't an awful lot of feist left in my feistiness tank."

"All right, honey," she said gently, kissing his bare shoulder. "I'm sorry. Did he show you any I. D.?"

"Maybe he did," Hal said uncertainly. "I really can't remember, Tans. He must've shown some cop I. D. to the dispatcher at the messenger place…"

"All right," she said briskly, relieved. "I can check into that. Let's get on with what he asked you. Just go through it the way it happened."

She listened closely, interrupting him only once: "And what did he look like when you told him it was Lasalle's handwriting giving the time of the delivery on the ticket?"

Hal thought a moment, then looked at her, nodding.

"You know, he did change a little. He seemed kind of discouraged up till then, but when I told him I'd lost my watch and I had to ask drops to write in the times-of-delivery, right then he seemed to perk up a bit."

"You're sure of that?" she pressed. "You're not just trying to make the story more interesting for me...?"

He shook his head.

"No, no, honey. I remember distinctly. He sat up straighter in the booth, and he even smiled. A big wide happy smile. And when I told him that ordinarily I'd be the one who wrote on the ticket, the guy damn near creamed his jeans... Oh, sorry, hon. I didn't mean to use language like that..."

She giggled, reached down, and grabbed his genitals, squeezing gently. He flinched and laughed.

"Hal, I'm really not that shocked, when you say something like that, I'm all growed up, really I am."

He nodded, grinning at her.

"Okay. I still can't quite get used to how bawdy women can be, sometimes."

"Oh, so now I'm bawdy, am I?" She gazed around the room and through the open bedroom doorway into the other room in his small apartment. "Then this must be our little bawdy house." She squeezed some more. "Is that what you're saying?"

When they stopped laughing and settled down quietly once more, Tansy thought over what he had told her.

"So he seemed...would you call it relieved? When you told him Jeff Lasalle had written in the time-of-delivery on the ticket?"

Hal shrugged.

"I guess. He might've been relieved."

"Did he go on with it much longer? Did he ask you many more questions?"

"No. That seemed to be all he needed to know. He got up, thanked me for cooperating, told me to finish my coffee, and left."

Tansy nodded, her eyes far off, thinking. Almost to herself, she muttered: "It's sure not a red-hot item, not anymore, over a week later, nearly two weeks. Still…"

Coming to a decision, she settled against him once more.

"I'll leave it up to the redoubtable Walter Noble. Let him decide."

"Decide what?" Hal asked sleepily.

"Whether it's still newsworthy enough to interview you for my program about the exact time of that script delivery you made that day."

Hal frowned uneasily.

"He told me not to talk to anyone else about it."

Tansy laughed.

"They always say things like that."

CHAPTER THIRTY SIX

"It's Dispatcher," Adams called across the office, at the same time reaching for the recording device and switching it on. "Line two."

Reynolds waited until Adams had everything ready to tape the incoming call, then he punched the number two button on his phone.

"Reynolds here."

"Dispatcher."

"About time you got back to us," Reynolds growled, watching Adams leave to see how the crew in the outer office were making out, trying to trace the call. Reynolds checked the second hand on his wristwatch.

"Things came up," Roper told him. "Stuff I wasn't expecting…"

Reynolds smiled grimly, thinking of Lasalle getting himself whacked on his way into that bank on Forty second.

"Look, Dispatcher, you're into us for fifty grand and a good bit of preparation," Reynolds recited, watching the second hand reach and pass the thirty second point. "We sent that fake driver's license and passport back to your motel down in Maryland, and then you were supposed to call. Except we don't hear word one from you…"

"I'll call back in a few minutes," Dispatcher chuckled, hanging up.

"Damn!" Reynolds snarled. He waited, watching the open doorway until Adams appeared in it, shaking his head.

"The bastard hung up just when we thought we had him located," he said.

Reynolds nodded.

"He'll be calling back. Tell them to be ready. One of these times, maybe he'll slip and stay on the phone a few seconds longer. Get in touch with your connections at some of the State Highway Patrols in this area…"

Adams grinned as he turned and disappeared, his voice coming back faintly: "Which states? Delaware? Virginia? Pennsylvania?"

On the next call, Reynolds got right to the point.

"Look, Dispatcher, give me a number where I can reach you. Otherwise, we might just as well take care of this job ourselves…"

"No way," Roper told him. "But I will call more often. That I can do. A week ago, I had to farm part of the pickup work to someone else. Then he had an accident. I had to do some checking…to make sure you didn't have anything to do with his accident."

Reynolds grinned.

"Did I?"

"Near as I can tell, the local cops where my contact lived got onto him for something. They also got the passport and driver's license you sent him."

"Forget about all that. The old job is cancelled. The one we might need you for is domestic. No passport needed. Maybe a driver's license."

"I'll call back," the voice said.

Click.

"Goddamn!" Reynolds shouted. "I could get to really hate that sound."

Adams appeared in the doorway, grinning, shaking his head no once again.

"I was listening in," he said. "What's this about a domestic job for that bastard? I haven't heard of any…"

Reynolds shrugged.

"Just trying to keep him on our string. Who knows? We may really need the guy…for loose ends. I sure would like to get some mileage out of our Dispatcher for that thirty thousand bucks he cleared from this deal."

"You mean use him instead of Tollman?"

Reynolds hesitated, then nodded.

"Yes. Tollman's getting antsy about being the shooter of choice lately, whenever there's a hit to be done."

"Can't blame the guy," Adams admitted. "He's worried that he might turn into a psycho, like he might get to like killing people." Adams shrugged. "I guess it could happen."

"I know, I know," Reynolds agreed impatiently. "But Tollmans' so good at these jobs. He knows just how to bring them off, and how to disappear afterward."

Rising, he paced the floor for a moment.

"Okay, at least we got Dispatcher back on the job. Sort of."

"You believe him?" Adams asked. "That business about checking to see if we might have had something to do with what happened to Lasalle? Who else but us could've…?"

"What's the difference whether I believe him or not?" Reynolds asked. "All we need is for Dispatcher to be available in case we need him. We also get ourselves additional time to maybe get a line on him. I always prefer it when I can put my hands on people like him who have to work for us."

"Maybe is right," Adams chuckled. Then, frowning, he thought a moment before asking: "Why do you suppose he got in touch with us again? I'm assuming he doesn't really trust us."

"For the rest of the money," Reynolds replied. "What else? A hundred thousand more bucks, that's why. That's the fucker's business, isn't it? That's how he makes his dough."

"Okay," Adams said agreeably. "Could be. I suppose not trusting the people he works for, like us, is part of the day's gig, for someone like him."

"And don't forget this," Reynolds added. "He hasn't done all that well, money-wise. He got the twenty five G we wired him offshore at the beginning. The actor kept ten thousand dollars of the twenty five thousand cash we paid him in Maryland. That left fifteen of that, plus the twenty five thousand we wired offshore. Total to Dispatcher, forty grand. Then he hands ten thousand to the actor in the church, so then he's down in the thirty grand area. Dispatcher's got some recouping to do."

"Sounds right," Adams admitted. "Unless Lasalle always carried a spare ten thousand dollars around with him."

Reynolds glared at him in disgust, causing Adams to grin.

Then Reynolds frowned.

"Why would Dispatcher hand over ten G to his helper, though? That's what I can't figure out." After a moment, he glanced at Adams. "Getaway money?"

Adams nodded.

"More than likely. Which would mean Dispatcher knew something was going down, and he was handing the actor powder money." But then Adams shook his head, adding plaintively: "But how could the son of a bitch know what we were up to? Or even suspect?"

Reynolds spread his hands.

"Perhaps with someone like him, maybe he goes by instinct. Maybe something bothered him, and he got the wind up, gave the ten G to his front man so Lasalle would stay away from the bank where he'd stashed part of the dough we handed him in the Chesapeake Motel. Except the damn fool didn't stay away."

"Okay," Adams sighed. "We'll just have to play Dispatcher by ear, and hope we can get our hooks into him, one of these days."

"We will," Reynolds said grimly. "And I can't wait for the day."

CHAPTER THIRTY SEVEN

"Yes, Roger Brent," the young woman told the records statistician. "I believe he's in his mid-forties…"

"Was," the clerk reminder her primly. "Call that twenty five years ago. Yes, here he is…"

"I've been doing studies in government," the visitor said, leaning on the edge of the counter, watching the records clerk's fingers fly over the computer's bank of keys. "Roger Brent seemed perfect as an example of the ones whose careers are cut off prematurely, or who burn out."

"His was certainly cut off prematurely," the clerk observed, never taking her eyes off the monitor screen in front of her. "What a shame, getting shot like that, in broad daylight…"

"And by mistake, too."

"Congressman Melford is a lucky man. All right, what do you want to know?"

"The article I'm working on is…well, I'm trying for something a bit deeper than mere statistics. What was Mr. Brent like? His potential, the way he studied when he was attending classes here at Margarita College. I don't just mean how high his marks were…"

"Yes, I understand. All right, that would be evaluation," the clerk said, her fingers rapidly tattooing the keyboard again, then swinging the screen around so the visitor could read what was on it. "This is page one of three. When you're ready for the next page, just hit the Enter key."

"Thanks you."

"I'll be right over here, in case you need help."

Outside, later, the nearest available pay phone was located in a lunch counter. Undergraduates were beginning to drift in for their midday meals.

When the other end picked up, the young woman identified herself, and then said, "Marge, I'm here at Margarita College. – Yes, they had a good deal of that kind of information on the subject. – Okay, I'll transcribe my notes and fax you a copy of everything I got this morning…"

* * *

Around the time Marge was receiving the fax from the stringer out in the Midwest college town, Roper was listening to the tape he had retrieved from Watkins Construction containing the conversation Reynolds and Adams had, after Roper had hung up, the last time he had called. There were several items of interest to him, in addition to following their efforts to figure out his, Roper's, motives for getting in touch with them once more.

One fresh item was the name Tollman showing up again. That was the one who had done the Roger Brent job. Apparently this Tollman was beginning to spook at being the one in the barrel, whenever a hit was going down.

The other item of interest was from an earlier tape, in which Reynolds had told Adams to make copies of a report, including an additional one for their friend at the front office. So who was this friend, and where was their front office?

Roper was getting bits and pieces of information from all his bugs and phone taps, both there at Watkins Construction and at both men's homes, but while it was beginning to form a picture for him, he wished he could get more of it faster.

After codifying and filing copies and originals of the various tapes, Roper buckled down, trying to figure out if easing into the Watkins office was the best way of getting the name of the messenger, over in New York, the one whose testimony could really gum up the official version of Lasalle's murder. He had just about decided that was the only practical way, short of praying for the name to drop into his lap, when his attention was caught in the middle of the Tansy Burns evening programs.

"The New York police are reported to have interviewed Harold Walker, an employee of the GlobeSpan messenger Service. It seems Mr. Walker delivered a soap opera script to actor Jeffrey Lasalle at almost precisely the same minute that Mr. Lasalle was alleged to have attempted to assassinate Congressman Timothy Melford in front of an Upper East Side hotel. The attempt took place across town from where Mr. Lasalle lived on West Forty Second Street, between Ninth and Tenth Avenues. Since it would have been physically impossible for Mr. Lasalle to have been in two places at approximately the same time, both receiving and signing for a package delivered at his apartment, and mistakenly shooting the Congressman's aide, Roger Brent, a mile away to the northeast, the police have very good reasons for digging deeper into the confusing affair. A weapon was found under the body of Mr. Lasalle, after he refused to keep his hands in the air, when Federal agents were attempting to arrest him. They were forced to shoot him, there on the sidewalk. Ballistics tests have since proved that the murder weapon Mr. Lasalle carried was the one which caused the death of Roger Brent. All this simply compounds the confusion. A police spokesperson at New York's Nineteenth Precinct could not comment when we called, because it is an ongoing investigation. Amalgamated Cable News will stay with this story, and we'll keep you apprised of further developments..."

Roper laughed at himself. He had spent the better part of an afternoon planning how best to get into a safe or a file cabinet in the

Watkins office, to photocopy the police report about the messenger, and here Tansy Burns hands him the very information he needed on a platter. No sweat.

Harold Walker, GlobeSpan Messenger. Let us now appraise not-so-famous men.

However, after thinking it over, Roper decided he'd be best off going into the Watkins office, anyway: he was building a case here, and he could still use pictures of the Precinct Report spelling out the business about the written-in time-of-delivery on Walker's messenger ticket.

So Roper didn't get to take the night off, after all.

CHAPTER THIRTY EIGHT

Roper wasn't the only one interested in Tansy's report.

Next morning, Laurie Buchan appeared in the doorway of Earl Gordon's office at DOI.

"Want to hear a recording of Tansy Burns's show last night?"

Earl grinned.

"Now that you mention it, yes, I'm sure I would."

She handed him a tape.

"That isn't all of it. The first sentence or two got past me, before I realized I'd better record this little item."

Earl slid the tape into his machine and punched the play button.

"The New York cops questioned a Harold Walker," Laurie said. "He messengered a package for Global Something to…"

She stopped speaking when the sound came from the machine.

"…seems Mr. Walker delivered a soap opera script to actor Jeffrey Lasalle at almost precisely…"

Lauire watched Gordon's face as the tape played on. At its conclusion, he reran it, listening closely, nodding several times.

"Okay if I make a copy of this?"

"Keep that copy," she told him. "I've still got the original one I made."

Rewinding the tape, he proceeded to make another copy anyway. While it was running, she asked him: "What do you think?"

"I think we ought to start looking for more information on all of it. That was a convenient little solution to the screwed-up assassination that took place in front of that hotel, is part of what I think."

"My thought precisely," Laurie smiled.

CHAPTER THIRTY NINE

Roper had a half interest in an upstate real estate company for tax purposes, just so he could show he had some income from somewhere. He never bothered his partner except to use him as an occasional mailing address, where Marge could send her reports to him, and her bills. The partner forwarded the Edward Dickson stuff to a Post Office box, where it began Roper's customary circuitous journey through several storefront mail-boxes, until finally it reached Roper himself.

Marge had sent him more material than he expected. Instead of a quick rundown on Roger Brent's boyhood years in a Tucson suburb and his four years at Margarita College in the upper Midwest, Marge had included lists of everyone in his classes, together with a brief notation beside many of the names...the sort of thing a high-school yearbook would include below the picture of each student.

Congressman Melford and Brent were easy to find, but Roper had to go by Norma Melford's first name to discover that her maiden name had been Tyler. She was easy to recognize, even some twenty-odd years ago: dark-hair, big eyes, thoughtful look on her face. Not unlike newspaper photos he had seen recently, in connection with Roger Brent's slaying.

Tossing aside the lists and pictures, Roper studied the boyhood material on Brent, then his college years. So-so marks for the first two years, but during his junior and senior years, Roger Brent had apparently settled down and worked hard, winding up at the head of his class…although Tim Melford still turned out to be valedictorian. Figured. The future politician was apparent all through Melford's college years, and probably long before that, too.

Putting it all away, Roper studied the copy he had made of the Police Report on that New York messenger-witness. He had already gotten Marge to locate the guy, and one of her street people had stopped Harold Walker on the sidewalk for a light, so Roper could observe him, from where he lurked nearby. That way Marge's men didn't see Roper.

For the next hour or so, Roper had shagged Walker until he had a pretty good idea of the sort of day he put in messengering, with an occasional stop-off for coffee and a breather.

And he had a pretty good idea of the sort of person Hal Walker was, too.

What he was going to do with all this information he was gathering, Roper hadn't a clue. But it was the only way he knew how to go about finding out just what was going down with those two employers of his, Reynolds and Adams: dig up as much as he could about anyone and anything connected with the double-cross they had pulled on him when they whacked Jeff Lasalle.

Because that was what it came down to: their Tollman hit-meister could have blown away Roper himself in front of that bank, if Tollman was the one who'd done that one, too. Only the fact that Roper had learned long ago how to be real careful in this business of his, only that had kept him from getting the bullets Lasalle had caught.

Now he was simply going about another part of that business, trying to find out what the opposition was up to, so next time he'd be ready, if they tried to create a next time.

And, of course, collect the money they still owed him.

CHAPTER FORTY

The car engine gunned behind Hal. The sudden ripping roar of the motor was so loud that his hands jumped on the bike handles.

Just in time, he swerved to the right. A low black car went zooming past, screeched its brakes at the next corner, made a snarling angry turn, and then it was gone, although he could hear its engine-growl diminish with distance until it was no longer audible.

Hal ended up angling off the road pavement and partway up a driveway, barely able to keep from crashing into someone's front yard hedge before bringing the bike to a stop. He was shaking from the suddenness and loudness of the incident.

By then he was way too late to get the black car's make, or its license plate number.

"Not that I would've been able to remember the damn license number," he admitted to Tansy on the phone, when she called him that evening.

"You poor guy," she sympathized. "Why do you bother with that messenger job? Come work for me full time, that personal assistant gig we were trying out."

"What, and quit my incompetent gigolo business?"

"Now, Hal, don't talk like that. You're not a gigolo."

"No? What are they calling it now?"

"Hal, are you unhappy about…us?"

"No, that isn't it."

"What is it, then?"

"I guess I've been so angry for so long at the working-over that detective-agency sub-culture gave me years ago, to force me to go through the motions of picking up…well, you. And those actresses."

"You don't have to bother with them now, do you? Now that you and I are…?"

She left it unfinished, so Hal shrugged and said into the phone: "I really have no idea. Nobody ever gave me a copy of the instruction manual for any of this crap. Except for you, I'm still flying blind. Why don't you ask them?"

"Ask who?"

"The detective agency people, the ones who bodyguard you, while we're together."

"Hal, I've never had any contact with private detectives," she protested.

"O' course you haven't, darlin'," he jeered. "You don't know nothin', right? Story of my life, lately."

"Hal, please don't take out your anger on me, will you? – Hal? Are you still there?"

"Yes, Tans. You're right. I won't take it out on you. Sorry I shot my mouth off."

"Good!" she said cheerfully. "I'm glad you don't blame me for… whatever they did to you. Tell you what, I'll ask my public relations people to find out about it, if you're still expected to try to pick up any other…gals, now that you and I are…have made contact."

"All right, Tansy. It'll be interesting to get some information that doesn't just waft through the atmosphere, and somehow I'm supposed to figure out what it means by some sort of osmosis. I never was really tuned in to all the signals those savages out there use to communicate with one another, and I mean, this was long before any of this idiocy began."

She laughed.

"Gotta go. Time I was made up for tonight's show. You wouldn't believe how long it takes to make me look good on-camera."

"You're right," Hal said. "I wouldn't believe it. You always look good."

"See? You're learning how to communicate with us people out here. You also lie quite capably, too. Bye."

CHAPTER FORTY ONE

"Walter, I feel responsible for the guy," Tansy told her boss. "You said yourself that it was a good piece of news-work on my part, finding and getting Hal Walker's part of the Jeff Lasalle story."

"Sure," Walter Noble agreed, "but that doesn't mean we have to wet-nurse the man, afterward. If you think he's being…what? harassed?…tell the cops. Someone in a car blasts past a guy on a bicycle. What's that? Happens all the time…"

"Walter," she interrupted desperately, "what good is telling cops? They might be the ones who are giving him this treatment."

Walter stared across his desk at her.

"Tansy," he chided, "aren't you going overboard, just a little? Cops don't operate like that. They don't have to."

"Then what am I supposed to do?" she cried. "Wait until one fine day he gets wiped out? Then what? Do we all sit around here and say, 'Yes, maybe we should've done something to help him.'?"

The editor shrugged.

"I say it again, Tansy: I can't wet nurse everyone we get a story from."

"At least let me get an extended interview with Hal Walker," she pleaded.

"I don't have to bring him into our studio or anything. I'll do the interview in my apartment. Billy and Jerry and myself. A couple of hours, and it's done."

Walter thought about it. Tansy watched him anxiously.

"Just give me an okay," she added softly. "You don't even have to promise to run it on-air. If the interview isn't up to standard, we'll just file and forget it."

Reluctantly, Walter nodded.

"Okay, babe. You want it, you got it. But it better be good, or it just won't make it to air."

"Fair enough, Mr. Noble," she smiled, hurrying out before he added any restrictions.

As she began making preparations in her office for the interview, Tansy felt scared and a little sick to the stomach, too. She wasn't certain she was doing the right thing, or even the smart thing, trying to get Hal's story out in detail, completely. All she could do was hope that if Hal really was being signalled to keep his mouth shut by someone, maybe by those Feds involved in the killing of Jeff Lasalle, one way to get them to lay off might be to remove any reason they might have to bother Hal Walker in their effort to keep him from saying anything more about it. And the best way to do that was to get Hal's part of the story out by giving it as wide a coverage as she could. Then, if there were a regrettable *accident,* which just happened to kill that particular messenger, there would certainly be a demand for a thorough investigation of the entire situation. And a too-close look into the shooting deaths of Roger Brent and Jeff Lasalle might be the very last thing some people might want.

First, she would have to get Hal out of that city up there, before he had any other close calls. Once she got him down here in Washington, she, Billy and Jerry could wind up a quick interview in a couple of hours.

After that? Hal might still be at risk until Walter made up his mind whether or not to air the interview.

What could she do with Hal until it aired?

Tansy shook her head impatiently. She would deal with that problem when she came to it. Right now, she still had to arrange for the interview. She reached for the phone.

CHAPTER FORTY TWO

The first thing Norma had to do at the Arakistan Ambassador's reception was guide Tim over to Senator Thaddeus G. Westbrook.

"Ah, Mrs. Melford," the senator wheezed, slipping an arm around her waist while he shook Ted's hand. "You look as lovely as always."

His huge hand slid skilfully down her back and he got in his grope. Laughing easily, Norma slipped free, thankful she had gotten that out of the way for the evening.

"Senator, you are one of the world's greater flatterers."

"Greater," he repeated. Turning to Tim, he pointed out; "Nice usage, don't you agree, muh boy? Not the greatest, but certainly one of the greater ones."

"Norma majored in English Lit in college," Tim smiled.

They drifted off, then separated, circulating.

Norma greeted Henry and Janene Graham, chatted a moment, then kept moving.

"Ah, Graham," rumbled Senator Westbrook. "And Janene, my dear."

Lucy Westbrook and Mrs. Graham paired off, allowing Westbrook to ask: "How are things with you, Graham?"

"Still keeping lids on, Senator."

The two stood side by side, observing the people mingling in the Arakistan Embassy's courtyard.

"How tight is the lid being kept on that recent New York brouhaha?"

"As tight as needs be, Senator."

Norma Melford drifted by. Both men observed her with appreciation. She smiled at their wives and turned to join them, complimenting their dresses.

"That's part of a keeper situation, isn't it?" the Senator asked softly.

Graham nodded.

"It's keeping…nicely."

They watched as Khalid Rafiz approached, a smile on his handsome mustached face.

"That's what keepers are for, after all," Westbrook rumbled, taking another sip of his brandy. "To be kept. Nicely kept, if possible, but kept nonetheless, nicely or not."

Rafiz came up, greeting both men, shaking their hands heartily, first the Senator's, then Graham's.

"I am so delighted you could come, gentlemen," he cried. "I speak for the Ambassador as well. Delighted!"

"Wouldn't miss yore little shindig fer nuthin', Mr. Rafeez," the Senator said, jovially. He took another swig at his brandy.

Graham could see that the Senator was starting to enjoy the festivities.

"Delighted to be here," Graham told the smiling attache.

"What is to be kept, nicely or not?" Rafiz asked, gazing curiously into the face of each of them in turn. "You were saying, when I approached…something about keepers."

Westbrook chortled. Graham smiled.

"One of Mr. Graham's secrets, probably," the Senator replied. "I forget which one."

"Mr. Graham has so many secrets, I'm sure," Rafiz smiled understandingly. "And no doubt he keeps them all admirably."

"He's a keeper, sure enough," Westbrook chuckled, his vast stomach heaving.

The attache stared at the big man, puzzled. Then he shrugged diplomatically at the joke he was not privy to. He seemed to remember something: "Oh, I meant to ask, Mister Graham, how did that chap of yours manage…?"

Someone passing behind Rafiz brushed against him. Both men turned and apologized to one another.

When Rafiz faced the two again, Graham asked him: "Which chap was that?"

Beyond the Senator, Norma was able to hear every word the three men spoke, and she could also listen and join in with the two wives' conversation, whenever one of them said anything.

She heard the diplomat's reply to Graham's question: "The man whom I most fortunately prevented our frontier guardsmen from dealing with, as they usually do, whenever anyone attempts to penetrate that particular sector of our southern border."

Graham's eyes slid momentarily to the Senator's face, then back to the attentive attache's.

From the corner of her eye, Norma noticed.

"Ah, yes," Graham answered carefully. "He recovered quite well. Oh, and he asked me to thank you for…what you were able to do for him."

Rafiz nodded, his eyes serious now.

"I am so happy to hear of his recovery. A winter in those mountains can be…" He shook his head. "Arduous. Most difficult. He was lucky to have reached our frontier at all."

"Indeed, he was that," Graham agreed. "Again, our heartfelt gratitude to you, Khalid."

For a moment, Norma waited, holding her breath, while the silence between the three men stretched out. Then the Senator broke it, saying: "He's keeping splendidly, Rafeez. That chap is also a keeper, aint he, Graham?"

As he agreed silently with the big man, Graham's eyes appeared mildly concerned, but Norma could see that he refrained from saying anything. It was obvious that Westbrook was enjoying his brandy. She could also see that the attache was puzzled, as he studied the faces of both men.

"There is that keeper thing again," he observed. "Is it a secret code, perhaps? If it is, of course, I will say no more."

Westbrook roared with laughter, clapping the younger man on the shoulder.

"No, my lad, it's not a code. Just one of those…jokes? The kind you can keep and savor and tell, again and again. In short, a keeper."

"And your man is keeping up nicely, is that it? Yes, I think I see. Your language isn't quite as outrageously wild and varied as the Isstrylian dialects, but I see that your many variations on the words kept and keep and keeper might very much enjoy a waltz with their Matilda, and might even hold their own, quite…nicely."

All three men laughed. With a twinkle in his eye, the attache apologized for rushing off, but his duties required that he greet the Ambassador's other guests.

When he had gone, Graham asked in an undertone: "Senator, could I get you a cup of scalding black coffee?"

Westbrook rumbled wheezily with laughter.

"It'll take a good deal more of this Arakistani white lightning to put me under, muh boy."

"I just thought you might have been slightly overdoing the keeper business."

"That Khaleez dandy has no idea in hayull what I was talkin' about," the senator scoffed genially. He turned his head. Norma just managed to avoid letting him catch her eye, as she said something pleasant to his wife, who was standing behind him and to his left. Westbrook turned back to Graham.

"Rafiz is no fool," Graham was pointing out. "Besides, we do owe him for what he did for Marau…for our chap, that time."

Westbrook grunted.

"Henry," he said ponderously, "I cain't he'p thinkin' that if he hadn't helped that chap of ours, we wouldn't be stuck with…keeping things contained, now would we?"

Graham eyed the older man with a trace of a smile twisting his lips.

"Senator, you are one tough old rooster."

Westbrook chuckled.

"Gotta break an occasional omelet to make a aig, muh boy."

Graham smiled dutifully, touched the senator's arm, and moved off, murmuring in parting: "I'd better polish some apples, too."

Norma waited a few seconds, then she did the same, wondering what all that business about keepers and keeping was about. She realized that she would probably never know, not if it had anything to do with where Graham worked, even if her husband did serve on the House Oversight Committee, to which Graham had to report regularly. Committee testimony was a good deal less than detailed about day-to-day nuts-and-bolts secrets of an agency like Graham's.

CHAPTER FORTY THREE

Reynolds slammed the phone down as Adams entered the office.

"Son of a bitch!"

Adams grinned.

"What's the matter?"

"Stoddard and Caldwell, up in New York. They were putting a tap on that messenger's home phone, while he's at work."

"And?"

"Seems there's already a phone tap in place."

They stared at one another.

"Who do you suppose…?" Adams began.

Reynolds spread his hands helplessly.

"Anyone's guess," he said. "The cops?"

"Wouldn't they have told us?"

"Not necessarily," Reynolds said sourly.

"I'll put in a call or two, Adams said. "Ask around up there, in the department."

"Good idea. That messenger bastard is starting to get on my nerves…"

Reynolds stopped in the middle of his sentence, and stared off at nothing.

Adams paused in the doorway on his way out and watched his co-worker.

"You don't suppose," Reynolds ventured, "that this messenger and the actor, Lasalle, might've had some kinda scam of their own going, do you?"

"No way of knowing," Adams said cautiously.

"Drugs?" Reynolds speculated. "How do we know that package Walker delivered to Lasalle's apartment was really a soap opera script? Or only a script? Drugs don't take up much space in an envelope big enough to hold a script."

Adams thought about it and nodded. "Could be," he admitted.

"Maybe the New York cops had a tap on Walker for something like that, and our gig just stumbled into the middle of an already existing situation."

Reynolds' eyes were lighting up as he built on the idea.

"If it *was* that way," Adams pointed out, "then maybe that's a plus, from our point of view."

"I was thinking along those lines."

"If those two did have another grift going," Adams elaborated, "we could use proof of it to divert attention away from the fuss that seems to be building about the way Lasalle was shot, there in front of the bank."

Reynolds nodded, watching him, waiting to see where he was going.

"Now," Adams continued, "if it turns out that either or both those twerps had something cooking, it gives our guys an out, and the FBI, too. One more doubt tossed into the mix, like the time of delivery written in on the delivery ticket by the actor, instead of the messenger."

Reynolds nodded.

"I see your drift, and you're right, George. Every extra confuser we can throw into the pot to screw things up, the better we look."

Nodding decisively, he slammed both palms flat down on his desktop.

"Okay, get in touch with your contacts on the New York cops. Find out if they're the ones who put that phone tap in Walker's apartment. Of course, tell Caldwell to be…diplomatic…when he's asking them for details. Same with you. Suggest to them we'd like to put in a phone tap ourselves, and what do they think of the idea. Start with that. We'll see where it gets us"

"Good thought," Adams said, turning to leave once again. "I'll impress that on Caldwell. It'll look good, too. Like we're being real cooperative with them on their home turf. They like that sorta thing."

Both men chuckled as Adams went into the outer office.

Reynolds called after him: "If the cops up there make it complicated, I'll come up and do the dealing myself. Let me know."

Adams' faint "Right," came drifting back to him.

To himself, Reynolds muttered: "I could use a change of scenery. I'm sick of being cooped-up in this goddamn office all day long."

CHAPTER FORTY FOUR

It had seemed like such a simple idea: all Tansy had to do was get everything ready for her evening program in the New York facility, then call Hal at his messenger place and have him meet her at her hotel, where they could spend some time together before her five o'clock show. And perhaps she could convince him to accompany her to Washington the next day, to do the interview.

But on some days, everything goes wrong. The shuttle up from Washington was delayed, it took her forever to get the segments of her show in shape, and by the time she could put in a call to Hal, he had gone home for the day.

Catching a cab, she apparently reached his place before he did, so she had to use the duplicate set of keys he had given her in a worn brown leather key case.

Letting herself in, she made a cup of tea while she waited for him. When she heard faint sounds at the front door of his apartment, she waited for him to unlock the two door locks and join her.

But the sounds continued.

Was he having trouble unlocking his own front door?

Smiling, she went down the short corridor and was about to unlock the door from the inside, when a man's voice out there growled.

"Come on, man. You've been in and out of this joint all these months, and today you can't do it?"

"Sometimes it's the humidity," another voice replied irritably. "Quit leaning on me, okay? That aint helping any."

Tansy stopped and listened. Scraping noises continued on the other side of the door.

They're picking the lock, she realized.

Thinking fast, she cried loudly: "Hello! Who is it?"

After a moment's silence, one of them asked: "Is this the Gomez apartment? Package for Gomez."

"No Gomex here," she called.

"Uh-oh!" the other voice muttered. Then, louder: "Sorry, lady. We got the wrong floor."

"That's all right," she replied.

Standing there, she listened and heard them move off. When everything out there was quiet, she found herself wondering if this might be some more of the kind of thing Hal had been experiencing lately. Maybe they…whoever *they* were…intended to break in, and when he showed up… What?"

She didn't want to think about that. Turning, she emptied the remnants of her tea into the sink, washed and dried the cup, saucer, and spoon, put them away, and left.

Going down the stairs, Tansy hoped she had given those men sufficient time to get far enough away so they wouldn't see her on her way out of the building.

She chided herself for not changing her appearance, before quitting Hal's apartment.

Taking a scarf out of her loaded tote bag, she covered her head with it, slouched a bit, and walked stodgily down the street without raising her eyes until she turned the corner onto the avenue, on her way to the nearest El station a few blocks down.

Once there, it seemed to take an eternity of waiting, but eventually Hal came down the steps, along with other arrivals on the train that had carried them out from the city.

"Hey, Tansy!" he cried when he saw her. "This is a nice surprise."

Taking him aside, she told him about the would-be intruders.

Hal shrugged.

"What's the problem?" he asked, dismissing her worries. "For all we know they were your people."

"My people?" For a moment, Tansy was confused. "Why would any of my crew be picking locks on your door…?"

"Not those people," he laughed. "The detective agency's people."

That stopped her confusion. She kept forgetting about them.

Hal watched her for a moment with an amused glint in his eyes, and then he said: "Tansy, those private police types have been in and out of my apartment for years. They've probably set up a complete set of bugs and phone taps and video surveillance. I've never been able to find anything, but nowadays the equipment available for that sort of thing is apparently undetectable. A bugging mike could be no larger than the point of a lead pencil. Video would have to be a bit bigger, I suppose, but it still might not need an opening in a wall larger than a pin-hole. I took a few looks around the place, years ago, but I gave up worrying about it long ago. I had to accept the loss of my privacy because there wasn't and isn't a damn thing I can do about it."

Tansy listened to what he was saying, but all the while she was thinking. When he stopped trying to reassure her, if that was what he'd been doing, she said: "Hal, let's take a cab downtown to the hotel where I stay. I've reserved a room for you already. After I do this evening's show, here in New York, we can catch a flight to D. C. and…"

"Tansy, I haven't got any of my stuff with me," he protested.

"What stuff do you need?"

"Shaving stuff. Toothbrush. Stuff."

She laughed and hugged him.

"Any *stuff* you need, we'll buy. Okay?"

"But it'll only take a few minutes for me to pick up some of it at my place, and then we can head down…"

"Hal, you haven't been listening to me, have you?" she whispered fiercely. Taking his upper arms in her hands, she shook him. "A half hour or so ago, at least two men were trying to picklock their way into your apartment. One of them accused the other of having been in and out of there dozens of times…"

"There!" Hal cried triumphantly. "See? What did I tell you?"

She stared at him, astonished.

"Hal, how can you face such an outright invasion of your privacy this way: Don't you feel any…?"

"Tansy," he told her quietly, "any outrage I might have felt I had to get used to, a long time ago. How can *you* pay private detective people to invade my privacy the way they've done, just to force me to pick you up, exactly the way you want?"

"You know," she murmured, "I don't believe I've ever thought of it that way before. I just took it for granted that it…you…were in place, that you didn't mind." She shrugged. "That you were used to it."

"Oh, I'm used to it, all right," he assured her, a bit wildly. "The problem here is that you can't get used to it, even though you're one of the gals who have been paying to have it done to me, you and those idiotic actresses."

"All right," she admitted, forcing herself to remain calm. "I'm sure you're absolutely right about everything you said, Hal…"

"Damn right I'm right."

"…but let's stick to right now, shall we? Let's get downtown, keep you away from that apartment of yours, get you down to Washington tomorrow, and maybe even do that interview. Once we've got that on tape, and, God willing, on-air, perhaps at least some of this stuff you've been catching lately will go away."

"I've been through a lot worse," he said, as she took his arm and started looking for a cab. "When this lover-boy business began, years ago, I found myself biting my tongue in my sleep, that's how hard those people ran me ragged with their bothering tactics. Real sweethearts, those private dick bastards, them and their street-trash helpers! Anything short of that kind of working-over is a milk run."

"All right, Hal, all right," she said soothingly, squeezing his arm. "Taxi!"

Tansy bundled him into a cab and they got out of there. She sank back in the seat beside him, drained, exhausted from the hell her afternoon had turned into. Her entire day, in fact.

CHAPTER FORTY FIVE

Roper was in the second day of checking out the messenger. The day before, he had used a car, a renter. Today, he was in a leased van. Both days, he kept the telephoto lens camera at the ready, not so much to record whoever he might see, but to be able to study their faces later, in the pictures.

Hal Walker lived in a five-story walk-up, half a block down a side street from the main drag that had an El train running overhead.

On one corner of the intersection, a fast food outlet's parking lot offered Roper cover. Another corner had a super-market, also with a parking lot. From each, a good enough view of the subject's building was available along the side street, and being able to move his vehicle from one lot to another and back several times in the course of a day of watching was quite helpful: it reduced the possibility of getting himself spotted simply by hanging around too long in one place.

He saw Walker leave for work around mid-morning, took yet another picture of him, then settled in to watch.

Like the day before, there was little to see, until well past midday, when Tansy Burns, the cable TV newswoman, showed up in a cab.

Roper got a couple of shots of her, as she was going in the front door of the building, side shots. He would have to be ready, if and when she emerged, to get a full-face picture or two.

More waiting. Tenants coming out of the building, later returning after shopping, or whatever. A couple of workmen in a pickup truck went in, coming back out a few minutes later. Roper didn't even bother taking pictures of them, until they emerged. Then he remembered, snapped a couple of quick ones, and watched as they got back into their pickup, made a U-turn and drove toward the corner where Roper was parked in the supermarket's parking area.

Unexpectedly, the truck turned in. It jolted Roper. He hadn't been expecting that. He had a road map in front of him, so when one of them glanced in his direction as they drove by, he had the map up and his head lowered in time to prevent a good look at his face. But the fact that he'd been caught off-guard irritated him. Getting old? Could be.

The pickup truck swung around, faced back the way it had just come, parked in one of the painted parking slots, and then it just sat there.

It took Roper a moment to catch on.

They're taking a plant, too, he realized.

So he had to put on a little act: stowing the map, turning his head to look across the avenue at the fast food place, starting the van, driving out of the parking lot he was in, and going down partway along the avenue under the El to the fast food's farthest entrance driveway, and turning there into its parking area. Then he drove behind the burger building and stayed there a full five minutes, to give the two in the pickup time to forget about him, if they needed to. Then he drove out from behind the restaurant and parked as far from the avenue as he could and still be inside the parking lot.

There was no sign from the two men in the pickup. Neither turned his head to look in Roper's direction.

Good enough. He got the camera up and took a shot of the pickup's license plate, then zoomed in as tight as he could on the little window in the rear of the cab, and waited until both men were facing one another. He wanted a decent profile shot of them. It took a pretty long wait, but when he had three quick shots, he relaxed. Later, he could try for full faces, if he got the chance, but at least he had their profiles.

He didn't have long to wait. Tansy Burns came out of the subject's building and walked this way, turning the corner while Roper was still trying to get some full-face shots of her. He watched her as she walked. Nice legs. He also noticed both men in the pickup turned their heads and watched her, too, until she was out of their line of sight, hidden by the corner storefront on the main street. Then they faced forward again.

But not for long. After waiting a few minutes, the two climbed out of the pickup, strolled toward the avenue, and stood on the sidewalk, there near the corner, looking down along the avenue in the direction the Burns woman had gone. After half a minute, one nodded, and both of them went back and got into their pickup, drove out of the parking lot, along the side street a half block, parked in front of the subject's building, and again went inside, one of them carrying a small tool case.

"Bingo!" Roper murmured.

He had gotten good full-face shots of both men, when they walked out of the parking lot and back, so it had worked out well enough, in spite of his lapse in alertness, there at the beginning. He decided to make it a policy to take pictures of anyone except people who were obvious tenants of any building he was surveilling. Those two workmen should have qualified as candidates for getting their pictures taken.

Roper jotted down the time they entered the building this second time, just as he had done when Tansy Burns went in and out, earlier. Later, he was surprised to notice when the two came back out again, it was over an hour after they'd gone in.

Almost four o'clock.

Rather than sit there waiting for the messenger to come home from work, Roper decided to tail the pickup truck. It was obvious from their undisguised attention to the departure of the newswoman that they were zeroed-in on her messenger story-source. Or were she and Walker more than just witness and TV newsie?

When the one at the wheel of the pickup dropped the other off, Roper noted the address of the house that one entered, but stayed with the pickup. When its driver finally parked and went into his place, Roper got that address, too, and then called it a day.

Maybe Marge could get him some useful information on that pair, with the addresses and license plate of the pickup truck and the pictures he had taken of them to help her.

Roper spent the next day again staking out Hal Walker's building, but he didn't see him leave for work at his usual time in the late morning, and he caught no sign of Tansy Burns, either. Nor of any more "workman" types.

He did notice one man enter the building, and because there was a certain look to him, Roper got pictures of him, going in and out. The FBI look was what he thought he'd spotted, but on second thought, he changed his mind. The man didn't look lawyer-y enough to be a Feeble.

CHAPTER FORTY SIX

Earl Gordon got nowhere trying to contact the messenger, who had called in sick at his job. When Earl stopped by at Hal Walker's apartment, no one answered.

Back at DOI's downtown regional office, Earl made some phone calls, trying to get in touch with the detective named Crayton, the one who had broken apart the smooth execution of that gun-planting routine the Feds had pulled on the scene, when they'd wasted Jeff Lasalle.

It took awhile. Crayton was no longer assigned to the Midtown South Precinct, and no one there was willing or authorized to reveal Crayton's current assignment. Earl had to keep going higher and higher in the department until finally a Lieutenant Brock listened and gave him a number in Brooklyn where the detective could be reached.

It turned out to be Crayton's home phone. His wife assured Earl that she would pass along his number when her husband got home from work, and he would return the call.

It was a relief when Laurie Buchan called.

Smiling, Earl leaned back in his chair in the cubby-hole of a partitioned office he was using.

"Good to hear from you, stranger," he said. "Where've you been lately?"

"Doing some regional work," she replied. "Nothing big, just tidying up loose ends on completed cases. Right now I'm in a college town where Roger Brent started out an okay-enough student for his Freshman and Sophomore years, and then caught fire for his final two years, enough to end up at the head of his class in all subjects..."

"Good for him," Earl murmured. "You're really intrigued by this case, aren't you?"

She laughed softly.

"Well, I know how much help you need in a thing like this, so anything I can do..."

"Don't say that where the chief can hear you," Earl warned.

"Oh, I meant to tell you something," she said. "A curious thing seems to keep happening in the course of my dipping into the early years of Mr. Brent."

"How do you mean, curious?"

"Everywhere I ask for information about him, birth certificate, place of birth, grammar school he attended in Tucson, and now up here in Margarita College, every place I go, someone has been ahead of me."

"Ahead of you?"

"Exactly that. Someone has usually been there first, asking for information about Roger Brent. In one instance, it was supposed to have been someone from the local newspaper. In another, a freelance writer intending to include Brent in an article about promising political people whose careers have untimely endings, either through discouragement, burnout, career disaster, or death by misadventure, like Roger Brent."

Grinning, Earl asked: "Laurie, are you sure you aren't imagining some of this? Sounds perfectly natural that a local paper would want to work up some detail on the early years of a prominent man who grew up in their baili..."

Laurie interrupted him, irritated by his attitude.

"Earl, whenever I could get a name, from whatever official I spoke to, I followed up on it. I could never find the person who preceded me on this trail."

That stopped Earl.

"Interesting," he murmured.

"She giggled.

"It is, isn't it? No one was sent out by the local Tucson newspaper. The name that was left up here at the college may not have been recalled correctly, but the name I got from them doesn't check out, either. I feel as if I'm walking in someone's footsteps."

"You know, Laurie," he pointed out, "in a reverse way, your finds confirm our decision to search Roger Brent's past. The chief doesn't have too much other stuff for me to work on right now, so he's letting me dig a little. How long he'll allow me that kind of leeway is anyone's guess, of course."

"At least I'm developing some background on Brent," said Laurie. "I tried to reach Arthur Merritt, his lawyer down in Tucson, for a list of the personal things in Brent's apartment, and a copy of the probate of his will. I had to settle for leaving a message on Merritt's machine."

"They hate to give away copies of wills," Earl said gloomily.

"Anyway, I'm raking in everything I can on Brent, and on Tim Melford and Norma Tyler, who later became Melford's wife. Oh, and on a girl who was her dormitory roommate their freshman year here, girl named…Linda Stevens. Things like pictures, grades, extra-curricular activities…just to give us a clearer picture on where Brent was coming from."

Earl chuckled, shaking his head in admiration.

"You're amazing!"

She laughed.

"Next, I'll start delving into Brent's political work. I'll need the chief's help there, and yours, too, Earl. You know, like setting up meetings with Congressman Melford and his wife, getting the names of people Brent worked with on a regular basis. That sort of thing. A man doesn't get murdered just for nothing, Earl, the way Brent seems to have been."

"You're assuming Brent was really the target, not Melford," said Earl. He stated it, rather than asked.

"Don't you?"

He shrugged.

"I'm trying to keep an open mind. At any rate, Laurie, it sounds as if you've taken on lots of work for the near future."

She chuckled.

"Sorry if I've run on. How've you been doing up there in New York, Earl?"

"Well, I saw the outside of that messenger Hal Walker's apartment door, earlier today…"

They both laughed.

Just before quitting time, the phone rang.

Picking up, Earl recited the extension number he was using and his name. Then the caller identified himself. Earl sat straighter, leaned forward, and picked up a pencil to take notes.

"Glad you could get back to me, Detective Crayton…"

CHAPTER FORTY SEVEN

The night before, when Tansy and Hal reached her building, she breathed a lot easier than she had all the way down from New York. She finally had Hal safe in the little apartment adjoining hers in Arlington.

She had been extremely careful getting him there, taking a cab, and the two of them slipping inside the building through its front entrance.

Up on her second floor, the corridor was empty, so she took a chance and unlocked the door of the efficiency apartment, and Hal ducked quickly inside at her urging.

"I'll be in to see you in a minute," she whispered. "In the meantime, don't move any curtains, don't look out any of the windows, don't touch the venetian blinds. It's all attached to a system of lights set to turn on and off by prearranged setting…so the apartment looks as if it's occupied by someone and doesn't get burglarized."

Hal grinned and nodded, shut the door and locked it.

Next door, in her own apartment, Tansy had to play with the kids awhile. When they buckled down to do their homework, she had time to take a few food items next door, using the hidden closet-ends and the door connecting them to get there.

When she appeared in the living room, Hal almost jumped out of his chair in front of the TV set.

"Where'd you come from?" he gasped. The front door to the little apartment was in plain sight at the far end of the entrance foyer, so he knew she hadn't come in that way.

Tansy laughed and apologized, explaining, and showing him the two closets.

When he had taken it all in, Hal grinned and shook his head in amazement.

"Tansy, you're stark staring mad, you know that, don't you?"

"You've got to admit," she pointed out, "there aren't many places this safe where you can stay, under present conditions."

His smile disappeared. He nodded. Then he thought of something.

"I wonder if the private detective shits know about this secret cubbyhole of yours?" After thinking about it a moment, he nodded. "Probably they do. Not much gets past those people."

Tansy took some of the things she'd brought and put them into the refrigerator, and the rest into the compact kitchen's pantry, over the sink. Then she returned to her own apartment, showing Hal how the closet business worked, and giving him a duplicate of the one key which worked all the door locks to the small apartment.

Inside the closet, she murmured: "See you in the morning."

Kissing him, she closed and locked the connecting door.

He called: "You can't spend the night in here with me?"

Sighing, she unlocked the door.

"Hal, I feel funny about that. My husband is right next door, here, and the kids, too. Anyway, you'll only be here overnight, or at most just a couple of days."

He nodded.

"You're right. Here, let me lock this door behind you, for practice."

Closing the door, he inserted his new key, turned it, and slipped out of the hidden section of his closet, holding the hinged panel so it made no sound when it swung shut behind him.

He thought there ought to be a few more items of clothing hanging in the regular closet, to make it look good…but, as Tansy had said, he would only be there a day or two.

That had been the night before. This morning, she told her husband about their new neighbor.

"Your friend from New York is a witness in that murder case?" Paul asked. "Tansy, hon, aren't you bringing some of your marbles a bit close to home? We agreed you'd try to be discreet…"

"I know, Paul, and you're absolutely right," she agreed. "I just couldn't think where else to hide him, until I got the interview. If I work things right, I'll bring Bill and Jerry in here sometime today, and get it done. We should be right out in a jiff."

"You're going to show our furniture in a TV interview?" he asked, incredulously.

"No, no, I'll use a blank wall as backdrop," she assured him hurriedly. "Paul, it will be all right. Trust me."

"Of course," he said. "I'll do everything I can to help. If you need me to come get the kids out of your way, just phone that special number I gave you."

"I'll do that. Don't worry. It'll go smoothly. And Hal will be out of there before we know it."

At work, she did her best to clear up her evening news chores and have it all ready before noon, but breaking stories kept happening, ones she had to include in her half hour segment, so the time was pushed back later and later, until it was too late for her and the two crew men to get out to her place to do the interview that afternoon.

"We'll go out there right after the show, okay, guys?"

Bill glanced at Jerry, who shrugged. Tansy hugged both of them

"I owe you," she said fervently. "I owe you big time, both of you."

Which was why it was after six that evening before the three of them trooped into her apartment right in the middle of supper. The two kids were delighted. Tansy and Paul had their work cut out for them, trying to get the youngsters to finish eating before they could watch the two men set up their equipment in a kind of workroom off the front entrance hallway.

When the children were finally out of the way, getting ready for bed, Tansy slipped away. A couple of minutes later, she reappeared with Hal Walker.

"This is our subject," she told Bill and Jerry. "You remember Hal Walker, my new assistant, before I knew he was a witness to that story, awhile back?"

They both nodded.

"Does this backdrop look stark enough?" Bill asked, waving at the whitewashed workroom wall.

They cleared away all the stuff from where it usually leaned and sat against the wall. Now, with the harsh lighting, it looked almost spooky.

Tansy studied it, then nodded.

"Good," she told them. "Gives it that expressionistic look."

Grinning, Bill winked at Jerry.

"That's what I was going for," he said. "The old expressionistic look."

Tansy laughed, helped move a couple of chairs near the wall, and sat Hal in one of them. When everything was ready, she took the other chair and started in.

CHAPTER FORTY EIGHT

Stoddard used a payphone to call Reynolds, finally reaching him at his home in Wheaton.

"I try to get a little time at home with my family," Reynolds grumbled. "Just once, I'd like to not get a call…"

"Sorry, Mike. Just a quick question. We're planted outside that newswoman's home, in Arlington?"

"Has that messenger come back out yet?"

"No. He's been in there all last night, and today, too. They must have him stashed in a guest room. But what I called you about is, right now she's got her two crewmen in there, too."

"What crewmen?"

"Her cameraman and the sound guy. Think they're taping an interview with your witness?"

"The little bastard!" Reynolds snarled. "When the hell is that goddamn creep gonna go away?"

"We could intercept them when they leave," Stoddard suggested.

"Intercept who?"

"Her crew. Confiscate any tapes they have…you know."

Reynolds thought about it, then growled: "Better not. If we do anything at this stage of things, it better be legal. The wolves may be gathering." Another pause before his voice came back on the phone again: "Tell you what, Stoddard, I'll call the Man. Get back to you. Wait a minute. You're not calling from a cell phone, are you?"

"No, Chief," Stoddard hastily assured him. "Pay phone."

"I hope Caldwell's maintaining the stakeout," Reynolds said.

"Of course, Mike. But if you're gonna get back to me, how… I mean, this pay phone is four-five blocks away from Burns's building."

"Maybe I won't have to get back to you," Reynolds said. "If the word is for you to do nothing about grabbing any tapes, no need for a call. If it's the other way, I'll be sending someone over there with a warrant. Nice and legal."

Stoddard chuckled.

"Okay, Mike."

"Good that you called," Reynolds said. "Shows you're thinking."

CHAPTER FORTY NINE

The interview took less than an hour, but Tansy had a lapful of notes, and she used them to cover everything she could think of. She tried to get into every angle, so there would be little if anything more anyone would need to know about exactly what Hal Walker had done, the day he had delivered the soap opera script to the apartment of Jeff Lasalle, that crucial afternoon in New York.

When she was finally satisfied, Tansy made a horizontal slicing gesture with her hand.

"Cut!" she said. "That should do it, fellas."

Utterly done in by the relentless questioning he had been put through, Hal looked drained. While they packed their gear and prepared to leave, he observed dryly: "Now I know why those witnesses to mob rub-outs always say 'I didn' see nothin'.' They want to spare themselves from being put through this sort of meat grinder."

The three pros laughed.

The kids had been permitted to stay up, so they could say goodnight to their Mom's camera- and soundmen. Then Tansy helped Paul bundle them off to bed. She kept Hal in the workroom where they had conducted the interview, but once the apartment was clear of the kids, she hustled him through the place and next door through the two-way closet connection.

"Get ready to leave with me," she told him. "I'm going to try something."

Dumbly obedient, Hal nodded. "Out through the basement garage…?"

"No. You'll come back in here. Just get your hat and coat. I'll explain on the way."

Just as she was hustling Hal through her apartment, Paul emerged from the kids' rooms. It was an awkward microsecond. All Tansy could do was introduce the two men across the room, and hurry Hal on out the front door and down to the street. Turning into the short alley beside the three-story building, she triggered the garage door open with the remote.

"I want to see if we can lose anyone who might have followed us here last night," she explained, as she slid behind the wheel of her car. "I don't want anyone to know you're here until that interview the guys are taking to get processed is shown on-air."

"Does that include your detective agency street people?" Hal asked, seated beside her in the car's passenger seat, watching with amused eyes as she backed the car out almost to the sidewalk.

"If we can manage it."

He laughed and shook his head.

"Good luck!"

She flipped the remote. The garage door slid down, locking when its bottom edge touched the pavement. The light inside the narrow garage automatically went out when the outside door closed.

Driving along the tree-roofed streets, Tansy stole a quick glance at Hal.

"You don't think we can do it?"

"Tansy, they're pretty thorough," he said, diplomatically. "How else can the private detective sub-culture assure customers like yourself and those actresses of complete service, bottling up some poor schnook like me the way they do?"

"Well, we'll try, anyway," she said. "Not so much to escape them as to make sure none of those Federal people know where you are. I'm a lot more scared of the Government types than I am of your private detective sub-culture."

All Hal said was: "What's the plan?"

She told him.

Tansy had been thinking of a place all day, so when she drove along beside a wooded section near the Potomac River, she waited until she reached the curved stretch of road she was looking for, and said tensely: "Get ready. When I pull up, open your door, but don't get out. Just pull it shut and drop down out of sight, as if you *had* gotten out. Crawl in back between your seatback and mine, and keep low from then on."

"Got it," he grinned.

It went smoothly. She pulled up to the side of the road beneath arching trees overhead. No traffic was in sight in either direction. No one was visible in any of the windows of the line of houses across the street facing the stretch of woods.

Hal pushed open the passenger door, swung it wide open, leaning out so he could hold onto the door handle, then pulled it shut, without moving from his seat. Ducking below window-level, he was on the floor and crawling back over the pulled-down seatback on his side.

Tansy had already started the car moving forward when he closed the passenger side's door.

In the rear-view mirror, she saw a car come into sight as she accelerated. Its headlights dimmed, and it stopped at the curb. As she drove on around the curve in the road, she glimpsed its brights going on again, as it began moving once more.

"A car just stopped, back there," she called to Hal in back. "It dimmed its headlights, but when I started pulling away, they switched the brights back on."

The road in front straightened. The trees on her right fell away, and the river was visible in the distance, beyond the Memorial Highway.

"There it is again," she said, after checking the rear view mirror. "It's still tailing us."

"Okay," he murmured. "But what have we accomplished with all this?"

"I'm hoping whoever that is, behind us, will think you got out of this car and disappeared in among those trees back there, while I was stopped."

"They're still tailing you, aren't they?"

She checked the rear view mirror again.

"Yes."

"So...?"

Tansy shrugged nonchalantly.

"I'm assuming the people in that car are right now cell-phoning backups, who will start watching for you to emerge from among those trees you supposedly ducked into."

She could hear him chuckle.

"All right, Tansy. It might even work. What happens next? Won't they be able to see me go into your building after we park the car in your garage..."

"No. There's a locked door at the back of that lovely little garage of mine."

"I thought that stairway in the extra apartment led down into the basement."

"Uh-uh! Garage. That key I gave you unlocks the door at the bottom of the stairs, and the door on the landing above. You get back into your hideaway apartment, and no one's laid an eye on you."

"Ingenious, Watson."

Smiling, she went on: "As for me, when I drive inside the garage, I close the door behind me with the remote, get out of the car, lock it carefully for the night, reopen the outside garage door, emerge into the alley, and with the remote again, I close the garage door once again, from the outside this time. I go around to the front of the building and enter by the street entrance...and so to bed."

She could hear him laughing on the floor in the back of the car behind her.

"Out of the mouths of innocents," he chortled. "Who knows, Tans, it just might do the job."

CHAPTER FIFTY

Headed back to the studio, Bill was driving the CAN van when a car passed them, just short of a main intersection. Instead of going on, it cut sharply in front of them and came to a jolting stop.

"Jeez!" Bill yelled, slamming the brakes on.

Jerry was almost catapulted through the windshield on the passenger side. He got his hands up in time, though.

"What the hell's with that guy?" he snarled.

Angrily, Bill shifted into reverse, just as two men jumped out of the cut-off car. In the glare of the van's headlights, Bill saw that both had guns in their hands.

He blinked, but continued to reverse, gunning the motor now, throwing the vehicle sharply to the rear, away from the car blocking half the street in front of it.

"Take it easy, man!" Jerry shouted. Then he noticed the two handguns out there. "My God, what's goin' on here?"

"I don't know," Bill growled, "and I'm not hanging around to find out. Damn! I wish you were driving. I'd be able to get some pics of those bastards."

Both men fired. The windshield shattered, showering bits of broken glass on the two men.

"Duck!" Bill called, crouching lower behind the wheel.

"Don't worry," Jerry muttered, sliding down onto the floor in front of his passenger's seat. "Let me know when it's over."

Bill grinned. He felt crazy, as he shifted into low gear and set the van plunging forward toward the two gunmen. They kept shooting. Bill flinched, hunkering as far down in the seat as he could.

There was a heavy thudding sound from in front of the van.

One of the shooters went whirling through the air, spinning off to the left. It distracted Bill momentarily. He barely had time to swing the steering wheel leftward, trying to avoid hitting the blocking car. He couldn't avoid it, not completely. The van's bumper crunched into the left rear of the car. The impact slowed the van's progress considerably.

Stubbornly, Bill kept grinding forward, swerving farther leftward, pushing the car out of his way until it was turned almost completely around.

Finally, the van's bumper scraped loose and the wide avenue was open in front of him. Getting up some speed, he turned a corner into the bigger roadway just ahead, and got the hell out of there.

When the van's speed picked up, Jerry peered up from where he crouched beneath the dashboard.

"Is it over?"

Bill laughed wildly.

"Yeah, tiger. You can come up now."

Jerry popped up and took the passenger seat once again.

"Hell, I'm a sound man, not a fury man," he said, grabbing the cell phone and tapping in a number rapidly. "Hello, 911? Listen, we just got bushwhacked…"

Bill kept checking the rear view mirror, but there was no pursuit. So when he turned onto Lee Highway, he slowed somewhat and drove along at a more reasonable speed.

Switching off the cell phone, Jerry crawled in back.

"Where you going now?" Bill called over his shoulder.

"Gonna call in the story," Jerry replied, already spinning dials back there. "Let Walter know what just happened."

"Good idea."

When he reached Glebe Road, Bill swung into it, listening to Jerry talking to Walter Noble at the studio.

Jerry interrupted what he was saying to their editor to yell: "Bill, did you get a look at those two guys?"

Bill tried to remember.

"Not much of a look. I was pretty busy at the time. Darkish complexion…that's about it."

"Not black?" Jerry prompted. "Did they look black?"

"No, they weren't that dark. Maybe…what?…Mexican? Central American?"

To the editor, Jerry said: "They could've been anybody, Walter. – It happened so damn fast, neither of us got a good look at either of them…"

CHAPTER FIFTY ONE

"It's Stoddard again."

"Look," Reynolds grumbled, "I told you I'd get back to you if there was…"

"We lost him," Stoddard interrupted.

Shivering in the wind coming from the river in the distance, Stoddard stood waiting for Reynolds' next words.

"How could you lose him?" Reynolds snarled. "You're supposed to be pros. How could a rank amateur like him…?"

"The Burns woman was only out of our sight for a second or two," Stoddard explained hastily. "When we caught sight of her car again, she was stopped at the side of the road. I dimmed my headlights and swung over, to park. She was pulling the passenger side's door shut. Before I even came to a complete stop, she pulled away again, so I had to start moving after her. It was blocks away before we came close up behind them, when they slowed for a traffic light…except now there weren't two of them anymore. Now it was only her in the car, behind the wheel. No one was sitting beside her anymore."

He could hear Reynolds breathing at the other end of the line.

"You mean that bastard just got out of her car and disappeared into those woods? I can't believe this!"

"Looks like that's what hap…"

"What did you guys do, just let it happen? Damn it, Stoddard…"

"No, Mike," Stoddard defended himself. "I called the other car. Caldwell turned his car around and went back. Later, he told me he dropped one of his men at this end of the stretch of trees, and the other one at the far end of the trees. He drove on around the wooded area and took a plant over near the Memorial Highway."

"Okay," Reynolds said, almost reluctantly. "You did right. Did you pick him up again?"

"Afraid not, Mike. He never came out of those trees."

After an interminable interval, Reynolds breathed: "The bastard pulled it off. Him and that news bitch."

"I stayed with her," Stoddard went on, "but I dropped off the man with me, and told him to get back there by cab and help Caldwell and the other two…"

"But it didn't do any good," Reynolds said flatly.

"No results yet. Caldwell said they stayed with it for an hour. Still nothing. Either that Walker is still in among those trees, or he got the hell away."

Reynolds sighed.

"All right. No loss. He'll turn up again. Where's he gonna go?"

"Funny thing, though," Stoddard said hesitantly.

"Even funnier than what you've already told me?" Reynolds asked sarcastically.

Ignoring his tone, Stoddard plowed on: "There wasn't a soul in sight in front of the houses across the road from those trees when Tansy Burns dropped that guy off, but Caldwell told me just now that by the time he got back there, it looked like some kind of flood of people got loose along that stretch of road."

"What're you talking about?" Reynolds asked irritably, obviously thinking about something else.

"From those houses across the road from the woods," Stoddard explained. "One guy was all of a sudden out walking his dog. A gal started jogging around the edge of the trees, at one end of the wooded stretch, and at the other end Caldwell says he saw a guy doing the same, jogging around the woods, headed toward the Highway and the river."

"Just neighborhood people," Reynolds said, dismissing it.

"That's what I thought," Stoddard agreed. "But…why all of a sudden that kind of…damn near a crowd? At that time of night? Some of them were still stirring around, when I got back there a few minutes ago."

"You left off tailing the newswoman?" Reynolds growled.

"No, Mike, of course not. Taylor and Gruner were still outside her place, when she got back. I stayed and watched her drive into her basement garage, come back out, go in her building by the front entrance, and I told them to stay there until I could have them relieved. I rejoined the search here at the woods, awhile ago, and… that's pretty well it."

"Okay," Reynolds sighed. "At least you stuck with her and put her to bed."

"Mike, I wasn't expecting them to pull something like this."

"That's why they pay us, man," Reynolds told him. "To be ready to deal with the unexpected, not just the same old routines. You did pretty well, Stoddard, considering."

"Now what?" Stoddard asked, feeling slightly better, but still on edge. He didn't like the unexpected to happen, not on his shift.

"Keep an eye on those woods for the rest of the night," Reynolds ordered. "There's five of you there. Just check out those joggers and dog walkers, make sure our witness isn't trying to pretend he's one of them. You can handle that, the five of you."

"Sure, no problem."

"In the morning, I'll have a few more men join you guys, and you can all make a pass through those trees, just to make sure Walker isn't holed up in there among them. I personally think he's long gone, but we'll pick him up again. No real loss. Okay?"

"Got it, Mike. Sorry I had to keep breaking in on your time off."

"Forget it," Reynolds said. "It happens. Trouble is, it keeps happening."

They chuckled at the lame humor and hung up.

CHAPTER FIFTY TWO

Tansy and Paul were in bed when the phone rang. She reached for it on the end-table between their twin beds, groping for her notebook, at the same time.

"Something tells me this is for me," she said sleepily.

Paul chuckled, turning onto his side and watching her.

The phone said: "Tansy, this is Walter. Sorry to call at this weird hour, but I thought you ought to know…"

"Know what, Walter?" Tansy switched on the end-table lamp.

"Your crew were cut off by a car, after they left your place…"

"Cut off?"

"Two men tried to hijack them. Shots were fired. Handguns. But Bill was driving. You know how he is, behind a wheel. They got away, but those two shooters shot the shit out of the company truck. The windshield was obliterated…"

"Are Bill and Jerry all right?"

"Yeah, they're okay."

"Thank God!" Tansy breathed.

"They called 911, but the cops were too late. The shooters were gone. Neither Bill nor Jerry got the plate number, so… can't blame them, of course. Who memorizes a license plate while they're dodging bullets?"

"Of course," Tansy agreed. "Lucky they got themselves away without being shot."

"Now, Tansy," the editor said seriously, "maybe they were just trying for the truck. Lots of valuable equipment in that van. But there may also be a connection with that interview with the messenger you and the boys did, last night. I thought I better alert you, just in case."

"Yes, I can see how either reason might have brought on that sort of thing," Tansy agreed. "Thank you, Walter."

Hanging up, she looked across at her husband.

"Two men tried to hijack Bill and Jerry in the van. They shot pistols. The windshield was shattered. No one was hurt and they escaped, but…Walter thought he ought to warn me, in case there is any connection to the interview I did with…" She tilted her head toward the room at the back of the apartment and the adjoining apartment, beyond the two closets. "…him."

Paul was sitting now on the edge of his bed. He nodded.

"It could be," he said quietly.

"Then again," Tansy suggested, "he also thinks it might have been the equipment in the truck. It must be worth a fortune. I never give it a thought, but all that electronic gadgetry back there… thousands of dollars worth of stuff."

"That could be, too," Paul agreed. "Still, your witness being that close, right next door, it's bringing your job pretty near home, isn't it, Tansy?"

She nodded miserably. "I know."

"I'm thinking of the kids," he added.

"Me, too."

Neither said anything for awhile. Then Paul shrugged.

"We'll talk it over in the morning," he said. "Get some sleep, sweetheart."

She returned the notebook to the end table and both of them got back under their covers once more. Paul switched off the light on the end table between their beds.

Presently, Paul murmured: "We can always take the kids out to my folks' place. McLean isn't that far."

Tansy stared up at the ceiling in the darkness.

"Mmmm," she murmured.

"I could drive them to school from there, go on to work, and take them back to McLean in the afternoon."

She went on staring up into the darkness.

When she didn't reply, he said, "Okay!" briskly, then: "We'll talk about it tomorrow. Don't worry, hon. They probably *were* after all that electronic equipment, as Mr. Noble suggested."

She nodded silently, but somehow she didn't think that was what those two shooters had been after. What puzzled her was why anyone had to go to all that trouble just to intercept the videotape of Hal Walker's interview. If it was stolen, all she had to do was shoot the interview all over again.

It took Tansy hours to get back to sleep. She kept wondering if she should tell Hal what had happened. She decided not to. Someone ought to get a decent night's sleep around here.

CHAPTER FIFTY THREE

Roper could see the Congressman and his wife in their relaxation room, surrounded by windows at the rear of the second floor of their Georgetown townhouse.

In the darkness, he ran up a periscope narrow enough to pass for a car radio antenna. Seated in the back seat with one eye on the mini-screen his camera was picking up, he couldn't have asked for a more intimate view of the husband and wife political team in their quiet moments together, relaxing, reading, occasionally working a computer, talking once in a while, even watching a TV set in a far corner.

But he couldn't hear what they were saying.

So far, the phone tap he had put in had produced nothing useful. Apparently their daughter and a few local tradesmen were the only people either Melford or his wife called on the regular phone. They seemed to prefer their cell phones. Roper might as well have saved himself the trouble he had gone to, tapping the landline phone, for all the good it had done him.

He'd have to install a bug. There was no other way. He'd been putting it off, but it became more and more obvious that he needed to know more about these people. A bug was the only way. And that cozy second-floor-rear enclosed balcony of theirs was the perfect place to put one or two bugs. At least one or two. They seemed to go there to unwind, to catch up with work, or simply to watch and listen to television.

Having made the decision, he ran the antenna-periscope down, switched off the mini-cam, and got out of there

CHAPTER FIFTY FOUR

Laurie and Earl waited while Jack Farris watched the Tansy Burns interview unfold on TV the following evening. Neither could read much into Farris's expression. He was too old a DOI executive to give himself away with a lot of grunting and grimacing, while he was taking in the basics of a case on which his subordinates wanted him to allow them more scope and freedom.

All day long, the cable news outfit had been plugging away, promoting their *secret interview,* which was scheduled to air that evening, an interview with a key witness in a recent murder case involving both the FBI and, allegedly, the CIA. Radio spots announced it, the television morning shows gave it a ten second mention, even some newspapers gave it a few inches on page three or four, as well as back in the TV section.

Now the three of them watched Tansy bore in on the hapless messenger, Hal Walker, relentlessly putting question after question to him. As the interview ground on, you could see him getting groggy. Somehow, though, he held on. When the wrap-up finally came, his story held together, Tansy was saying good night, and was turning the show over to her co-host, Parkhurst.

Farris switched the set off and swung his chair around to face the two of them across his desk.

"Okay, so the Spooks and Feebles got caught with their mitts in a cookie jar," he admitted. "But why would our department want to dig deeper than the New York cops have done?"

"With all due respect," Earl ventured, "the Feds tend to overawe local police. Even in New York."

"And it's beginning to look as if there may be a third party involved in this whole imbroglio," Laurie put in.

"That shoot-'em-up last night?" Farris asked. "The TV truck?"

Laurie nodded.

"Tansy Burns sneaks an interview taping in her own home," Laurie said. "Then, a few minutes later, two men try to stop her crew from getting the video tape back to their shop for processing..." She shrugged and spread her hands. "it could be a random hi-jacking..."

"But you don't think so," Farris stated.

"No, I don't. Not unless the two men who got away are found, and turn out to be run-of-the-mill law-breakers. Then I will believe."

"And now you want what from me?"

Laurie glanced across at Gordon, who nodded and said: "We've been doing background checking on both Congressman Melford, his wife, Norma Melford, and his murdered aide, Roger Brent. We've reached a point where we need to know more than just where they were born and went to school, and when they all met each other, twenty-some years ago. We need to..." He stopped, sighed, then continued: "I have to talk to someone in the Company. And I don't mean mechanics or field agents. Someone at least partway up the ladder. Maybe even as high as Graham..."

Farris chuckled.

"Fat chance! Graham is a policy man. He talks to diplomats, or to Chairmen of Oversight Committees. He doesn't have to talk to no stinking Department of Information investigators."

"It doesn't have to be Graham," Laurie pointed out. "Just someone who can give us real answers, is all we need."

Now Farris laughed out loud.

"Real answers? From the Spooks? First of all, they couldn't find a real answer to anything if they fell over one, just like most of the so-called *big secrets* they can't find, the ones that are supposed to be their main job."

He sat there, thinking about it, shaking his head.

"Well," Gordon ventured in a quiet tone, "could you try a few of them, over there in Langley?"

Farris came out of his thoughts and studied their faces, first Gordon's, then Laurie's. Shrugging, he said, "Try? Sure. Why not? But I can't guarantee much."

They both rose.

Laurie said: "We'll keep on with what we've been doing, but my nose keeps telling me that double-killing in New York has a bad odor all around it."

Gordon grinned.

"It stinks to high heaven, frankly."

Farris agreed.

"I know," he said, "but all I can tell you is that I'll send some probes across the river."

"Good enough, Chief," and "Thanks, chief," they said, as they left his office.

CHAPTER FIFTY FIVE

Tansy got home late. All the fuss and excitement of editing and cutting her interview with Hal had taken most of the day. When it finally ran during her five o'clock half of the program, she was drained and limp. Not even the look of congratulation in Walter Noble's eyes had been able to get more than a momentary rise out of her.

"If that doesn't put a real investigation onto the front burner in the Jeff Lasalle shooting, I don't know what will," Walter told her. "You did a grand job, Tansy. I'm damn glad you kept after me about running it."

Now, she put in a phone call to Paul's folks' home. He sounded perfectly normal, as always. Only her own life was in turmoil.

"The kids've been fine," he assured her. "They think it's a kind of vacation, coming out here to Grandma and Grandpa's house, instead of going home right after school."

"Did you get any flack at your job?"

"None at all," he chuckled. "There, I pretty much write my own ticket. Practically own the place."

She smiled. "I must try that sometime."

Afterward, she phoned Hal next door.

"Want to come over here for supper?"

"Love to. Right away?"

"Make it in a half hour. I want to look pretty for you, instead of like a drowned rat, which is what I feel like."

"Rough day, huh?"

"Brutal. But they ran your interview on-air. Now all we can do is wait and see what happens. Half an hour."

She had time to bathe and rest for a few minutes, before putting on light makeup. At the half hour, she heard the faint sounds from the little room at the back end of the apartment: the door panel closing inside the closet, the closet door being slid open. Then Hal emerged from her straitened den and she smiled at him, continuing to chop salad for their supper. When he slid an arm around her shoulder, she burst into tears.

Later, after they made love and then ate supper, they sat side by side, watching TV, with wine and cheese crackers.

When the ten o'clock news finished, she switched the set off with the remote, and they sat awhile in silence.

"I saw the interview," he said presently.

"What did you think?"

"You sure know how to pry the right answers out of a fellow."

With a wan smile, she nodded, but her eyes remained dark and thoughtful.

"I just hope it helps put an end to any . . . threats against you . . . by whoever might be making them."

"Maybe I was exaggerating," he said, stroking her shoulder gently. "About that car nearly clipping me that day. And some other things, too. Maybe it was being done by your private dicks, not the Feds, or whoever."

"Why would they?" she asked. "The PR man handling it for me says generally in a case like yours, as long as you and I are . . . seeing each other, the private detectives won't be pressuring you to pick up anyone else."

"Decent of them," Hal grinned. "Let's hope you're right, that there aren't any aftershocks from that interview. I mean from cops, or whatever Federal people might have a finger in this pie . . . or should I call it this can of worms."

He stopped speaking, his head turned, listening.

"What is it?" Tansy asked, watching him, frightened.

He looked down at her quizzically.

"Didn't you hear it?"

"Hear what?" She listened intently, but couldn't hear a thing except a car passing the intersection at the opposite corner of the building.

"A cough. Out there." He pointed toward the living room windows overlooking the street.

"What does a cough mean?" she asked apprehensively.

"Pressure by sound," he said, staring off a lot farther than at whoever was below the living room windows. "Bothering. The crime nobody knows anything about, especially cops and Feds and the rest of those idiots. The Chinese invented water torture. The French invented silence as a form of torture. The Americans came up with . . . noise. Characteristic, huh? Noise that never ends, noise that goes on and on, day and night for weeks, months, noise the victim has been trained by repetition to know is intended to bother *him*. A wonderful people, Americans, in some ways. But I could see a hundred million of them blown off the face of the earth, and it wouldn't bother me even a little bit, not after what they put me through all those years ago, for whatever pig of an actress started this idiocy for me."

"Don't, don't," she whispered, caressing his face with the palm of her hand. "Don't let it do this to you. Hatred never helps . . ."

Hal laughed harshly.

"The hell it doesn't," he said quietly. "Hatred helps a lot. It's kept me going all these years."

His eyes were burning. His jaws were clenched with the strength of the feelings inside him.

When he finally looked down at her face, he relaxed. Grinning wryly, he said: "A cough means that while you may have helped me give the Feds the slip, your detective agency scum are still out there, doing business as usual. C'mon. honey, let's go to bed."

"Yes," she said, rising, "but not here. Next door. I'd feel strange if we . . . here."

"Sure. I understand." He led the way through the two closets, using his key on the door connecting both.

Later, in bed, he listened to Tansy's even breathing beside him as she slept.

Odd, he thought, to have a double bed in this smaller place, and twin beds in her big apartment.

Then he grinned.

I draw no conclusions, he thought. I see no evil. I am a chimera . . .

At the front end of the building, he heard the sound of someone in the street coughing. Shaking his head ruefully on the pillow, he murmured: "We never sleep."

They sure didn't seem to. They did sleep, of course, but probably in shifts. Private detective street trash were definitely the opposite of shiftless.

CHAPTER FIFTY SIX

"Mr. Dickson? This is Marge."

"How're you doing, Marge?"

"Got some info on those two subjects you asked about."

"Quick work. What's their story?"

She laughed. "Truth is, they've probably worked for me, at one time or another, up there in New York."

"How's that?"

"On farmed-out jobs, I mean," she explained. "They're both electronic techs . . ."

"Computers?"

"Well, truth be known, they tap phones and install bugs and video cameras. Or check for them. The works: sweeps, repairs, service . . ."

"Okay, Marge. Good enough. Any more stuff come in to you on those out-of-state looksees.?"

"They are running kind of thin, by now, Mr. Dickson. Roger Brent and Mr. and Mrs. Melford left the mid-west almost a quarter-century ago. I've pretty much dug as deep and wide on the backgrounds of all three of them as anyone can."

"All right, then," Roper said. "Wrap all of it up and send me a report. We'll close that down. And the pair of bug-and-tap men, too. That's really all I need to know about them."

"Fine and dandy, Mr. Dickson."

Hanging up, Roper went over it in his mind: the messenger's apartment had either already been bugged and wired, or those two he had spotted had been putting new stuff in. It could be Feds hiring private enterprise to do its verboten work, but more likely it was someone in the private sector. But who? And why a nobody like that messenger?

Should he have Marge or another private dick outfit see if there were still taps and bugs in Walker's apartment?

Roper decided not to. After that Tansy Burns interview the other night, Hal Walker's connection as a witness to the whereabouts of Jeff Lasalle on the afternoon Roger Brent was murdered, that was now pretty much public knowledge. If anyone tried to whack that messenger now . . . like maybe Reynolds and Adams . . . it would cause a major stench. From here on, Walker was pretty much out of the case.

CHAPTER FIFTY SEVEN

"I don't believe it!" Adams breathed. "After the whole world took in that interview on TV the other night, Blanchard wants us to waste the guy? Is he out of his mind?"

"Relax! He left it up to us," Reynolds pointed out. "As far as I'm concerned, all the higher-ups want is for us to discredit that messenger bastard. If we plant some cocaine on him and get him taken into custody by the DEA, fine. If we've got to kill him by accident, the way we had to do with Lasalle, okay, I can live with that."

"All right," Adams said disgustedly. "Planting the coke on him is the way to go. It could discredit anything Walker says or ever did say. And it's the one sure way to squash anyone, high or low. I kinda like to keep the extreme prejudice thing down to a minimum, frankly."

"So do I," said the third man in the office.

Reynolds nodded in agreement.

"You're right, Tollman. That's why I want you to handle this. You'll do your best to *not* blow away this renegade witness of ours. I'm counting on that."

Tollman grimaced.

"You're also counting on me to put the hit on him if he doesn't stand still for the frame-job we hand him."

"Tollman," said Reynolds earnestly, "the only reason I want you heading this up is because you're the best man we've got right now."

"Your best man for killing people," Tollman said bitterly. "No, I don't want in. I'm not going to turn into some kind of psycho just to keep your efficiency score up near the top of the chart."

"We're not trying to turn you into…" Adams began to protest.

"There are lots of other men in the Company," Tollman said, rising and starting for the door. "How about using one of them for a change?"

Both men stared at the door after Tollman slammed it shut behind his departure. Reynolds looked at Adams and shrugged.

"Well, he came up with the drug-planting scheme, anyway."

"He wouldn't have," Adams pointed out, "if we hadn't been trying to find a way he wouldn't have to hit Walker. We'd've thought of it ourselves, sooner or later."

Adams got up and came around from behind his desk, pacing across to the window and back.

"I tell you, Mike, I'm getting pretty tired of Tollman's prima donna ways around here. If he don't like the heat, why doesn't he get the hell out of our kitchen?"

Reynolds nodded, blowing gently against a steeple he made of his fingers at the top of the arch where his elbows were planted on his desk.

"Anyway," he said, straightening and putting his hands flat on the desktop, "we've still got the problem Blanchard stuck us with: who do we get to supervise the job on the messenger?"

"Stoddard's got seniority," Adams said.

"Yeah, but has he got . . ." Reynolds spread his hands. "That extra something?"

"Maybe not," Adams admitted. "Not yet, anyway."

"How about Caldwell?"

"What about that Dispatcher guy? The hitter we . . ."

Reynolds shook his head.

"No," he said decisively. "Let's save him for a real job. This is only a bust-and-plant situation. There shouldn't be any need to kill that schnook of a messenger."

Adams chuckled.

"No, we'll just plant some crack on the poor bastard and send him to the slammer for fifteen-to-life. Me, I'd rather get whacked."

"That's only up in New York State," said Reynolds. "If we ever need to make contact with Walker again, we just wait till he and the news cunt get together, the way they've been doing. Then we bust him in an easy-drug-law state, and all he gets is, what? three to five? A milk run."

Adams laughed.

"Right. Now all we have to do is find him again. How the hell did he ever get out of that stretch of woods the other night?"

"I think I figured that out," Reynolds said.

"They never found any footprints," Adams marveled. "Not even with the dogs. Nothing. Not a sniff.".

"Maybe he never went into those trees," Reynolds suggested.

Adams's eyes widened. He thought it over.

"Meaning the son of a bitch snookered us and is still holed up in the broad's apartment?"

Reynolds shrugged, grinning broadly.

"It would explain why her husband took the kids to his parents' place in McLean."

Adams nodded.

"It sure would."

CHAPTER FIFTY EIGHT

When Roper listened to their taped conversation a few days later, he couldn't help but shake his head at their plans for the messenger who seemed to have eluded them.

"What a bunch of sleazeballs!" he muttered.

By now, Roper had uncovered the connection between the crew working out of the Watkins Construction office and the CIA. Marge's reports on the various types who went in and out of Watkins had turned up not only home addresses, for most of them, but had also revealed that now and then one or two had gone more or less directly from Reynolds and Adams over to the big think-tank at Langley.

Okay, Roper had thought, everybody's got to come from somewhere . . .

The rest of the exchange on the tape, both with Tollman, and later between Reynolds and Adams, had been most enlightening. That thought about where Walker might still be holed up could prove out. Roper decided it would behoove him to pay a visit to Tansy Burns's home, down there in Arlington.

He also had a new name to pass along, so Marge could add it to her collection of addresses: Blanchard. And Roper was particularly interested in him because he seemed to be the one who rode herd on the two hammerheads at Watkins Construction. "Blanchard wants us to whack the guy . . ." Adams had said.

One name at a time, Roper was getting there. Now all he had to do was figure out where there was.

Before making copies of the most recent tape his bug of the Watkins office had netted him, Roper reran it, listening closely to the sound of Tollman's voice. To the best of his knowledge, this was the first time he had heard a recording of Tollman, but there was a faint echo of familiarity about that voice of his. It was as if Roper had heard it before.

While he made copies of the tape, he made a mental note to replay some of the earlier tapes he'd made of those two, going back to the beginning, in the Chesapeake Motel, with their face-to-face meeting with Jeff Lasalle. Maybe that phone call from the motel manager had been Tollman . . .

CHAPTER FIFTY NINE

Nick Blanchard glared out his office window.

"Graham, I don't like giving in to someone like Earl Gordon."

The speaker-phone was on, because Blanchard couldn't sit still and carry on this conversation.

"Nick, every so often, we all have to give a little," came Graham's voice soothingly from the machine.

Turning to face his desk again, Blanchard rocked back and forth on his heels.

"What does Gordon think he's investigating, anyway?" he asked harshly. "Jeff Lasalle was a hired professional killer. We know he was, because we hired him. The crew tried to make an arrest, and he went for a weapon. What's to investigate?"

"Easy, Nick, easy!" Graham chuckled. "You don't have to convince me. You don't even have to convince Gordon."

"Then why do you insist that I speak to the turncoat son of a bitch at all?"

"Because he's with the Department of Information, and right now, that's where it's at. Tell him whatever you feel you can. Convince him that you've got taped phone calls proving that Lasalle was a killer for hire. If he demands access to them, just say it's classified information. If it ever gets to a court, or before one of the Oversight Committees, that's another story. Don't concern yourself about that, though. By then, I'll be the one on the hot seat. Right now, it's your turn. Get used to it. It's good practice."

Blanchard shook his head in exasperation, but he could think of no way out of the impasse.

"All right, Graham," he finally growled, "but if you think I'm walking any planks over this Operation Marauder cleanup, guess again. Mrs. Blanchard didn't raise her little boy to be a Judas goat, not for you, not for the company, not for any…"

"No one's asking that, Nick," Graham assured him gently. "Just sit Gordon down across the desk from you, answer whatever questions you can, and stonewall the rest . . ."

"No, sir," Blanchard said decisively. "I'm not letting that has-been come prancing into my office, and let everyone here know I've been forced to knuckle under to any of those wimps over at DOI."

"What, then?" Graham asked dryly. "Do you prefer to meet him in a waterfront tavern? Walls have ears, Nick, except in places like your office or mine."

Grinning, Blanchard said: "I'll use the old park bench ploy. That's all someone like Earl Gordon is worth."

"Do whatever you think is best, Nick. Let me know how it goes. And go there wired."

"Don't worry, I will. It's the only way I can be halfway sure I don't find myself getting early retirement like that Marauder guy . . ."

"Gently, Nick, gently," Graham cautioned. "Even walls that don't have ears just could."

"If they do, it might not be a bad thing for me," Nick replied. "I don't intend to be mustered out for the good of the service for running a rogue operation, not without taking plenty of company right along with me, maybe including you."

There was silence at the other end. Blanchard clenched his teeth. He wished he could pull those last words back, but he could not make himself even try.

'I mean it, Graham," he went doggedly on. "I've seen that sort of thing done to too many others, some of them good men . . ."

"Nick, I don't blame you at all for feeling that way," Graham said placatingly. "Just meet with Gordon. Answer his questions. Let me know how it goes, and send me a copy of your tape of the exchange. Then we'll talk about it afterward, you and I . . . in a waterfront tavern somewhere."

Blanchard couldn't keep himself from chuckling.

"Here comes the famous Graham soft-soap routine, huh? I've got to learn how to manage that."

"Takes time learning that, Nick. Scads of time. Good luck with Gordon."

* * *

Graham stared gloomily at his phone for a moment, then reached out, picked it up again and tapped in four extension numbers.

"Graham here. Could you send up a file?" He recited the file number from memory.

When the file arrived, he stared at the tag: MARAUDER. The usual EYES ONLY was stamped prominently on the tab of the folder.

Opening it, Graham read through it quickly. The grim expression on his face deepened. Toward the end, he shook his head, closed the file and slammed his fist down on top of it in the middle of his desk.

"All those lives! Thrown away!" he murmured, his voice thick, almost choking. "For what, some motley crowd of international political idiots?"

Sighing, he used the phone again, telling his aide in the outer office to have the MARAUDER file returned to records.

CHAPTER SIXTY

"It's good of you to make time for me," Laurie said.

"Not at all, Miss Buchan," Norma told her, pouring tea.

They were in the rear balcony room on the second floor, overlooking the garden behind the house, which was surrounded by its twelve-foot-high brick wall.

"It's peaceful here," Laurie said, looking down at the garden below. She found herself keeping her voice low. The gentle approach seemed appropriate with the Congressman's wife.

Norma nodded, following Laurie's glance out one of the row of westward-facing windows.

"Yes," she said. "My refuge. I've even begun to do a little work in the garden, since . . . since Roger died."

"It must be helpful," Laurie said gently. "Tell me about him. Not recently, but about . . . oh, his college years."

"Truth is, I wasn't really aware of Roger Brent until the end of our sophomore year at Margarita College. Of course, when he and

Linda Stevens had that terrible car crash, I couldn't help but become aware of him. The poor guy!"

"Were he and Miss Stevens engaged when she died?"

Norma's forehead wrinkled slightly with her effort to remember.

"I never really knew. There was a rumor, in the last week of the school year . . . but when she was killed in the car wreck, the point became more or less moot."

Laurie nodded, referring to her notes.

"The reason I asked was that I've heard different stories," she said. "One was that the two were engaged, another that they barely knew each other."

Norma smiled and nodded.

"Probably somewhere between. Linda and I were roommates in the dorm, our Freshman year, but for most of the Sophomore year, she lived in town, part of the time with Sam Mason, an All-American type, big man on campus. The year before that, Linda would have laughed at the idea of taking up with a straight-arrow like Sam, but . . ." She smiled at Laurie and shrugged. "When you're young, as she and I were, you try different things, just to find out about them. Today you're an intellectual. Tomorrow, you're into riotous living. Next week, you're cheering yourself hoarse watching Sam Mason throw touchdown passes in football games."

She sighed and gazed out the window. Tall trees in the side street beyond the wall arched high overhead. The afternoon sun peeped through leaves that were being rustled by gentle breezes, speckling the carpet with shifting shapes of sunshine and shadow.

"Sam Mason," murmured Laurie, jotting the name in her notes.

"I don't know what happened between them," Norma said, turning to face her visitor once more. "I only caught distant rumors about them. Then, suddenly, Sam wasn't on campus anymore, even before graduation day . . . he was a senior when we were sophomores. There was something about his R.O.T.C unit being called up. Or maybe he and Linda had a fight and Sam just . . ." She spread her hands helplessly. ". . . simply overreacted. Those simple straight-forward types can be that way. More tea, Miss Buchan?"

"No, thank you, Mrs. Melford."

"Anyway, the next story that went around campus about our own special golden girl was that she had taken up with an utter non-entity." She smiled across at Laurie. "Yes, our Roger Brent, who at the time would have been what is now being called a nerd. You can imagine the effect that would have had on everyone. Talk about going from one extreme to another!"

Norma shook her head at her recollections, smiling slightly. Then the smile faded, and she sighed again.

"None of all that lasted very long, however. Little more than a few weeks. Then, the terrible night of their car crash! Some reports said Linda was at the wheel, and of course she wasn't wearing any safety device. They didn't have them, back then. Other stories had Roger doing the driving. Whatever . . . when they were found, he was unconscious, thrown clear of the wreckage, but without a scratch. Linda . . . that beautiful, lovely girl . . . Linda was catapulted through the windshield. The glass tore her to pieces. The damage to her face was so extensive that they had to have a closed casket."

She fell silent, staring off into the distance beneath the trees towering high overhead.

Laurie maintained a discreet silence, waiting. She wondered which of the Melfords used the computer off to one side, near where Norma was sitting. Perhaps both used it.

Returning from her reverie, Norma smiled apologetically.

"As for the rest of us, Tim and I found each other in my junior year, his Senior year. Roger buckled down to hard work and turned into a first rate student, top of his class in his last two years there. I don't know what did it. Perhaps Linda's death, the suddenness of that. Perhaps guilt he may have felt because of it. Whatever the reason, he plunged into his studies as if that was all there was left in life for him. In a way, perhaps it was. He never again became involved with another girl. Never even looked at one. I often thought that perhaps he was afraid of bringing about another girl's death, the way he may have imagined he caused Linda's. Maybe he thought he was jinxed, and he didn't want to jinx anyone else, or cause any more harm."

Laurie nodded understandingly.

"Some people do react that way," she agreed. "Involve themselves in work, anything to keep busy. It helps them get past rough spots."

"The important thing is that he survived," Norma said with satisfaction. "I suppose you could even say he flourished, if getting good grades and developing a first-rate mind can be considered flourishing. But I've often wondered . . ."

"Wondered what?" Laurie asked, when she could no longer wait for Norma Melford to finish what she had started to say.

"I wondered if he and Linda really were engaged, however briefly. And if they were, did she get engaged to Roger Brent to get back at Sam Mason for deserting her, for disappearing into one of those ugly little wars this country of ours was so prone to get itself involved in, back then?" Abruptly, she sat straighter and smiled helplessly at Laurie. "Well, I don't think we'll ever know, will we? Now that Roger, too, is dead, there's no one left who could tell us . . . unless Sam Mason knew."

"Any idea where Mason is now?" Laurie asked.

"Good luck trying to reach him," Norma laughed.

"He's still alive, isn't he?"

Norma looked at her, startled.

"As far as I know he is. Last I heard, he was a field agent for the CIA, somewhere in the Middle East."

CHAPTER SIXTY ONE

Roper was glad he'd gotten a bug or two and a small video camera into the Melford's glass-enclosed balcony. Now he could not only watch Norma Melford and the woman from the DOI who was interviewing her through his antenna periscope, but he could listen to them, too. And he could hear most of what they were saying, too, always a plus. More to the point, he was getting them and their words on video-tape, so anything he might miss now, he could go back and pick up later, when he retrieved the tape it was all running onto.

His efforts to check on Tansy Burns' Arlington apartment, to see if she was hiding the messenger, hadn't panned out. He had been prepared to put in two or three days, staking the area out, but he wasn't parked up the block fifteen minutes before he began getting bad vibes. He felt as if he himself were being watched. When the feeling got through strongly enough, Roper pretended he was a salesman who had parked there to bring his appointment book up to date. When he tossed aside whatever he had faked he was working on, he started the renter and got out of there. Within two blocks, the watched feeling was gone.

All the same, Roper made damn sure he lost anyone who might have begun following him, before he returned to the place he was basing himself in, whenever he was down in the D.C. area.

That's all he needed, to find himself bracketed by detective agency street people who were watching Hal Walker, like those two tap-and-bug mechanics he had spotted going into the messenger's place, up in New York.

He wondered idly who might be having a private dick watch kept up on Walker. Maybe the newswoman herself? Tansy Burns might be trying to protect her interview witness, now that she had thrust him into the national spotlight. She might have hired the private police to watch over the guy awhile.

Now, sitting in the renter in a side street, watching and listening to Norma Melford and her visitor, Laurie Buchan, Roper again felt as if things were on track. The Tansy Burns stakeout hadn't panned out, but here he was with Marge turning up a home address in Falls Church for Blanchard, and now this past history linking all these people with Roger Brent.

The two women were talking about Linda Stevens, a girl Brent might or might not have been engaged to, after she broke up with Sam Mason, whoever he was. Maybe both would turn up in the mass of pictures and information Marge had sent him of those college years both the Melfords and Brent had put in, a quarter century ago.

The visit was breaking up. The Buchan woman rose and followed her hostess back into the house, out of sight.

Roper ran the periscope-antenna down, switched off the receiver on which he had been listening to their conversation. He decided to return later to pick up the video tape. It was up near the top of the brick wall that surrounded part of the side yard and all of the rear yard of the corner property. He didn't want to take the time right now to retrieve it, because he wanted to follow the Buchan woman. It would save him having Marge find out where she lived if he could do the tailing himself.

He was acquiring quite a collection of addresses of these Federal people. They lived all over the D. C. area.

Tailing Laurie Buchan was a good idea, but she didn't lead him to wherever she lived. Instead, she returned to downtown Washington to the building that housed the Department of Information, where she worked. Roper already knew she worked there from her first words introducing herself to Norma Melford, so his tail job didn't produce a thing, except maybe hone his skills at it.

When he saw her enter the DOI building, Roper jotted down the license number of her car plate, and drove back to Georgetown to pick up the videotape and replace it with a fresh one.

On his way, he decided that when he called Marge to have her find out Laurie's home address from her license plate, he would also have her put a tail onto Nicholas Blanchard. For a few days, anyway. See what it turned up, if anything.

CHAPTER SIXTY TWO

Laurie looked up from her office computer and smiled at Earl Gordon.

"Did Blanchard agree to meet with you, Earl?"

Earl nodded, closing the door behind him and slumping into the visitor's leather armchair beside her desk.

"Finally!" he breathed.

"Someone must have done some heavy-duty leaning on those people across the river," she mused, tilting her head toward Langley.

"I was thinking of going right on up to Graham at the top, if I had to," Earl said. "Turned out it wasn't necessary. Just as well. I'd prefer to save ammunition like that for a real emergency. I don't consider a talk with Nick Blanchard that big of a deal."

Laurie smiled, turning back and continuing with what she was doing.

"Just some detail work," she told him over her shoulder. "Entering the list of things Roger Brent's attorney gave me . . ."

"What list is that?"

"Things he left various people in his will. Mr. Merritt has been very cooperative and helpful. When I get it all entered in the file, I'll download it and send you a printout."

"Okay," he sighed. "You never know what'll turn out to be vital. I'm still swimming in a swamp."

"When's your meeting with Blanchard?"

Earl checked his watch.

"Less than an hour. I'd better get myself organized."

Groaning, he rose and started out.

"Let me know how it goes, Earl," she called after him.

"You got it."

The meeting took place on a park bench near the Washington Monument. The only other human creature within a hundred yards was an elderly man sitting on another bench, throwing crumbs to birds. He had a bamboo cane resting on his lap, and a big plastic bag containing an apparently inexhaustible supply of crumbs.

"Glad you could see me," Earl said, trying to keep his voice neutral.

Blanchard shrugged.

"A man's gotta do what a man's gotta do."

Earl's mouth tightened. He'd been afraid that was the way their talk was going to go, and that's pretty much the way it went.

Every piece of information Earl managed to draw out of Blanchard was like pulling a rhino's horns out with a pair of tweezers. He got them out, but by the time he did, it was messed-up and really bloody.

To Earl's initial questions about the Lasalle case, Blanchard said: "I'm as aware as you are, Gordon, that the Company isn't authorized to operate domestically, but the real world *we* live in isn't always so neatly compartmentalized. Something that happens overseas can extend to these shores . . . and vice versa."

"Granted," Earl conceded. "The world isn't perfect for any of us. Tell me about the shooting of your hired killer, Jeff Lasalle."

Blanchard grimaced.

"That hit wasn't supposed to happen. One of our people yelled to Lasalle in front of the bank: 'Put your hands in the air.' Lasalle no sooner complied, than another damn fool yelled: 'Show us I.D.'"

In disgust, Blanchard threw up his hands. He had to force himself to calm down before he continued: "So Lasalle is getting two orders at the same time: one is to put his hands in the air, the other to reach for identification."

"And when he did that last, that's when your men fired?" Earl asked, jotting notes.

Blanchard nodded.

"Bam! They blew him away. It wasn't supposed to happen, Gordon. Believe me."

"I do believe you. You said earlier . . ." Earl referred to his notes, although he was wired and recording every word both of them spoke. He assumed Blanchard was doing the same. ". . . that because of the special nature of the operation, you decided to hire an outside professional killer."

Blanchard nodded again in reply.

Nods don't record at all, but Earl didn't press it: "The theory being that . . . ?"

He made it a question.

"The theory was that if whatever went down couldn't be handled, we could waste a provable hired murderer."

"Provable how?"

"Our field men met him in a motel room. To set things up and pay him a second installment of front money. Both our men were wired. They had another agent in the motel manager's office. That one phoned the room, pretending he was concerned about the two men he'd seen enter Lasalle's room. That way they got Lasalle's voice on the phone tape, to compare it with earlier phone talks the team had with the hitter they were hiring. There seems to be some doubt about whether the earlier voice-print matches up with Lasalle's voice-print on the agent/motel manager's call to the room. But that may be because it was such a brief exchange."

"Can my department have a copy of those voice-print tests?"

"Certainly, if you subpoena them," Blanchard said, staring at Early with quietly hostile eyes. "There's no other way we're giving them up, not to you people at DOI, not to Treasury, not to the Attorney General even . . . not without a full-fledged legal brannigan. And that means subpoenas. That was the deal I struck with Graham . . ."

"Which means I can't check on anything you tell me."

"Those are the rules of this talk," Blanchard said stubbornly. "If you want to quit right now . . ." He made as if to rise.

"No," Earl said with a smile. Wouldn't you love me to break this off at this point, before I've gotten anything out of you? he was thinking.

Reluctantly, Blanchard settled back on the park bench, and it went on.

The shabbily dressed old man feeding the birds kept the bottom end of his cane pointed at the two men, getting most of what they said on the recorder in the cane's elaborate handle, picked up by the ultra-sensitive mike in the tip of the cane.

A lot farther away than a hundred yards, Roper made sure he parked his renter outside the perimeter within which Marge's mike men and picture-takers had planted themselves, but Roper wanted to take his own pictures with his telephoto lens. He got a good look at the two men on the distant bench. One of them he had seen up in New York, going into Hal Walker's building the day after the two tap-and-bug guys had been there, the one he thought was a Fed when he first laid eyes on him, but on a second look hadn't been so sure. Even now, he still didn't have that buttoned-down look the feebles and spooks always wore around the Capitol.

The other one was Blanchard. This was the first time Roper got a look at Blanchard. He took pictures of both of them, glad that he had called Marge, and that she had clued him when this meeting was going down, and where. Promising her he would stay well clear of her people, he had hustled over.

It was always best if you could see men like those two in person, the way they sat, how they moved, walked . . . everything. A lot better than pictures. Even video pictures.

Finally, they rose, nodded to one another, and walked off in different directions.

Marge had already provided Roper with Blanchard's home address, so he let her tail stay with Blanchard, while he joined in the follow-job Marge was having done on the other one, Earl Gordon. The license plate on Gordon's car would eventually provide Roper with a home address, but if he could find out where Gordon lived right away, it was that much more information he had in hand that he didn't still have to get from Marge.

Always economize whenever it's reasonably possible!

As with the Buchan woman, it didn't work out that way. Since it was still only mid-afternoon, the DOI man didn't go home. He simply went back to where he worked, in the same building Roper had followed Laurie Buchan to, after her visit with Norma Melford. Marge had already uncovered her address and had passed it along to Roper. Now her people would have to watch and follow this Gordon dude and find out where he lived, too. Roper had no more time to spend on it himself.

Peeling off, he let the hired people do the drudge work of waiting for the DOI man to emerge from work, get back in his car, and go on home; unless Marge developed a home address from Gordon's license plate before evening, through her contacts at the DMV.

Roper decided to check with her before day's end, in case she did.

But most important of all, Roper had another name to play with: Graham. The man Blanchard had made a deal with, before he would talk to Gordon. Which meant that Graham was higher up the food chain than Blanchard . . .

One name at a time . . .

CHAPTER SIXTY THREE

"All right," Reynolds told the three men gathered around his desk. "This is the floor plan of the Burns woman's building."

Caldwell asked: "Aren't you bringing Tollman in on this?"

"No, he's out of it. He's put in for a transfer to the planning section."

Caldwell and Stoddard exchanged glances, grinning.

"Ambitious guy!" Stoddard murmured.

"Basically, the ground floor doesn't concern us," Reynolds continued. "Boiler, furnace, oil storage tank, a garbage collection area, and over here a private garage area, walled-off from the rest of the basement. There's a connecting door, but it hasn't been opened in years. The super doesn't even have a key for it, anymore. Tansy Burns rents the garage."

Reynolds pointed at the four corners of the plan spread out on his desk.

"On the first floor, above the basement, all four corner apartments are pretty much like the second- and third-floor layouts: good-sized apartments, each L-shaped, extending halfway across the front and halfway along the sides of the building. Same with the two apartments in back. Except for the first floor, that is, behind the Burns woman's apartment: that's a small efficiency apartment. The building owner used to occupy that, but he moved out."

The three men studied where Reynolds was pointing, over at the right side of the floor plan. Adams didn't bother. He had studied it already, so he was less attentive to the orientation than the others.

"Burns's apartment and the little one reach more than halfway back from the front corner of the building, but the apartment at the rear corner, away from the street, that one isn't L-shaped. The small apartment takes up the space they shaved off that one."

Reynolds pointed to the lower right-hand corner of the plan.

"That rear apartment just runs straight across its half of the back of the building to its common wall with the other rear apartment, which is L-shaped. As you see, the efficiency takes up the space that would have been the upright extension of the corner apartment's L."

"No one's in the efficiency apartment?" Stoddard asked.

"That's right," Reynolds said. "Your stake-out indicates there's one of those adjusted light systems in there . . ."

Stoddard nodded.

"That means the lights turn on and off at exactly the same times, day and night, as if the place was occupied. To keep burglars away."

"Exactly," Reynolds agreed. "So we can forget about that little apartment. You'll have a couple of the Drug Enforcement guys outside in the driveway, to watch the Burns apartment's windows, in case there's an attempt to escape that way. The rest will go in the front way, through the street entrance, up the stairs, and right there, adjacent to the top of the first floor steps, is the entrance to the Burns apartment. You won't even have to go down that side of the hallway to the other two apartments on that side of the first floor. Put one man back there, just in case, but the rest just go straight in. Got the layout?"

They studied the floor plan, nodding thoughtfully.

"I still wish Tollman was going in there with us," Stoddard murmured. "In case there's any shooting . . ."

"There isn't going to be any shooting," Reynolds said forcefully. "Walker is just a witness, not a hard case of any kind. Just arrest the guy. Let the DEA people do that, too. Leave everything to them. They know how to come up with an arrest so they find plenty of stuff on the perpetrator, certainly enough for an arrest. Which is all we want: just something to smear that messenger bastard so his testimony won't be worth a damn anymore. We're trying to clean up that mess with the actor, up in New York. Okay?"

They all nodded, decisively. It was okay. They could handle it.

CHAPTER SIXTY FOUR

With Tansy's family living with Paul's folks in the next town, she and Hal spent a lot more time together at night than they had before now, but she still had to get up each morning and go to work. Hal did his best to wake up and join her for breakfast, but she laughed and sent him back to bed.

"You're only in the way, sweetheart," she told him.

When she was ready to go, Tansy came back in through the two closets. Bending over to kiss him goodbye, she whispered: "I brought a half-full container of milk over for you. It's still fresh. I just bought it yesterday. I'll get an extra container for you tonight, if I can remember to."

"That's all right," Hal assured her. "I can go out and pick up two containers . . ."

"No, no," she cried, alarmed. "I want you to stay out of sight. Give it a couple more days, to see whether those federal agents, or whatever they are, are still looking for you."

He nodded.

"You're right. It's just that I'm going a little stir-crazy, cooped up in here all day and all night."

"It won't be much longer," Tansy assured him. "I've got my editor in touch with our legal people, to find out what kind of rights you, as a witness I've interviewed, might have. I don't know if that will be much help to you, but it's better than no lawyer at all being on your side. Maybe soon you can act like a free man again."

"Honey, I haven't been able to act like a free man for years," Hal grinned wryly, "and it has nothing to do with Feds. I wouldn't know how to handle real freedom."

Tansy nodded, couldn't think of anything to say to that, and left. Hal rolled over and went back to sleep.

It was mid-morning when a huge crash out in the corridor brought him awake in a shocking instant.

"Federal agents!" a voice roared.

Another crash.

"Open the door! We have a warrant to search this apartment . . ."

Scrambling out of bed, Hal tried to get dressed, still half-asleep, his heart pounding.

More smashing sounds.

He got his shoelaces tied and looked around in a panic.

Where should he go? Out into the corridor was no good: they'd spot him, and he'd be in jail in no time. If he lived long enough to get to jail!

He couldn't help thinking of what they had done to that actor in New York.

Easing up beside a window, he took a careful peek out around the edge of the curtain.

A man in a shiny black leathery-looking jacket stood gazing up at the windows of Tansy's apartment, toward the front of the short driveway. The man turned his head and glanced back this way.

Hal caught his breath and froze, tilting backward slightly, away from the curtain.

When he dared to take another peek, the man was facing the other way, toward the street end of the driveway. A big yellow DEA was across the back of his black jacket.

I wonder if that's a flak jacket, Hal found himself thinking.

Then he remembered the closet.

Suppose they broke into Tansy's apartment next door and one of them went barging into the closet on her side of the wall? That hinged end-panel would swing inward if anyone just breathed on it.

Frantically, he hunted for his keys, found the one that opened all the door locks in this little apartment, and carefully slid the closet door open wide enough so he could step in there. Pushing aside the hinged panel, he entered the secret part of this closet and eased the key into the lock of the connecting door. It turned silently, and the door opened, just as silently.

Stepping through, he could hear hammering sounds in one of the distant rooms of the bigger apartment, which were increasing in volume, followed by a crashing noise, then heavy hurrying footsteps.

They had broken the corridor in, and now they were inside Tansy's apartment.

Sweating, Hal carefully slid the top bolt on the panel into its iron bolt-hole, then he did the same to the lower one.

When the hinged door-panel in Tansy's side of the closet was secured by the two bolts, Hal got himself quickly back through the connecting doorway and closed the heavy door behind him, locking it with the key as soundlessly as he could manage.

Sighing with relief, he got out of the closet on his side of the common wall and carefully slid the closet door shut.

Now if one of them took a look inside the closet on her side of the wall, and even pushed against the hinged panel at the secret end, it wouldn't bounce obligingly away from the push and reveal the connecting door, In fact, it might even feel like a plywood panel in a closet ought to feel, to anyone who shoved it.

But he was still stuck in this place, waiting to see if they broke in on him next.

Then he remembered the stairway leading down to the garage below.

He started for the door that gave onto the landing at the top of the stairway. But before he could even put the same key into its lock, he heard a woman's voice outside in the corridor.

Hurrying to the front door, Hal leaned close to it and heard the woman saying: ". . . but should we leave the building, officer?"

"No, ma'am. Just remain in your apartment. Don't let anyone in through the windows, not even if you know them. We'll let you know when this emergency procedure is completed."

Hal continued listening. He heard the door of the apartment behind his close, as the woman there at the back followed the DEA man's instructions.

After listening awhile longer, he still couldn't hear anything useful from the front end of the corridor, just deep men's voices. Except for an occasional word that was louder than the rest, he couldn't make out most of what they said.

Shrugging, he decided to act as if he was a tenant of the building, too, just like the woman in the apartment at the rear end of the corridor.

"None of this has anything to do with me," he muttered.

Going into the kitchenette, he proceeded to fix himself some breakfast.

With the TV on, he ate slowly, but try as he might, he couldn't blot out the sounds of those heavy footsteps beyond the wall with its two closets. The footsteps seemed to shake the entire building. It was only after he had cleaned up his breakfast dishes and put them away that it occurred to him to place a call to the ACN network and leave a message for Tansy.

To whoever took his message, he said: "Tell her it's got to do with her apartment."

CHAPTER SIXTY FIVE

Earl Gordon was leaving the cafeteria when he spotted Laurie sipping coffee and reading the Washington Post at one of the tables. He swerved over that way.

"Hi. I was going to return the copy of those notes you made," he said.

"Of my interview with Mrs. Melford? Here, Earl, sit. Let me get this stuff out of your way." She swept her papers off the table onto the chair beside hers.

Earl took the seat across from her, sliding a folder over.

"Keep that, why don't you?" she suggested. "I've got the original copy."

"Okay." He retrieved the folder.

"Anything in there of use to you?"

"Quite a lot. Especially that business at the end, about Sam Mason being in the CIA. I recall attending a lecture given by an instructor named Mason, when I was starting out in the Company. One of those practical hours they made us sit in on, now and then:

what it's like in the field. I think his name was Mason. Might even have been the one Mrs. Melford spoke about."

Laurie watched him, a smile in her eyes.

"Are you going to follow up on it?"

"Huh?" He returned from wherever his thoughts had taken him. Seeing the amused look in her eyes, he grinned. "I've thought about it."

"So soon after your last request?"

"Good point. I don't want to push those people, over there in Langley, so this time I may work the 'old boy' routine . . ."

Thinking about it, he stood, decided, and nodded.

"Yes, that's probably the way to do it: call one or two chaps I worked with, reel in some lines, collect one or two 'owe-mes.'"

Laughing, Laurie began collecting her things.

"That's probably the best way, so soon after crow-barring the talk you got with Blanchard out of them. Wait for me, I'm going up, too."

As they left the cafeteria together, she added: "You might put in an official query about Mason, too . . . for the record."

He grinned. Nodding.

"What devious dodges we have to keep thinking up!"

CHAPTER SIXTY SIX

Walter Noble hung up the phone just as Tansy Burns stormed into his office. She looked furious. He wasn't surprised.

"How'd your place look?" he asked.

"As if a hurricane hit it," she snapped, throwing her tote bag onto the floor and flinging herself into the leather-covered chair facing the editor's desk. "They chopped through the front door of my apartment with an ax. An ax! Inside, the place looks like it was struck by . . . I don't know . . . a whirlwind!"

"I was just talking to our legal people," Walter said. "They're getting right on it."

"They're a bit late," Tansy said bitterly. "It'll take months to get my apartment looking the way it should . . ."

"It's First Amendment I'm thinking of," Walter interrupted. "Coercing a witness. Trying to pin a crime on your messenger so his testimony will be next to worthless . . . We have to forestall those tactics they're using. Did anyone you spoke to out there claim they found anything?"

Wearily, she shook her head.

"What was there to find? Hal Walker isn't hiding in my apartment . . ."

"I was thinking of drugs," Walter said patiently. Rising, he went around his desk and over to the door, closing it.

Tansy stared at him, her eyes round with astonishment.

"You don't think they'd dare accuse me of using drugs, do you?"

"I hope not," Walter said, going back behind his desk. "They could. Nothing is easier than for the Drug Enforcement people to . . ." He shrugged as he sat down. ". . . oh, plant a little glassine envelope. They do it all the time. It's the reality of this New Prohibition they've sneaked into place by way of the Food and Drug Administration's rules and regulations. What should be a good thing gets turned into a nightmare. Al Capone would have loved operating now. Instead of having to unload a ship full of hundreds of cases of liquor, nowadays all you have to do is get some Columbian peasants to swallow ten or fifteen little plastic bags of cocaine or heroine and hope none of the bags are eaten through by stomach acids before they get . . . evacuated."

Tansy couldn't believe her ears.

"But . . . me? You actually think they would try to frame me?"

"The thought did cross my mind. I'm damn glad they didn't try."

"My God!" Tansy murmured. "So am I. I never thought of it before. And yet, you're absolutely right. It would be so easy for them to do something like that. It's downright scary."

He nodded, his face grim.

"That's what we get for living in a country that refuses to face the reality that people can get drunk now with a needle stuck into their skin, not just by slugging down a shot glass of scotch whiskey. Until ordinary people deal with that, these idiotic wars on drugs will continue." He shook himself, and straightened in his chair. "All right, they didn't try pinning any planted evidence on you. We can be thankful for that. Now get to work and organize your story about it for tonight's five o'clock."

Tansy lunged to her feet and picked up her tote bag.

"I can't wait!" she growled, her jaw set and her eyes blazing.

"Tansy, I'm sending your crew out there for pictures and quotes, if they can get any from those DEA people. Oh, and I'd better have Burley send one of his legal staff with them . . . in case the Feds give Bill and Jerry any flak."

Tansy nodded, but she wasn't really listening as she hurried out, headed for her office and the computer, so she could get started on what she wanted to say on her evening show.

CHAPTER SIXTY SEVEN

"**B**lanchard, have you taken leave of your senses?" Graham growled into his phone. "You bring in those DEA neanderthals and turn them loose on Tansy Burns's home?"

"It was just supposed to be a quick bust," Blanchard replied defensively. "In and out, the guy in cuffs, maybe a little white stuff found in his pocket . . . no big deal. Then let them try to use his testimony to cloud that Lasalle mess up in New York . . ."

"Nick," said Graham patiently, "are you dealing with reality at all? Tansy Burns is a newswoman. Every evening she goes on cable TV and talks for half an hour about anything she wants to. Care to make a rough guess what her five o'clock show tonight will be dealing with?"

At the other end, Blanchard sighed.

"Chief, we're just trying to dampen the damage that's been done . . ."

"I understand that," Graham replied, "but you're producing exactly the opposite result."

"What do you suggest?"

"Pull in your horns," Graham advised quietly. "Tell your DEA people to use the wrong address routine. It happens. Effusive apologies to Ms. Burns and her family . . ."

"And what about that messenger?" Blanchard cried angrily. "Do we apologize to him, too?"

"If necessary. Stop worrying about him. Time passes. People forget. By now, hardly anyone remembers Jeff Lasalle and how he died. Every time you engineer something like this morning's disaster, you're simply reminding everyone all over again. Soft-pedal it, Nick, including Hal Walker. You can even have the DEA offer to give him twenty-four-hour-a-day protection, in case anyone is trying to intimidate him, or tries to influence his testimony."

Blanchard snorted.

"You really mean that? You think people will be fooled by a routine that corny?"

"Nick, believe me, people will believe anything. You just have to tell them what you want them to believe long enough and often enough, and sure enough, eventually they do. It's the basic principle behind advertising."

CHAPTER SIXTY EIGHT

For the first twenty minutes or so of her half of the program that evening, no one could have told from Tansy Burns's smooth delivery of the local news that anything unusual was about to happen. But six minutes before Renn Parkhurst would take over for his part of the show, Tansy looked directly into the camera, and now her eyes were not intent and serious and sometimes even mildly concerned. Now her eyes were steely, and her voice, when she delivered her first words, was flat enough to send a chill down some viewers' spines.

"At around ten o'clock this morning," she began, "my home was broken into by U. S. Drug Enforcement Agents. They smashed in the front door of my apartment with an axe and a sledge-hammer, demolishing the door completely. They left my apartment a shambles in their search for . . . whatever it was they thought they would find.

"The news isn't all bad, however. My family was lucky in a couple of ways. One, my husband and I were both at work when our home was invaded, and both our kids were at school. None of us had guns stuck in our faces. The other break was that the DEA didn't plant any illegal drugs in our home.

"You say they wouldn't do such a thing? Agents of our government? Mr. and Mrs. America, it's done all the time. Any highway patrolman who stops any car on any highway can just happen to 'find' a little plastic bag with white powder in it on the back seat or on the floor of the car. Who do we complain to? The cops? They *are* the cops!

"Where did all this insanity come from? It came when the Food and Drug Administration began ruling that this drug and that drug is illegal and harmful to consumers, and must be forbidden. To enforce that rule, they needed a drug Enforcement agency. So now we have the New Prohibition that sneaked in the side door here in America, and even the rest of the world, too, and all with the very best of intentions of the various nations' Food and Drug Administrations trying to protect us from the effects of harmful drugs.

"Nowadays, anyone's home and fireside can be invaded to save us all from the danger of illegal drugs. True, it's more likely to happen if you are dark-skinned or black, but as I found out today, it can even happen to me, and I'm about as white-skinned as you can get without a special permit.

"All right, it's possible that this is part of an effort to get back at me for recently interviewing one of the Government witnesses about an FBI shooting, up in New York City a few weeks ago, which may also have involved the CIA. It's nice to see the DEA cooperating with the other law enforcement agencies, isn't it? . . . but not in my neighborhood, okay?

"In a way, it may be partly our fault: we can't stand the thought of people getting drunk or high by sticking needles into themselves, instead of doing it the old fashioned way, by drinking a shot glass of whiskey or a schooner of beer or a glass of wine. We've had ten or twenty thousand years to get used to those ways, most of us. But we had better get used to these new ways with needles and pills, Mr. and Mrs. America, or the sort of insanity I experienced today will continue, and perhaps get worse for the next fifty or hundred years, or however long it takes for us to get used to it."

All the while Tansy was speaking, her words were being reinforced by footage of her apartment's broken-in front door, then later, of the overturned and ripped-apart furniture inside.

Walter Noble watched and listened closely, as he directed the segment himself. Part of it he had written himself, with Tansy. He stayed right on top of it all the way through, cueing in the inserts illustrating the formation of the Food and Drug Administration with quick-cut shots of newspaper headlines, then footage of various highway patrolmen stopping speeders by roadsides and searching them on the spot, without warrants.

"What have I learned from this experience?" Tansy went on. "I've learned that perhaps we should stop this nonsense. It isn't working. Don't war on drugs. Tax drugs . . . and use some of the revenues to fund rehabilitation for those people who have been wiped out by their foolish use of whatever chemical they stuck into themselves, and to fund nursing care for the ones who can't ever recover. Use those revenues to educate the young about the dangers of taking drugs. But the main point is this: wake up, Mr. and Mrs. America. It's still your country . . . though just barely. And I hope you do wake up, while there's still time. It's later than you think. The enemy is not only at the gates, he's smashing in our front doors. My front door. And the enemy is us, in more ways than Snoopy ever dreamed."

Tansy had been leaning forward tensely, all the while she spoke. Now she sat up straight again and leaned back. The angry look left her face, and she smiled the warm friendly smile her audience was accustomed to seeing, during her part of the program.

"But enough about me," she said wryly, almost disparagingly. "I think it's about time to turn this show over to Renn Parkhurst . . . before I tell you what I *really* think."

One member of the crew laughed at that, although they were never supposed to. Walter grinned and let it go. It might be exactly the touch needed to wind up the intensity of the segment Tansy had filled with so much passion.

"Switch to Parkhurst . . ." Walter sang out to the technicians at the bank of monitor controls.

Renn Parkhurst was almost finished with his half hour of the program when he glanced aside and said, "This just in . . ."

He brought a sheet of paper into view of the camera and read from it: "Word has just reached Amalgamated Cable News that a spokesperson for the Drug Enforcement Agency has been authorized to extend the Agency's sincere apology to Ms. Tansy Burns and her family for the damage this morning's raid did to her apartment and any inconvenience done to her and her family. They had the wrong address . . ."

CHAPTER SIXTY NINE

"Jenner, I'm very glad you called me about it," Graham said.

The two men sat in a wood-paneled bar frequented by upper-echelon attorneys savvy in the ways of Washington. Jenner sloshed his drink around in its glass, nodding thoughtfully.

"Earl Gordon's a good enough man," he said, "but the Company comes first. I decided if he's asking around about Sam Mason, it might be just as well to let you know he was, and leave it up to you to decide whatever you want me to tell him. If anything."

Graham nodded his approval.

"Best thing is to soft-pedal the facts on Mason. Don't stonewall Gordon, but don't give him much in the way of detail, either."

"In other words, you don't want him to think there's anything special we're trying to hide about Mason."

"Precisely. You've run a check on Mason. He's still on active duty overseas. So, of course you can't leak anything more than that to anyone. Without clearance."

Jenner's glance flicked sideways to the other man's face.

"And you'll see to it that Gordon doesn't get clearance."

Graham's head tilted a bit.

"Not necessarily, Jenner. Leave it relaxed and open. I may want to arrange clearance, somewhere down the line."

"Okay, good enough," Jenner said. "Let Gordon know the bare minimum, not enough to think we're specially covering up anything about Mason, but not giving him access to any more information on him than we'd give to anyone.'

Graham nodded.

"We'll see if he wants it real bad. That way, Gordon will let us know how important the information he wants is to him. It will also give me a bone to throw him if I don't want to give him a piece of some other bone."

Both men chuckled.

CHAPTER SEVENTY

Reynolds left the payphone and rejoined Adams in the car. Adams watched silently as Reynolds settled into the passenger seat beside him.

"What did he say?"

"Blanchard?" Reynolds shrugged. "We're to go easy on the messenger. The DEA is offering Walker bodyguard coverage, day and night, to make sure no one tries to damage his credibility as a witness . . . as if anyone would try!"

"God forbid!" Adams laughed.

"The rest of it was just . . ." Reynolds shrugged again, his mouth tight, his eyes staring through the windshield.

"Just what?" Adams asked, when his partner's silence dragged on too long.

"Just lay off both of them, Walker and Burns." Gently, Reynolds pounded his fist down onto the smooth rounded edges of the dashboard in front of him.

"But you don't cotton to that."

"No, I don't."

"So? What do we do?"

Reynolds thought about it awhile, then said: "I think we should start a quiet watch on Ms. Tansy Burns. Nothing to alarm her, but . . . watch . . . and wait."

"Any particular purpose?"

"Something Stoddard said once, or one of the men, about Burns."

"What was that?"

"Oh, about maybe her and Walker were getting it on."

Adams' eyes widened. He thought it over.

"Okay. It would be worth finding out about . . . if they are."

"Damn right it would," Reynolds said emphatically. "If we can prove something like that with a few tapes of pillow talk, or, if we work it carefully enough, a video camera planted in a bedroom . . . well, it might not be anything we could use in court, but it sure would be a threat to hang over that bitch's head. No one in her racket wants that kind of publicity."

CHAPTER SEVENTY ONE

By the time Tansy arrived home that evening, her husband had overseen the repair of the doorframe by the landlord's contractor. They both watched, as the new door was installed. When they were satisfied with the snugness of the fit in the frame, they made sure the lock worked, and then thanked the landlord for the trouble he had gone to for them. As soon as they could, afterward, they got out of there and drove up to McLean.

"I simply couldn't spend the night there," Tansy explained, "not with the mess those DEA thugs left."

"Can't blame you for that," Paul agreed. Then he chuckled: "For all that smash-and-grab routine they pulled this morning, they still don't have a clue that your witness friend is right next door."

"Sh-h-h!" Tansy whispered, her eyes darting around the inside of the car.

Her husband turned his head and looked at her curiously.
"Why not?"
"What if they've bugged this car of ours?"

For a moment, he looked as if he would laugh at the thought, but he didn't. Instead, he shook his head.

"Tansy, I hate to hear you talk that way. This is all getting to you, and I hate to see that happen."

She nodded.

"I guess it is. That's one reason I need a night away from there. Distance myself from the scene."

Next morning, she had Paul drop her off at their Arlington apartment, where she sent him on to his job, while she and her regular cleaning woman did the best they could to straighten up the mess the intruders had created, the day before.

"It will still take weeks before it looks decently again," she told Hal, after the woman had left for the day.

"What do we do now?" he asked her. "I'm running low on milk."

For some reason, Tansy began to laugh. She kept on laughing until Hal joined in. They ended up falling all over themselves in hysterics, laughing their heads off in bed.

They spent most of the morning making love and fixing breakfast dishes and making love yet again.

When it was finally time for Tansy to leave for work, she told Hal: "Stay here for the rest of today and tonight. I'm going to find out if my PR contact can make sure the private detectives keeping you under observation are also protecting you. If they are, it should be safe for you to get on home again."

"I think they are," Hal said. "It's probably part of the job they do, not only making sure I don't get away from *them*, but that nobody else messes up this ongoing meal-ticket I've been providing them with, all these years."

She grinned ruefully.

"You poor man," she said.

Kissing him, she headed for the closet, calling over her shoulder: "When I know for sure you'll be safe, I'll call you . . . although I still wish you'd just go to work for me and move down here."

"I might just as well," he laughed.

He watched as she slipped inside the closet and slid the door shut behind her.

"Lately," he called, "I'm spending most of my time down here in Washington, anyway. Might as well make it official."

He heard her giggle before the connecting door closed behind her in the secret area beyond the closet's end-panel.

Turning, Hal wandered over and switched on the TV set in time to hear a news announcer's voice say: ". . . with the Drug Enforcement Agency's assurance to Mr. Walker that they will gladly provide him with round-the-clock bodyguards to make certain there are no attempts from any source to influence his testimony in the ongoing investigation of the killing of the alleged hired assassin, Jeff Lasalle, in New York, several weeks ago . . ."

"Okay," Hal muttered to the TV set. "Now who do I get to protect me from you guys influencing my testimony?"

CHAPTER SEVENTY TWO

Sometimes Roper felt like a phone company repairman, the way he had to move all over the place, "servicing" the various phone taps and bugs he'd installed.

The most recent taps were those of the two DOI people, Gordon and Buchan. There were no problems out of the ordinary with either installation, just normal precautions watching each of their buildings awhile, then moving in at the right time, putting in the tap, and getting back out, as quick as possible.

With Graham, he'd had a different situation. Once he finally secured a home address for the man, he tried to get the lie of land in his usual preliminary survey of the subject's neighborhood, prior to zeroing in on the actual house. But the shield of protection around Graham's house had been such that Roper could almost feel the smell of ozone burning and his hair standing on end with electricity, the moment he came within range of the safeguards in place.

Knowing when he was clearly outgunned, Roper got out of there. He'd have to do without a tap on Graham's home phone.

As for most of the other taps, so far they had proven to be unfruitful. The people involved, Reynolds, Adams, Tollman, Stoddard, Caldwell, the two DOI people, Earl Gordon and Laurie Buchan, even Congressman Melford and his wife Norma, all seemed to be professionally close-mouthed on their unsecured phones. Household calls, intimate stuff with their various family members, there was plenty of that, but anything having to do with work, there was hardly ever anything at all.

That was the trouble when you dealt with highly trained pros: they handled an unsafe phone as if it was a live grenade in their hands, very carefully.

Still, it was like the mining business: you had to process tons of shale for every nugget you came up with. Roper just wished he could rake in a few more nuggets than he had so far.

Which may have been why he was so gratified, when he listened to the most recent tapes he'd picked up from the taps on the home phones of Earl Gordon and Laurie Buchan.

Roper played both tapes simultaneously when he realized what hers contained: he stopped hers, ran it back to the beginning of the call she made to Gordon's home, and on a second tape player, he found where Gordon's part of the conversation was caught.

"Bingo!" Laurie chortled, when Earl picked up his phone.

"Bingo the game?" he asked. "Or just Bingo! like in 'Eureka, I have found it'?"

"Like in Eureka," she replied. "Whether I've found 'it' or not, I know not, but I may have found something."

"I'm glad one of us has," Earl said, sounding dejected. "I'm still stymied by the key question in all of this: why was the attempt made on Melford's life, or was Roger Brent's killing intentional? We're still noplace on that fundamental motive."

"Perhaps this will help," Laurie said. "I was running family trees through the computer. Melford: nothing. No connection to anyone else. Norma Tyler, his wife's maiden name. Nothing there, either. Roger Brent, same: nada. Then I ran Linda Stevens through . . ."

"And you found something!" Earl sighed. "It's about time we got a break. What was it?"

"Linda Stevens' mother had a sister, somewhat younger than she. The sister married a Midwest businessman named Blanchard . . ."

"Aaah!"

"Right," she chuckled. "Aaah! says it perfectly. Linda Stevens' aunt had three children, all boys. The youngest was named Nicholas. He now works in quite a hush-hush department, somewhere in the Federal Government."

"Say no more," Earl told her. "We'll save it for when you take it to Farris. These phones of ours . . ."

"Yes, you're right, of course," she admitted. "I just felt so terrific, I had to tell someone."

"Glad you did," he laughed, "and I'm glad it was me. We'll make an appointment to show your find to Farris, first thing in the morning. I think he'll be damn glad to see it. We've been puttering away at this case for so long, and my results, at least, have been disgustingly negligible."

"You've done fine," she assured him "Although you're absolutely correct: I think it's just the right time to bring Farris something. He's been unusually patient, especially with me, considering it's your case, and I'm just horning in on it."

"But your horning in has finally produced results. See you tomorrow, Laurie."

Roper switched off both players and thought it over, while he was making his usual copies of the various tape sections he considered worth copying.

So Blanchard might have had a motive to arrange an Extremely Prejudicial exit visa for Roger Brent. All it would need was a conviction on his part that the Congressman's aide had somehow been responsible for the death of his first cousin in the auto accident, a quarter century ago. Suddenly an opportunity presents itself to avenge Linda Stevens' untimely death, and Wham! Goodbye, Roger Brent.

Roper shook his head, though. It could be . . . but it seemed a bit far-fetched. Who waits over twenty years for something like that?

Still, one never knew. Some people can hold hidden grudges for a long time. Perhaps Nick Blanchard was one of them.

CHAPTER SEVENTY THREE

"It's kind of stretching it," Farris eventually said, after examining the material Laurie had presented.

Earl agreed.

"True. We're not coming out and saying that's the basic motive for arranging Roger Brent's untimely departure . . . but it's something to consider."

"At least in Blanchard we've got a focus," Laurie interjected. "One suspect we can zero in on."

Non-committally, Farris said: "I suppose we might use it as a wedge, however weak it is."

The other two exchanged a glance, but said nothing, waiting.

"On the Company," Farris explained. "I'll slide it into them. We'll see what happens, if anything happens."

"Wouldn't that be tipping our hand to them?" Earl asked.

"It won't be that big a tip," Farris replied. "So far, we haven't got a helluva lot, just this connection with someone linked uncomfortably close to that actor-maybe-assassin's murder, or execution. Specifically,

Blanchard. I gather he's running whatever operation pulled off the Brent/Lasalle hits. But an experienced pro in the Company like Nick Blanchard isn't going to jeopardize any operation by letting personal feelings influence his decision, especially one about who gets whacked. What we're looking for is why?"

Farris stared at each of them in turn.

"What is the operation those people are running? And why are they operating domestically at all? Even with a rogue outfit farmed out to handle the dirty work?"

"They did use the FBI and New York cops to do the shooting in Lasalle's case," Earl pointed out. "Or most of it."

"Granted. But we still need to know why? What's the operation? That's why I say we'll let them know what we've found so far on Blanchard . . . just to see if anything comes of it."

"Okay," Laurie said. "Makes sense, Chief."

"Which of us do you want to handle it?" Earl asked.

"Neither. I'll take care of it."

The meeting seemed over, so they both rose and turned to the door.

"Oh, Earl," Farris called. "One more thing. Anything come of that query you put in over there, among your old buddies?"

Earl grinned ruefully.

"Not much. One of the three I called got back to me on it . . . but not with much that was real."

Farris grimaced.

"More stone-walling?"

"Not exactly," Earl assured him. "I didn't get that impression. Jenner didn't seem forthcoming enough about Mason, but in a standard way: Mason's off on assignment overseas, so of course he couldn't give me any details as to where and what, for obvious security reasons."

Farris nodded with an understanding grin.

"They'll tell you anything you want to know . . . but it still comes to nothing."

"For security reasons," Laurie added.

"Okay," Farris sighed. "Can't fault them there. It's what they do. They can't run up banners announcing where they've inserted their people, and what they're up to. I'll let you guys know if I come up with any results on the Blanchard find, when I feed it to them . . . in the interest of inter-departmental cooperation."

CHAPTER SEVENTY FOUR

"Hi," she said. "It's Tansy. I'm calling from Washington."

"How's the fix-up work going?" Hal asked. "Got your apartment looking all right again?"

"It's getting there. We've all moved back in. Write down this number I give you, all right?"

"Wait," he said. "I'll get paper and pencil."

When he had found them in the kitchen drawer, he said into the phone: "Go ahead, Tansy."

She read off a phone number, including an area code.

"Got it," he told her.

"Do you have enough quarters handy to call me down here?"

"Yes. I'll use quarters I accumulate for laundry machines."

She laughed.

"Okay. Take your bike and ride half a mile before you use a payphone to call that number. It's a payphone, too."

"Any particular reason for all this . . ."

"I'll tell you when you call."

"In about fifteen minutes," he said. "Ten to fifteen."

In just about that time, he put quarters into a payphone after being told by the operator how many.

Tansy's voice said, "Hello? Hal?"

"Hi. What's the big secret?"

"My public relations people got back to me on whether your private detectives provide protection for you. Yes, they do."

"I kinda thought so."

"It's part of their job. But there's something else they told him."

"What's that?"

"They had to remove the tap they had on your phone, as well as the bugs and a video camera that was active in your apartment." She was silent for a moment. "I'm sorry, Hal."

"What for?" He was genuinely surprised.

"Oh, that your privacy had been invaded so . . . so completely."

Hal laughed, watching traffic going along beneath the El tracks overhead.

"Tansy, I told you already: I got used to all that a long time ago. But it's nice to know I can leave the bathroom door open when I use the john from now on, and know I'm not on camera."

"Oh, my God!" Tansy wailed. "It can't be that bad!"

"Why can't it?" Hal asked in a flat voice. "Who's gonna stop them? Huh? The District Attorney here? The FBI? Tansy, none of them could find Godzilla's asshole unless it blew up right in front of their noses. So how are they gonna know about a thing as subtle as the bothering routines the private detective sub-culture has developed and made foolproof? Law enforcement people couldn't shoot themselves in the foot without blowing their own brains out . . . if they had any to blow out."

Tansy had begun to laugh around Godzilla.

"Anyway," she gasped, when she could finally stop the laughter, "the reason the private detectives removed all their bugs and taps and videos was because word reached them that some of those Feds were going to install their own phone taps . . . and maybe bug your apartment, too. They weren't sure about that part, though."

"So," Hal murmured philosophically, "my phone will still be tapped. These are just different intruders."

"You'll have to be careful what you say from now on," she cautioned him. "Those Feds might still be out to get you . . . in spite of all their hot air about giving you twenty-four hour protection."

"I'll be careful, Tansy," he assured her. "You're about the only one I talk to on the phone, anyway."

"And from now on, we'd better not. We'll have to figure out another way for me to reach you . . ."

The operator broke in, wanting more quarters. Tansy heard.

"Tell me the phone number there," she said quickly.

He read it off to her.

When she read it back and it checked, he said, "I'm hanging up. Call me back."

She did. They talked awhile longer, but the only thing added to the conversation was her suggestion that Hal list the phone numbers of nearby payphones, make a chart of their locations, and number them.

"Then you can send me a copy of your list and the identifying number you've assigned to each of the phone numbers. Then I can call you at home and just say the assigned number, and ten minutes later, I'll call you at that phone."

"Brilliant plan!" he laughed. "Okay, that's what we'll do."

CHAPTER SEVENTY FIVE

Roper pulled one of his spot-removals of the bugs and phone taps in Watkins Construction. All he could hope was that they did a sweep of the place while his gadgets weren't there, but he still had no way of knowing.

After giving them a few days, he put it all back. Next afternoon, when he switched tapes two floors below Watkins' office, there was nothing but humdrum stuff going on, so he relaxed and went off to service his other taps and bugs, which also contained ho-hum material.

The following day, he made one of his periodical phone calls to Watkins and was surprised to hear Reynolds say: "Glad you called, Dispatcher. We've got an assignment for you . . ."

Roper got all the details within his forty seconds of allowable time on any phone call, so he just told Reynolds "Got it," and hung up. If any of the material he'd been given required clarification, he could always call back.

The job was simplicity itself: Roper was to hold himself ready on a standby basis, calling in at fixed times to get detailed instructions as to who his target was to be, if any, and where said target might be found.

"If it turns out that your . . . dispatching skills are required," Reynolds had specified, "your price will be the hundred thousand, as per our original agreement . . . in addition to the fifty G you've already been paid. But for this standby period, you get paid only fifteen G. That okay?"

"Sure, that's reasonable," Roper had assured him. "Fifteen thousand to make a few phone calls, that's nice money. If the rest of the job develops, is the hundred thousand in addition to the fifteen?"

Reynolds had chuckled.

"You're a close man with a dollar, Dispatcher. No, you'll just get the remaining eighty-five thou."

"Deal."

Now all Roper had to do was find out what Reynolds and his Chief, Blanchard, were up to.

He got on the phone to Marge.

"Like you to put a follow job on a few of the people whose addresses you've gotten for me."

CHAPTER SEVENTY SIX

"We're doing it this way so it doesn't look like any kind of big deal," Farris told Earl Gordon.

"Understood."

"I have no clue as to why Graham caved in to my request for data on Sam Mason," Farris continued. "Maybe that business I fed him about Blanchard being a first cousin of the girl who died in that car crash years ago . . . Linda Stevens . . . maybe that prodded him. This give on his part could be Graham's way of asking us to lay off. 'We'll let you talk to Mason, so forget this other thing,' etcetera." Farris shrugged. "Whatever his reason is, I'll take it."

"Same here," Earl grinned.

"You're just going on a regular round of visits to a few of our regional offices." Farris went on. "Stop off at Seattle, then San Francisco, and wind up the business on those case files I gave you yesterday. On your way to the Denver branch, stop off in Colorado and see this Mason."

"So he wasn't on overseas assignment," Earl observed.

"No. He's retired . . . one of those gotta-be retirements. You'll call that number I gave you. That Jenner you contacted will take you the rest of the way to Mason himself. Apparently Jenner is one of Graham's trouble-shooters. Or trouble-calmer-downers, more likely."

"Okay."

"Anything you want to reach me about, contact your buddy, Laurie. Don't run her ragged, though. Her caseload is getting up there."

"You're not expecting any heavy-duty stuff to come out of this Mason's corner, are you?"

"Earl, the fact that Mason's been retired in his middle forties tells me something."

"You wouldn't care to share that something with me, would you?"

"Hell, you know what it is without my spelling it out."

"Spell it out, anyway. Today's one of my slow days."

Patiently, Farris explained: "It's like a map spread out right under your nose, Earl. He isn't taken into Langley to work on planning, where he'll likely move up in the Company as a matter of course. No, they retire him. And when someone like you goes to see him, you have to be led there by someone like Jenner, an old-line smoothie who knows the Company's dirty laundry like the back of his hand. In short, Mr.Gordon, they're protecting this Mason guy, from somebody. Either that, or they're protecting themselves from Mason. Maybe both."

CHAPTER SEVENTY SEVEN

Melford stood in the doorway, watching his wife in the glass-surrounded second-floor-rear balcony.

Norma gazed pensively out at the trees overhanging the side street beyond the brick wall. When she became aware of his presence, she turned and smiled at him.

"Hello."

Tim knelt beside her chair, kissing her cheek, then her throat, and finally gently pressing his lips against her breasts, first one, then the other.

Norma encircled his head with her arm and held his lips pressed to her left breast for a long moment, her eyes closed and her breathing deep and regular. When she loosened her hold, she pressed her lips to his and whispered: "Here, my dear, get up from there. Sit with me awhile."

"A pfennig for your thoughts," he murmured, pulling his usual chair over beside hers and sitting on it.

"Just wondering how long it was going to go on."

"How long was what going to go on?"

"The aftermath of Roger's killing."

"Ah, I see. Sorry. I'm still caught up in some of those hearings I've been locked into, in committee. You're referring to that Burns bust the DEA pulled off, a few days ago?"

"Yes. In her program that evening, Tansy Burns as good as accused them of doing it as payback for her interview of one of the witnesses to that shooting of the man who killed Roger . . ."

"Quite a blast she laid on them," Melford said, shaking his head in admiration as he recalled it. "I hear the Networks are hovering around her now, trying to find out if she'd be willing to jump ship from that cable outfit she's with . . ."

"When does it end, though?" Norma cried, her head turning away, repulsed by his practical take on things.

Holding her hand and kissing her wrist, he murmured: "Soon. It should end soon, my dear."

"But when?" she wailed, a note almost of desperation in her voice. "One minute they think you were the one that assassin was trying to shoot. Next moment they suspect it may really have been Roger he was after . . ."

"Who's they?" he asked, turning to stare at her. "This is the first I've heard of that."

"Oh, no one comes right out and says it," she admitted, "but the direction of some of the questions that Department of Information woman asked me pointed unmistakably in that direction."

"What woman?"

"Laurie Buchan, from the DOI. I told you about her."

"Yes, now I remember." Her husband shook his head. "Don't let it get to you, Norma. They have nothing else to do in their jobs except keep trying to find out about these things. Since I'm directly affected by the question of whom the assassin was trying to kill, Roger or myself, I say, keep at it, fellas. Leave no tern unstoned." He grimaced ruefully. "Sorry about that pun, or whatever it was. It was definitely for the birds . . ."

Smiling wanly, she put the palm of her hand on the nape of his neck, leaning her forehead against his cheek.

"You're so sweet, Tim. You could always make me smile, even at . . . even at a time like this."

"It will pass, my dear," he assured her gently. "All things pass, given time enough and world."

"You're chock-full of twisted poeticisms this evening, aren't you?" she chuckled.

He stroked her back with the palm of his hand.

"I guess you bring out the twisted poet in me . . ."

CHAPTER SEVENTY EIGHT

"Chief, I appreciate what you're trying to do," Blanchard said. "It just gripes me that you have to bother doing it for me."

They were having lunch in the executive dining room, with Blanchard as Graham's guest.

"It's not entirely for you, Nick," Graham assured him.

"I know that. I also know it's almost impossible for someone in my position to prove that there wasn't a personal thing influencing my decision to have Brent taken care of."

Graham nodded.

"Understood."

"I mean, how do you prove you hardly even remembered that this guy was the one in the car when a cousin of yours was killed, all those years ago . . . ?" Blanchard's voice was ragged with exasperation. "Who the hell drags that kind of weight around for a quarter of a century?"

"Okay, Nick, relax. It's never been a real possibility, to me or anyone else. We're letting Gordon look in on Mason for several other reasons, in addition to signalling Farris to turn off this nonsense connecting you with the Brent case. That decision was approved even before you were ordered to set up your rogue operation to take care of it."

Blanchard nodded, appearing to relax slightly, poking at his so-far-untouched pot roast dinner, but still not eating any of it.

Graham eyed him for a moment, before continuing to eat his own fish meal.

"One of those other reasons," he said presently, "is to prepare Gordon and his boss over at DOI, in case anything hits the fan in the Marauder situation."

"Chief, you don't intend to let them in on that, do you?" Blanchard asked incredulously.

"Of course not. But in case it does come out, they won't be totally unprepared."

Shaking his head dubiously, Blanchard thrust a forkful of food into his mouth, almost unaware he was doing it.

"Then there's the on-going status of Mason himself," Graham continued thoughtfully. "The Company doesn't put someone like him on the retired list and leave him there forever. We . . . oh, let's say we try to contain the situation. We keep him under observation for a period of time. Check up on him, now and then. No pressure. Just to see how he works through whatever made us retire him in the first place. Who knows, one of these years, Mason might even be able to return far enough to be taken back into the ranks deep enough so we could groom him for . . . perhaps a move into planning, if only as consultant."

Blanchard glanced at him, a mocking smile touching his lips.

Graham grinned sheepishly, nodding in agreement.

"I know," he admitted. "That almost never happens, but every so often it does. Mason just could be the one out of how many? who just might be useful again. We have to keep evaluating his progress."

"And allowing Earl Gordon to visit him is part of the evaluation?"

"Exactly. It eases Gordon into contact with him and with the reason he was retired, without exactly telling Gordon anything real. It also lets Mason know we're still dealing with him as a valued agent, not just a zombie we put out to pasture."

"Even if that's really the case," Blanchard chuckled.

"We don't necessarily have to keep him in that status. There's a next stage to his rehabilitation. I'll be interested to see how Mason reacts to Gordon's visit."

Blanchard nodded and continued eating, saying: "Good luck with it . . . and with Mason."

CHAPTER SEVENTY NINE

"One of your people just caught a flight to Seattle," Marge told Roper.

"Which one?"

"Earl Gordon. Should I arrange for anything . . . at the other end?"

"Yes. Stay with him."

"Okay, I'll have someone waiting out there, when he gets off his plane."

"Make it a several-faces tail, will you, Marge? Gordon's an experience man, I gather. We wouldn't want him to spot the generic two-hundred-and-fifty pound guy in the ten-gallon-hat and a purple-and-orange sports coat, like in a John Grisham novel."

Marge laughed.

"Several faces it is, Mr. Dickson. And I don't care how experienced Mr. Gordon is, he'll never know they're there."

"Good girl. I'll keep in touch on this one."

Roper sat with his hand on the phone, a grin cracking his face.

"All right!" he murmured. "Maybe this is the ice breaking in the river at last. It sure took long enough."

* * *

Marge was right. Earl Gordon never knew that the private detectives she had farmed the tail-job out to in Seattle, and later in San Francisco, never let him out of their orbit . . . but he was experienced enough to sense he was being watched.

It was a subtle thing, and it took awhile to make itself felt, but eventually he got that feeling: the uneasy awareness that he was never alone, no matter where he went outside his various hotel rooms.

He'd felt it before, when he was doing fieldwork for the Company overseas, so it didn't take too long for him to pinpoint and identify the feeling. He still didn't spot them, but he knew the watchers could literally be anyone, of any age short of a two-year-old infant . . . and maybe an occasional one of those just might be one of them, laughable as it might seem: infants in strollers can conceal video cameras and microphones.

However, Earl didn't let it bother him. He assumed it was Graham's people making certain no one else was dogging his footsteps. Which meant that it was simply part of their ongoing effort to keep Mason's whereabouts a secret from . . . whom?

Perhaps those two shooters who had tried to intercept Tansy Burns' crew that time . . . the X-factor people? The police had never made an arrest in that case. No on had any idea who those shooters had been.

Unless perhaps they were Graham's people? Doing lots of shooting, but not hitting anyone?

Shrugging off such questions, Earl kept going through the motions at the various regional offices, ostensibly "wrapping up" completed cases, and forwarding the final reports on each to DOI's Washington headquarters.

When he received Jenner's message in San Francisco, giving him the go-ahead for the next day, he took a final stroll on the Marina Green . . . and he also put in a payphone call to Laurie at her home,

248

bringing her up to date on what he'd been doing, and telling her he would be meeting Graham's man Jenner in Central Colorado, to be taken to his rendezvous with Sam Mason.

"Be careful," Laurie cautioned.

Earl chuckled.

"Hey, they're the Company, but they're still on our side . . . sort of. I hope."

"I hope so, too," she echoed quietly. "But you are doing a little job of investigating things they've been up to. Don't forget that."

"You may be right. I'll watch my back. How's everything at your end?"

"I'm just finishing supper."

"It's bright and sunny here by the Bay, where I am now," he said cheerfully. "Sails out on the water, the St. Francis Yacht Club, people flying kites, jogging, sitting on the Marina Green grass. A veritable idyll." Then the smile left his eyes, and he added: "Too bad so much that's dark lurks underneath all this sunlight and pleasantness I'm looking at . . . It's almost as if it's all on display, for contrast with reality."

"Don't fret about it, Earl," she advised. "Have a nice visit, and let me know how it goes, as soon afterward as you can."

"Will do," he assured her, before hanging up.

* * *

Next morning, back in Washington, Roper retrieved the tape on Laurie Buchan's home phone tap, so he heard about Earl Gordon's progress toward his encounter with Sam Mason even before the light plane dropped down from the skies and landed Gordon at Sardy Field near Aspen, where he was presumably to be guided by Jenner on the final stage of his roundabout journey to meet the mysterious Sam Mason.

CHAPTER EIGHTY

"This is nice," Elyse Branston said. "You're a lucky man to be groundskeeper of this place. I've always loved it up here."

Sam Mason grinned.

"You're even luckier. Your folks own all this land."

She shrugged.

"I'm so used to it that I never think we actually own it. There's too much of it. No one can really own all that magnificence out there."

She gestured at the surrounding forest.

They were standing at the railing on the upper porch of the log-built Alpine lodge, above the front entrance to the groundskeeper's dwelling.

From high up, a pinpoint of light across the narrow valley shone into her eyes, dazzling her momentarily.

Elyse blinked.

"What in the world was that?" she cried, startled.

He had noticed, although the light had only touched her for an instant. He noticed a lot of things.

Glancing at the tree-covered slope across the way, he said, "Probably my watchers. They're pretty close, today. Too close." He shook his head. "They aren't training them the way they used to train us. But then, there aren't all that many cold wars to be trained to fight in, not anymore."

Elyse scanned the far tree-grown slope, but couldn't see anyone. Turning back to Mason, she studied him for a moment.

"Are they your protectors?"

"I suppose you could call them protectors," he said, grinning ruefully.

"Well-l-l, are they friendly? Can you tell me that, at least?"

He studied the opposite slope a moment, before returning his attention to her.

His eyes were hard, but they were also lit with a touch of amusement, as he finished his thought aloud: "As I said, with all the brushfire wars contained, the only enemy left is us."

She looked puzzled.

"That sounds like something I heard recently," she murmured. She tried to recall where she had heard it, but couldn't. Shrugging, she smiled up at him.

"Do you have any idea how fascinating you seem right now?"

Puzzled in his turn, he eyed her with a trace of suspicion. He wondered if she was putting him on.

"I may be guilty of many things," he drawled, "but fascinating isn't one of them."

"Oh, you are, believe me," she laughed, taking his hand and squeezing it, trying to pull him away from the railing toward the split-log bench. "Here you lurk, in the middle of a wilderness, guarded by who knows what government bent agency, living high on the hog in this groundskeeper's lodge . . . God! If any of my women friends knew about you, I wouldn't be able to keep them away from here.

Mason laughed.

"If anyone but you turned up at this lodge your family loaned them . . ." He tilted his head across the valley toward the observation post, where the gleam of reflected light had originated. ". . . somehow I don't think I'd be around here much longer. They'd ship me off to someplace that was less crowded."

"Well, I certainly wouldn't want that to happen," she said. "Who would I spend an occasional carnal afternoon with?"

His grin was perfunctory, his thoughts obviously elsewhere.

"When is your visitor slated to arrive?" she asked.

Mason spread his hands.

"No set schedule. Just sometime this afternoon." He frowned, shaking his head. "It's odd. The last thing I would think they'd want is for anyone to see me."

"Are you in that deep a cover?" she asked in a hushed tone.

His glance was mocking.

"It's more like a witness protection program . . . but one is seldom certain who is being protected, the agent, or them."

She nodded. "It must be a strange world to inhabit."

Again he spread his hands, negligently this time.

"It's a living."

She watched him for a long moment, then smiled and shook her head.

"No," she said gently. "Not with you. In spite of this flip act of yours, it was never just a living."

His head swung around. His eyes were startled, as if he was surprised at what she had said. Then, averting his glance, he stared across the valley. Gradually, his gaze swept along it and down toward the lower country through a gap to the southeast.

After a prolonged silence, he murmured: "So many are dead who were young."

The sound of his own words spoken seemed to bring him back from wherever his mind had gone off to for a moment. Looking at Elyse almost shyly, he said, "Something I read somewhere."

She leaned against him at the railing, gazing across the sweep of treetops down the narrow valley to the gap, and the wider lower country beyond it.

"Come inside," she whispered. "Even if your visitor prevents me from staying the night, at least we can enjoy ourselves while there's still time."

* * *

Up at the observation post, Earl Gordon peered through the binoculars set up on a tripod.

Just inside the electronically operated gate fronting the groundskeeper's lodge, on the left, trees half-concealed the building. A car was parked near the entrance.

"Whose car is that?" he asked Jenner. "The sporty job."

Jenner glanced inquiringly at the man on post.

"The woman's," he replied. "She stays up at the main house." He gestured up the valley, toward the northwest.

"There's a place bigger than that?" Earl asked, stepping back from the binoculars to give Jenner a chance at them.

Both men laughed.

"It's ten times the size of that lodge down there," Jenner said, squinting through the glass. "The original Branston first built this lodge as a place where he could take his family for vacations and an occasional weekend getaway. I guess the really big bucks came later. That's when he built the new house up top."

With his naked eyes, Earl could clearly see the man and woman turn and leave the tiny upper porch under the steep roof sheltering it. The wooden door closed behind them.

"When do I pay him my visit?" he asked.

"Whenever she leaves," Jenner replied. "Unless you want to barge in on those two right now?"

Grinning, Earl shook his head.

"No. There's no hurry."

About an hour later, the two people emerged from the lodge on the side away from the drive beyond the gate. She came around to the front, where she had parked her sport car, and got behind the wheel.

Backing and turning around, she drove out of sight beyond the lodge, appearing on the drive a moment later, where she turned in the other direction, away from the gate, and disappeared in among thinner tree growth that still managed to conceal most of the long drive that led to the main house, higher up.

Jenner glanced at Gordon.

"Any time you like."

Earl nodded.

"I go down that path we came up on, then I make a right onto the road and follow it up to the gate. Push the button under the speaker to the left of the gate."

"Correct. Mason is expecting you. When you come out again, I'll see you from here, so by the time you walk down to the foot of this path again, I'll be there at the roadside to meet you in the jeep that brought us up here."

"Got it."

Nodding to both men, Earl started down the path he had climbed earlier in the afternoon.

CHAPTER EIGHTY ONE

Inside the gate, Earl walked along the asphalt-paved driveway for a dozen paces, until he was out from under the trees. There, he turned left onto a flagstone pathway leading up to the lodge, beside the driveway that circled the building.

The lodge stood on a rise. Three plank steps led up to a narrow porch, where a compactly-built average-sized man in his forties stood watching him.

"Mr. Mason?"

"Yes. You'd be . . . ?"

"Earl Gordon," he said, climbing the steps and shaking hands with his host.

Earl was surprised to find that he was a bit taller than the other man.

"Come inside," Mason said, turning and stepping into the open doorway. Pausing, he turned back to ask: "Unless your friends across the way instructed you to remain out here where they could see us."

Laughing, Earl shook his head.

"No, inside will be fine. It's getting a little chilly for me, this high up."

"I hadn't noticed," Mason said, going on ahead inside. "I guess I've become accustomed to it, the altitude and the cool nights."

Earl closed the door behind him. His eyes swept the big room before him: a wide stone fireplace, a Malacca walking stick leaning against one side of the fireplace, nothing on the mantle, a moose-head projecting from a wall opposite the fireplace, scattered Native American-looking rugs, comfortable furniture, but not much of it, and a wooden stairway climbing to the floor above.

Not luxurious, but comfortable. Earl liked it.

"Coffee? Or a drink?" Mason asked.

"Coffee, but only if you've got it already made."

"I have. I perc twelve-cup pots of it, and I drink it all, one cup at a time, until it's all gone. Then I make another pot, just as big."

"When did you last make it?"

Mason thought a moment.

"Yesterday, I think. Time tends to pass, up here. One forgets." He glanced inquiringly at Earl. "Still want a cup?"

"Sure. Yesterday isn't so long ago."

Mason grunted.

"Sometimes, yesterday can be eons ago," he observed dryly.

The coffee turned out to be not bad. Not stale at all.

They had the coffee in the kitchen, another all-log room, like the rest of the place. Earl sat at a smooth plank table, while Sam Mason leaned his hips against the edge of the sink.

Earl examined the man: solidly built, he moved smoothly in high-topped hiking boots, wore corduroy pants and a dark-blue checked flannel shirt. Light brown hair cut fairly short, pale blue eyes, a jaw that clenched more often than it should, making the muscles tend to ridge, even when he wasn't trying to flex them.

"I took one of your courses," Earl said into the silence. "I remember you, slightly."

Mason grinned, thinking back.

"One of those 'What it's like in the field' lectures? Did it ever turn out to be useful?"

"I was never sent into the field, while I was with the Company."

"And now you're with . . . ?"

"Department of Information."

Mason seemed amused.

"And they let you come see me?" He shook his head in mild amazement. "The ice must really be breaking up in the river."

"I suspect they're trying to keep me from going down any wrong paths in my inquiry."

"And this inquiry of yours, exactly what is it? And more to the point, what's it got to do with me?"

"We're curious about the way Roger Brent was killed."

Mason nodded, his gaze wandering off.

"Brent," he murmured. After a moment, he nodded. "Oh, yes, the congressman's aide."

Earl's eyes narrowed. He wondered if he was watching an expert put on an act for him.

"The accepted scenario was that someone tried to kill Congressman Melford," Earl explained. "But when we looked into the past histories of both men, the indication seemed to be that Brent himself might have been the true target."

Mason was watching Earl again.

"I see," he said. "It was supposed to look as if Melford was the target." He smiled, shaking his head. "They're always so goddamn devious. More coffee?"

"No, thanks. This is fine. How well did you know Roger Brent, Mr. Mason?"

Mason's eyes widened in surprise. "Know him? I never met the man . . . to my knowledge. Of course, what little time I spent periodically in Washington could have brought us together, at public functions. Still, he left me that . . ."

He gestured toward the fireplace.

Surprised, Earl leaned forward. "You're telling me that you never knew Roger Brent back in Margarita College?"

Mason's eyes became still. His jaw set.

"That's what I'm telling you, Mr. Gordon."

"You lived with Linda Stevens for awhile, though."

"What's that got to do with . . . ?"

"I'm trying to find out how you could be so intimate with a young woman for perhaps the better part of her sophomore year and your senior year, but shortly after you disappeared, Linda Stevens is killed in a car crash . . ."

Mason nodded, still watching his visitor steadily.

"What I'm trying to see in all this is some connection to me," he stated flatly.

"Roger Brent was the other person in the car crash that killed the woman you lived with for . . . how long? Several months? A full semester? Or was it longer than that?"

"Part of the Fall semester and most of the Spring. Then my ROTC section was called up for special training . . ."

He gazed at the opposite wall, a smile touching his lips lightly.

"So that's what the connection is? Roger Brent was in the accident that took Linda's life? But Mr. Gordon, that still doesn't expl . . ."

"How did you feel when you heard Linda Stevens had died so suddenly?"

"I felt terrible, of course," Mason said, spreading his hands palms up. "But by the time the news reached me, weeks had passed. She had already been buried . . . We'd been out in the boonies on exercises, so we weren't getting regular mail. I suppose no one thought to notify me. Why should they? She and I were only ex-roommates. We had a difference of opinion about some things, so when the time came for my ROTC call-up, Linda was probably as glad as I was to let our break-up come about through more or less natural forces outside ourselves. It solved our problem. At least, to me it seemed a convenient solution. I can't speak for how it might have been for Linda. With women, sometimes you can't be sure."

"The story we reconstruct," Earl said, "is that she turned from you to Roger Brent. It was even noised about that they were engaged. Then the accident takes place. He lives, she's killed instantly. Our question is this: was that a possible reason for the killing of Roger Brent under cover of a faked assassination attempt recently on Tim Melford's life?"

For a long time, Mason stared at him, until a grin slowly spread across his face.

"Jesus!" he murmured. "I don't believe those bastards. The things they come up with." Then a thought struck him. "Are you accusing me of being involved in this far-fetched concoction of yours, Gordon?"

"Mason, I'm not accusing anyone of anything," Earl replied evenly. "Simply trying to find out the most likely possibility."

"Okay, I'll accept that," Mason said. "And my answer to your implication is simple: I never knew nor heard of Roger Brent to my knowledge until I heard his name on television news shows recently, when he was apparently shot by mistake, instead of his boss, Melford. Does that answer your questions, Mr. Gordon?"

"Some of them."

"How about answering a few of mine?" Mason went on, his eyes hard, boring into Earl's. "Like, why would you dig up past history about me and an old girl-friend, almost a quarter of a century ago? Are you doing a job for your old pals in the Company, trying to connect me with Brent's death? Am I supposed to have managed it for revenge of some kind, because Brent's lousy driving caused Linda's death in that accident?"

"Not at all, Mason, nothing like that," Earl protested. "We know you couldn't have. You were nowhere near New York the afternoon Brent was shot . . ."

Mason laughed.

"That doesn't mean a thing. Long range whacking can be easily arranged." He straightened, lunging suddenly away from the edge of the sink he'd been leaning against. "That's what those bastards are up to, is it? Pin this on me. And you're doing their dog-robbing for them, is that the way it works, Gordon?"

"No, it isn't that way at all . . ."

Mason shook his head, snarling: "I wouldn't put anything past those sons of bitches in the Company."

"Neither would I," Earl snarled right back at him. "That's why I got out."

That stopped Mason. For an endless moment, he stood staring down at the seated man. Finally, he nodded and turned away, standing beside the old iron wood-stove, gazing out a window at the darkening sky off to the east.

When he spoke again, his voice was no longer strident with anger, but quiet, barely audible to Earl, halfway across the room.

"You're lucky," Mason said. "You were able to get out."

CHAPTER EIGHTY TWO

After buzzing Earl Gordon electronically out through the iron gate, Sam Mason ascended to the second floor and stood watching from the little balcony as his visitor strode quickly down the county road out of sight around the nearest bend.

Mason was still wondering what the visit had really been about. There had been no mention of the Marauder Operation, only this business about the killing of Roger Brent they had arranged. But try as he might, Mason could not make any connection.

Shrugging, he went back inside and downstairs, still thinking about the conversation, while he got a fire going in the fireplace. When it was well along and began to warm the big main room, he leaned against the side of it, staring down into the flames. When his gaze drifted and took in the Malacca walking stick leaning in the corner between the side of the stone fireplace and the log inner wall, he grinned.

"Any more than I can make a connection between you and me, Mr. Walking Stick."

Picking it up, he hefted it, weighing it, as if it was a sword he was attempting to familiarize his hand and wrist with, checking to see that it had proper balance and flexibility.

Leaning it where it had been, he went out to the kitchen to start supper. Before beginning, he picked up a wall phone and punched in the number for the main house. When Elyse came on the line, he told her that his guest had come and gone.

"Thought I'd invite you down for supper."

"I have an even better idea," she said. "Why don't you come up here for supper? I understand the cook has laid on something special. Or is it lain on?"

"Whichever goes down easiest," he chuckled, feeling better already. "What time should I get there?"

CHAPTER EIGHTY THREE

"How did it scan?" Graham asked, when Jenner called in his report that evening.

"Hard to tell. That Gordon fella doesn't give away too much. He's hard to read."

"Just give me an idea."

"Well, let's say he didn't appear ecstatic," Jenner temporized. "I gather he didn't learn anything from Mason that he didn't already know."

"Good. We don't want to stir anything up out there, too."

"What should I do with my team?"

"Remain in place there for another couple or three days," Graham decided. "Make sure there aren't any delayed reactions from Mason. Then head back here."

"Leave the regular crew, though."

"Of course."

* * *

"Hi," Tansy's voice said in his ear.

"I can barely hear you," Hal said. "This stupid traffic . . ."

"It still seems necessary, though . . . don't you think?"

"Yeah. I guess."

"Hal, we're heading out of town again, on assignment. Want to come along?"

"I'd like to, but the messenger place has been giving me a hard time. They don't cotton to my being missing so often."

"That settles it," she said crisply. "From now on, you're working for me. My personal assistant. If something better shows up for you, by all means take it, but until we're over this hump, that seems the best way to deal with it."

"When do you expect us to get over this hump you mentioned?" he asked slyly.

She giggled.

"You're awful."

"You're awful nice."

"Flattery will get you everywhere."

"Is your crew going along on this trip?"

"Of course. Hal, this is Television. Pictures! The first three rules of TV are Pictures, Pictures, Pictures."

* * *

"I told you that bitch was up to no good," Reynolds told Blanchard, when he heard about Tansy Burns's trip to Colorado. "You no sooner have that Gordon snoop from the DOI out to see Marauder, than all of a sudden she's headed out that way, too."

"Easy, Mike," advised Blanchard. "It could be a coincidence."

"Not with her," Reynolds insisted.

"You're still keeping her under surveillance, aren't you?"

"Sure, but the phone taps aren't working worth a damn. We might as well not bother."

"Why aren't they working?"

"She hired a private dick outfit to sweep. They're doing it on a spot-check basis, but it seems like damn near every second day.

We no sooner get a tap put in than they find it and neutralize the goldang thing. We aren't learning buppkies about Tansy Burns."

"Stay with it anyway, Mike," his superior advised. "And don't take it so personally. Burns is just part of a job."

Reynolds nodded.

"Yes, I suppose you're right. No repercussions from that guy? The one Gordon went out there to see?"

"Nothing. Apparently we threw Gordon a bone that had no meat on it. For my part, I hope it stays like that. Keep in touch. Let me know what Burns and her crew are up to out there."

"Oh, and for kickers," Reynolds put in hastily, "she's got that messenger along with her, Walker. He quit his job in New York, the part-time delivery work. Now he's . . . are you ready? . . . he's her personal assistant."

Reynolds guffawed.

At the other end, Blanchard chuckled dutifully.

"Nice work, if you can get it," he observed.

"And that Walker schmuck obviously can assist her where it counts, too," Reynolds cackled. "Okay, chief, I'll keep you up to snuff."

CHAPTER EIGHTY FOUR

"I thought you could use a nice dinner," Laurie told Earl. "Help you unwind after your jaunt out west."

"It's nice here," Earl said. "An enjoyable place. I guess I don't get out often enough to find a restaurant like this on my own."

"This place is one of my discoveries," she said proudly.

"Glad you shared it with me."

"So nothing developed?" she asked, taking a sip of wine, after the waiter removed their dinner plates. "With Mason?"

"Not a thing. I keep feeling I missed something, but I can't figure out what it could be."

"Something he said?"

Earl's eyes stared off at nothing, then he shook his head impatiently.

"Partly that, I guess. Once, he started to say something, but I overrode him. I have this bad habit of boring in hard, when I think I'm onto something."

"Gee, I never noticed that about you, Earl," she said, all wide-eyed innocence.

They both laughed.

"Good," Earl said. "I'm about due for a laugh. Too wound up lately, trying to puzzle out what it was I feel I missed . . . in my talk with Mason, I mean."

"It'll come to you."

"I hope so. If it does, I hope it comes soon. All this stuff we've been slogging through is taking a good deal longer than I'd like. We seem to be getting nowhere."

"Perfectly natural," Laurie pointed out. "In effect, we are trying to pin an unnecessary murder on Mr. Graham's Honorable Company. Why would they want to help us nail them in one of their sacred schemes rife with mayhem and skulduggery?"

"It's even affecting the way we think," Earl said, with an amused tone in his voice, watching her closely.

Noticing the look, she said: "I take it 'we' in this case means me?"

"A moment ago you said we were trying to pin an unnecessary murder on Graham and his Company."

Laurie's eyes widened.

"My God, Earl, you're absolutely right. An *unnecessary* murder, as distinguished from the murders that are necessary, and therefore perfectly okay to commit."

"We're beginning to think like them."

"Well, I am, at any rate." Now it was Laurie's turn to shake her head in mild bafflement. "Part of the gig, I suppose. How can we find a motive for murder unless we begin thinking the way a murderer would think?"

"Okay, enough of this shop talk," he said. "Let's get out of here and do something. Go somewhere. Anywhere."

"Where shall we go?"

"Anyplace where people like Sam Mason and Blanchard and Graham and Company are not likely to be."

Laurie nodded.

"You're right. As someone or other once said, long long ago, let's go and get tight."

"Exactly!" Earl laughed, looking around for their waiter. "Good and tight."

"Well-l-l, we don't necessarily want to overdo the good part, of course."

CHAPTER EIGHTY FIVE

They had to stay up late, so Tansy's crew could get some night footage of the slopes, and of the resort itself. Bill was trying to make it look as if they were shooting during the ski season.

Hal hung in there, wondering how Tansy and her two guys, Bill and Jerry, could be so painstaking about this work of theirs. All he was able to do was help them carry things and arrange stuff, anything to make it easier for them to get whatever they were trying for in their shots.

Finally, it was over and they were through for the night. They all repaired to their various rooms in the ski lodge. When the four of them came along the corridor, two men emerged from Tansy's room, carrying compact tool kits.

"See you guys later," Tansy murmured softly.

Hal and the other two nodded and went on to their own rooms, Hal's just beyond Tansy's, Bill and Jerry's rooms both around a bend in the corridor.

As he unlocked the door to his room, Hal heard Tansy ask one of the workmen: "Did you find anything?"

Hal glanced toward them. One of the men held up something, showing it to Tansy. Her mouth tightened, and she nodded with satisfaction.

"Good! You men are worth your weight in platinum."

They grinned.

"Tomorrow, too?"

"Of course," Tansy said, stepping out of sight through her doorway. "Whoever's doing this is obviously making a habit of it . . . so we'll simply make a habit of rooting their gadgets right back out. Good night, and thanks again, guys."

They waved and went off.

Hal slipped inside his room. Locking the door behind him, he shed his clothes and took a quick shower. He was almost finished when the bathroom door opened and Tansy slipped in under the spraying water beside him.

"Good to get cleaned up," she whispered. "It's been a long day."

"Too damn long," Hal grunted. "I'm not used to doing real work."

"Delivering messages is real work, isn't it?"

"Yeah, I suppose," he agreed, "but I'm used to it. I'm not used to this heaving and hauling for you and your two technicians. I never realized there was so much detail involved in taking a few background pictures for TV news stories."

She grinned.

"See? We really earn those high salaries."

"You sure do. Want me to scrub your back?"

"Yes. And my front, too, if you'd like."

"But of course," he laughed. "Never do things by half, I always say."

"Odd!" she mused. "I've know you awhile, now, and I've never heard you say that before."

Later, in bed in Tansy's bigger room, she whispered in his ear: "They found some bugs and a phone tap in here."

"I heard. Anything in my room?"

"No, just in mine."

"I must be slipping . . ."

"I'm so glad I told that girl Marge to have the detectives out here check for that stuff every evening."

"Right, what with you out working all day, that gives whoever is doing it all the time they need to install that crap. Are you getting pictures of whoever comes in here?"

She turned her head and stared at him.

"No. Funny, the thought never occurred to me."

"Well, you are kind of new at this sort of thing," Hal smirked.

She grinned at his zinger, but she was serious when she said: "I'll have to call Marge back in Washington and see what she thinks about that idea."

"Couldn't hurt."

*   *   *

Later that night, Earl woke suddenly and stared up at the ceiling of his bedroom. For a moment, he couldn't recall what had brought him so abruptly out of sleep. Then he did.

Struggling to penetrate the mists of sleep, he strove to pinpoint the thought, but found himself drifting back into sleep.

For a moment, he was tempted to make a mental note to deal with it in the morning, but something in his mind told him: Don't! If you let it go now, you'll never remember it in the morning.

Groaning, he threw the covers off and rolled over to the side of the bed, where he sat on its edge.

Make a note? His hand groped for a notepad beside the phone on the end-table, but instead he picked up the phone, switching on the light.

Finding Laurie's home phone number, he tapped it in and sat there, waiting, listening to his own breathing in the silence of the Washington night.

"'Lo?" her sleepy voice came on the receiver.

"It's me," Earl said. "I just thought of something, and I was afraid if I put it off till morning, I'd never remember what it was."

She chuckled.

"Earl, why not just admit you missed me so much you simply had to call in the middle of the night?"

He laughed.

"That, too, of course. I'm sorry now that I bothered you. It seems silly. So tenuous . . ."

"What is it? Tell me, before you forget it completely."

"Remember that list you got from Roger Brent's attorney, down in Tucson? What was his name? Matthews?"

"Merritt."

"That's it. Merritt."

"What list was that, Earl? I can't seem to recall any list. Still half asleep, I guess."

"A list of things Brent left in his will. I can't recall which item is bugging me, all of a sudden, but if I look over that list, maybe it'll trigger something in this alleged brain of mine."

Chuckling, she said, "All right. I'll make a copy of those bequests and have it on your desk, first thing tomorrow."

"Good for you. Sorry to bother you this way, Laurie. I should have made a simple mental note, and asked you about it in the morning . . ."

"No, it's all right, Earl. Two mental notes are better than one, anytime."

They hung up, laughing.

*　*　*

The call to Laurie's home phone was the only reason Roper got word of the list of the bequests. It was the first he'd heard of it, but after hearing about it on both their phone-taps, it put him on a plane to Arizona by mid-morning, which was just about when Earl Gordon got a look at the list of bequests Roger Brent had willed his heirs.

CHAPTER EIGHTY SIX

No sudden revelations struck Sam Mason in his sleep at three o'clock in the morning. It got through to him slowly, first as part of the process that went on in his mind over the next few days when he thought back on the conversation he'd had with Earl Gordon.

It simply didn't make sense for the Company to blow a cover this deep, in which they had buried him alive. Yet, by allowing a straight-arrow type like Gordon to just drop by for a nice little visit, they had done exactly that.

There had to be a reason. But what reason? What possible connection could there be between himself, out here in boonieville, and whatever dirty little erasure-job they had pulled on Roger Brent?

When the solution to the puzzle finally came to him, Mason was astonished that it had taken so long.

Picking up the Malacca walking stick from where it was always tilted in the corner beside the stone fireplace, he decided it had to be habit. He was out of the habit of thinking like a field man.

But examination of the cane made him doubt his sudden realization of his connection. This cane was his only link with Roger Brent, but Mason had received the cane long before the Congressman's aide had been "accidentally" shot instead of Melford.

At the time it arrived, Sam had been hard-pressed to figure out who Roger Brent might be. For a moment, he had been tempted to phone Merritt, the attorney down in Tucson who had forwarded it to him, through channels, of course. Then he had seen Melford making a speech on a TV news show, and the aide beside him had been referred to as Roger Brent. A little reading up in various news magazines and Mason had come up with the source of the odd bequest the Arizona lawyer had sent him.

Mason had shrugged and forgotten about it, assuming that the Company's technical people had X-rayed the cane to a fare-thee-well and found no hidden poisoned darts buried within it, ready and waiting to spring out one fine day and pin-prick him into a sudden case of no doubt well-deserved oblivion.

Now, he hesitated.

It seemed a shame to destroy the Malacca stick. The wood shone smoothly, and it felt light and sturdy to the hand.

Shrugging, he took it out to his workshop/cum/darkroom, where he proceeded to unscrew the metal tip at the bottom end. Nothing. The tip was solid metal, and there were no fine lines indicating that minute welding could have sealed anything inside the metal cap.

That left the handle.

A narrow metal ring with a gripping spur on the outer side, away from where the hand might grip its handle, encircled the top of the stick, just below the handle itself.

That was a possibility.

He tried to unscrew it. The handle refused to budge, even when he wrapped it in cloth cushioning and held the shaft in a workbench vise. He didn't want to try turning the handle too hard, or likely he would wreck the stick entirely with such brute-force methods. Instead, he got a glass on it and examined the handle itself.

His patience paid off: partway down the two-inch long spur, he saw for the first time the tiny head of a minute screw which held the spur in place.

"Finally!" he murmured, turning to his rack of tools sitting in trays along the back of the workbench.

But for all the varieties of screwdrivers his collection contained, Mason feared for awhile that he didn't have one small enough to turn the screw he had discovered.

After a search, he came up with a set that very nearly qualified as jeweler's tools. One of the smallest fit. When it turned the miniature screw, Mason felt a touch of excitement, the like of which he hadn't experienced in a very long time.

Once the tiny screw was out, the handle slid up the top end of the walking stick and off. Examination of the stick itself showed no hole had been drilled into it. Mason hadn't thought there would be. If anything had been hidden inside the stick itself, the procedures of the Company's X-ray techs would have revealed it.

That left the handle itself. Which revealed absolutely nothingl.

There were no tiny cracks in which a microfilm could be concealed, no infinitesimally small holes drilled . . . nothing.

Tossing the handle onto the workbench, Mason gave up. For whatever reason he had been bequeathed this cane at the instructions of the then-still-living aide to the Congressman, it hadn't been to convey any hidden messages. Apparently it had been sent for the reason he had initially assumed to be the true one: a good-will campaign gift of some kind, perhaps harking back to when Sam Mason had been a legal resident of the State which Congressman Melford now represented.

Shaking his head at the unlikelihood of even that possibility, Mason picked up the handle, intending to reattach it to the top of the stick. But he noticed a shiny substance on the inside of the spur that had secured the handle to the stick with the tiny screw.

Putting the magnifying glass on the shiny patch, Mason could see nothing but the opaque surface. Taking sandpaper, he made a gentle pass or two over the shiny patch, which was less than a third the size of his pinky fingernail.

After the gentle sandpapering, the surface of the patch no longer gleamed.

Scraping carefully once more, the shiny patch turned to powder. Something drifted to the hardwood top of the workbench. When he tried to pick it up with his fingertips, he couldn't. It was much too small.

Getting a pincers from his makeshift darkroom, Mason finally picked up whatever it was and examined it with the magnifying glass.

He smiled. Here was his microfilm.

Marvelling that it had been sitting there right under his nose all those months, Mason turned and entered the darkroom again, thinking: "All right, let's see what great big secret the late Roger Brent willed to me, prior to his untimely demise."

CHAPTER EIGHTY SEVEN

When Laurie looked up from her desk and saw Earl standing there in the doorway of her office, she smiled. "You found something."

Grinning, he nodded.

Sliding the list of Roger Brent's bequests across Laurie's desk, he said: "The Malacca walking stick. It's the only thing that meshed."

Laurie scanned the list, found the item and read its description and date. Puzzled, she looked up.

"But Roger Brent had his lawyer send the walking stick to Sam Mason months ago. Are you suggesting Brent had some kind of premonition?"

"Not at all," Earl laughed, sprawling comfortably in her visitor's chair. "Perhaps he was simply making certain it reached Mason. Remember, Sam Mason has been in the Company's custody for quite awhile. You don't just up and send him a gift whenever you want to."

"Then how could Brent manage to get this walking stick through to him? Did you say you actually saw the thing?"

"Yes. I'm assuming it's the stick mentioned here." He flipped a thumb toward the list of bequests. "As for managing to send Mason something, you and I know too well that in this town, the people who run things can usually get a lot done that no one else would even try."

"And an aide to Melford, who is on a Congressional Oversight Committee watching the CIA, would be in an excellent position to manage that sort of gift-giving."

"Especially an aide like Roger Brent. The one thing that seeps through all the investigating we've done is how extraordinarily capable he was at worming his way in and out of anyplace he wanted to in the Capitol scene, finding out whatever he wished to find out. Or manipulating people and their opinions and votes in ways that would redound to the credit of his boss, Melford. So finding a way to slip a gift like a walking stick past the watchdogs over at Langley to one of their hibernated former field agents wouldn't be that much of a problem, not to Roger Brent."

"That figures," Laurie agreed wryly, staring at the list. "I wonder what it contained. The walking stick, I mean."

Earl shrugged.

"Who knows? The Company's specialists would examine it every way from breakfast, to make sure there no messages, lethal or otherwise, contained therein."

"Maybe just the walking stick itself meant something to Mason and Brent," Laurie suggested.

Earl looked doubtful.

"All our research, back at Margarita College, indicates that the two of them never met. Mason was a junior and senior when Roger Brent was a freshman and sophomore. Sam left, and a week or so later, his old girl linked up with Brent, and shortly afterward, they had their car crash. When could Mason and Brent ever have met?"

"Earl," she said gently, "just because we asked everyone we could find who knew both men if they had met, and they said they hadn't, still doesn't mean they didn't."

He agreed.

"Yes, you're probably right. It's possible. But it is pushing the probabilities."

Laurie sighed and nodded.

"I can't deny that," she admitted. "What are you going to do about this?" She nodded at the list.

"Take it to Farris. I can't think of anything else to do with it."

"And what do you think Farris will be able to get out of those Company types with just a walking cane as leverage?"

"Laurie, it's a connection," he pointed out, picking up the list. "That's a good deal more than anything we've managed to come up with, to this point. Wish me luck."

"I do," she smiled. "You'll need luck. So will Farris."

CHAPTER EIGHTY EIGHT

Sam Mason sat in the main room of the lodge, staring at nothing, waiting for night to fall.

He had nothing more to do, no more preparations to make, just wait until darkness came, so he could slip out, after setting the lighting system he had jury-rigged, hoping it would work well enough to turn out the last lights in the lodge at the time he usually went to bed . . . since he didn't expect to be there, to turn them out himself.

He grimaced impatiently. Of course the lights would go off. It was a simple dodge, but it should give him an extra twenty hours or more of a start on them. Every extra hour counted.

The Malacca stick was back where he always kept it, leaning in the angle between the left end of the stone fireplace and the log wall.

Always leave everything the way the enemy was used to seeing it.

Sam had prepared dark clothes, careful to make certain nothing in them, no button, no trim, nothing even resembled metal, which could therefore be traced by their surveillance equipment.

Moccasins, too. They were rubber-soled and sturdy enough, but they contained no metal, no nails securing the soles or heels to the upper part, as some shoes did.

He checked the time. Only four o'clock. Another two hours, maybe closer to three. He didn't want to move out and up through the woods to the main house while it was still light enough for him to be spotted by those watching eyes out there.

Gotta hold onto the old patience. Wait. Wait.

Through the front window, he could see the narrow valley and the distant lowland.

From this angle it looked somewhat like the valley where Yussuf and his people had waited five or six hours longer than they should have, because he, Marauder, had assured them all was well, there was no need to start toward the mountains, the Monster and his tanks would never be allowed to come near them, the planes would see to that. Hadn't the message he had received at dawn promised as much?

Yussuf had looked down at him, behind the wheel of his jeep.

"All right, Marauder, we will not start yet. If your Company makes the promise, we will trust it to keep that promise."

And it was in that moment, sitting behind the wheel of his radio-equipped all-purpose vehicle, looking up at Yussuf's dark, lined face, it was then that fear struck Mason to the heart.

Could he promise this tribal chief that his people would be protected, that the Company had promised it would protect them?

Mason had taken out the copy of the message he had translated from the code they'd used to send it to him. Reading it over, his fear subsided within him. No need to worry. The message they had sent at dawn in response to his urgent query was a guarantee. Yussuf and his thousands of tribesmen would be protected if the Monster turned his tanks loose on them. The planes would come if they were needed.

Now Mason stared out at the woods climbing both sides of the narrow valley. No, it didn't look at all like Yussuf's valley. That had been flat and wide, almost devoid of trees, and had no cover at all.

"If they'd been here," he muttered into the silent room, "in this sort of terrain, they might have had a chance. If only they'd been here."

He shook his head in despair. Those wretched tribesmen! Just another collection of people for whom the planet Earth had not quite enough room. Somehow, they always found themselves caught between two or more other tribes, always far more numerous, never willing to share the land between them with this superfluous people.

"Quit it!" he told himself. "It's been going on like that for thousands of years. One man or one day can't change it."

Telling himself that didn't help, though.

Life for many people wasn't lived on a long-range basis. Especially not where Yussuf and his people struggled to remain alive, strove to keep from being crushed between the more numerous peoples surrounding them. They struggled on a day-to-day basis, trying not to be destroyed today, and then again tomorrow, and the next day. It was the only way they knew how to deal with their fate. And the problem they had faced on that day had been how much could they depend on Marauder's promise that they would be protected from the Monster's tanks if he advanced them, as he had threatened.

Remaining seated seemed to make Mason more vulnerable to memories and regrets. Surging to his feet, he paced back and forth in the big, silent, high-ceilinged room. Anything to keep busy, to keep from thinking, from remembering, until this endless day finally came to a finish.

It was exactly the way he'd felt waiting for that other day without end to finally draw to its close.

His hand itched to take out the two almost identical messages, to study them, to try to understand. Both messages exactly alike except for the time each had been sent and that one word, that all-important word.

But he kept his hands still. There was no need to look at the two messages again. He could recall every word they contained, especially in that last line, and the one extra word in one of the messages, a word which had meant the difference between life and death for thousands of people.

CHAPTER EIGHTY NINE

J ust after dark, Jenner received a call from the team watching the main gate of the Branston estate.

"Miss Branston just left in her car. Seems headed toward Sardy Field, or maybe up into town."

"Which car?" Jenner asked.

"The big one. The Bentley. The chauffeur's driving. Should we stay with her?"

"Of course. If she catches a flight out, let me know where it's headed. Get one of your men into that airfield, so we know for sure what destination they file in their flight plan. And make sure it's really the chauffeur doing the driving. We don't want our friend pulling a duck-out on us."

"Roger."

It was no big deal, but a half hour later, Jenner got another call: "They didn't stop at Sardy. They're headed east on the Interstate."

"All right, stay with them. Is it the chauffeur driving?"

"Looks like him. We'll make a positive I.D. whenever they stop."

"Good. Keep in touch with me on this."

Jenner checked with the various guard posts set up around the Branston estate. All reported no movement, no sign of Mason trying to bung-oh. Jenner relaxed.

When the following team reported that the Bentley had delivered the woman to the Denver airport, Jenner just ordered them to see her aboard whatever flight she took and pass the word along to whatever was her destination, so Company people there could pick her up and stay with her.

And, of course, send him a copy of the pass-along order.

* * *

Tansy and Hal got their boarding passes and rejoined Bill and Jerry to wait for their flight to be called.

Jerry went off to the men's room.

"All that mountain water, I guess," he said.

"Don't take too long," Tansy cautioned him. "We don't want to miss the flight."

"Take a look at this," Bill murmured, nodding toward a nearby woman.

Tansy watched as the man with the woman fussed over her. Then Tansy took a closer look.

"She looks familiar," she whispered.

Bill studied the woman, too, but shook his head.

"I don't register anything."

Tansy reached into her memory, then nodded with satisfaction.

"Branston. Elyse Branston. Well-connected, out in these parts."

"Mucho dinero?"

"Like this big," Tansy laughed, stretching her arms wide, as if she was showing how big a fish she had caught.

Hal looked the woman over, too, decided she was pretty, and watched as the man with her bent to listen, as Elyse Branston told him something, after which he nodded and went off.

Bill had a small camera out and was shooting, discreetly. He always kept some kind of camera handy, even if he did have to check the video camera with the other baggage on a plane flight.

"This red-eye must be gaining in cachet," Tansy whispered to Hal, "for someone like her to catch it. I would have thought she was the private jet type."

"What the hell!" Bill growled under his breath.

Without another word, he started off after the woman's chauffeur.

"What is it, Bill?" Tansy called to him.

"Tell you when I get back," Bill answered over his shoulder.

They watched as he followed the other man until both were lost on the far side of the vast terminal.

"Finally!" Tansy sighed, leaning against Hal. "Just the two of us. Let's sit down while we wait."

They relaxed, watching people scurry in every direction.

"You'd never think this was the middle of the night," Hal observed.

"It's a busy place, all right," she agreed. "I hope they've got their baggage-handling system straightened out. The last time I came through here . . ."

Just then Bill and Jerry returned.

Jerry was saying: "Bill, I didn't get that good a look at them. Once the shooting started, I just ducked."

"What?" Tansy asked, jumping to her feet. "What shooting?"

"That time Jerry and I almost got hijacked," Bill explained. "I think I just saw one of the two bastards who shot at us." He patted his small camera with satisfaction. "Got pictures of him, too. And of the guy with him."

"Did you report him to the . . . ?" Tansy began to ask, but Bill was already shaking his head no.

"Lost them outside," he told her. "They seemed to be following that chauffeur of your lady friend, there . . . or whatever he is. But the second they got a good look at his face, they seemed to lose interest and just went off into the parking lot, almost running."

"Odd!" Tansy said. "What connection could Elyse Branston's chauffeur have with those two?"

CHAPTER NINETY

"I suppose I was lucky to get to talk to Graham at all," Jack Farris told Laurie and Earl, next morning.

He was filling them in on it in Earl's office, having brought Laurie along with him. He'd been careful to close the door to keep their meeting reasonably private.

"Nothing substantial came of it, though?" Earl asked.

"Trying to get information out of Graham is like trying to extract anthracite coal by blasting at it with firecrackers."

Laurie smiled.

"He does seem to be a close-mouthed man."

"All right," Farris summed up, "we're still in touch with them, and it looks as if we're all cooperating nicely."

"It doesn't seem to me much of a quid pro quo," Earl noted sourly. "Not from our end of things."

"Well, Graham did say he'd check into the results of the tests they must have done on that Malacca cane. They wouldn't simply forward something like that to someone being kept as deep under cover as Sam Mason . . . not without some heavy-duty examination of whatever it was that was being sent to him."

Earl shrugged.

"Okay, I suppose we have to be satisfied with that." He was obviously not satisfied. "This is the weirdest case I've ever worked on. I feel like one of those Keystone Kops out in Boulder, Colorado, the way they had to deal with that meatball of a District Attorney out there, and the family whose kid was murdered. It's as if we're working with our hands inside lead-lined gloves."

Both Farris and Laurie laughed.

"Not kid gloves," Farris noted, "but lead-lined gloves. Good one. As for the case, keep on keeping on, you two. Maybe something will break in our direction, so be ready, in case it does. It happens, occasionally."

Late in the afternoon, there was indeed a break in the case, but it didn't come to Farris or his two investigators. It went to Graham, by way of a phone call from Jenner, out in Colorado.

"Marauder's loose, Chief," Jenner said in a subdued voice.

Graham sighed.

"All right," he said quietly.

"When he didn't come out all morning," Jenner explained, "I decided maybe we should send someone into his lodge, to take a look. It was mid-afternoon before we could manage to come up with some kind of delivery . . . as an excuse."

"And the lodge was empty," Graham stated. He felt as if he had already known what he was being told.

One of his hands picked up copies of Jenner's various reports from the night before, about the Branston woman being driven, not to nearby Sardy field by her chauffeur, but to the Denver airport. By now, she was in Paris, but she had accomplished what she had set out to do.

Jenner's voice was going on: ". . . so either he ducked over the mountains on foot, or . . ."

Jenner didn't bother finishing what he was saying.

Graham finished for him: "Or he was driven in her car to Denver."

"Yeah." Jenner's voice was almost inaudible. "Chief, I'm . . . I'm real sorry about this."

"It's done, Jenner. Leave a skeleton crew out there to keep a watch on the vicinity. Bring in local police, in case Marauder . . . in case Mason did what you first suggested, slipped over the mountains on foot. You can bring the rest of your people east. We might need every man we can get hold of. I'll get in touch with . . . the rogue operation we set up back here. They may have some work to do."

CHAPTER NINETY ONE

Graham had wanted Blanchard to bring along the two field agents handling the detail work on the rogue operation. He was familiar with the records of Reynolds and Adams. For whatever seemed to be upcoming in this case, they would need to know a fair part of what they were dealing with in Sam Mason.

The meeting took place on the floor below Graham's office, in one of the conference rooms. Up on a wall TV screen, Jenner had a map of the region around Denver, and he was using a pointer.

"We know that the man who drove the Branston woman was really her chauffeur, not Marauder," Jenner was saying. "At the Denver air terminal, the chauffeur dropped her and her luggage at the front entrance, then drove into the parking area, and stashed the Bentley. Walking back out of the parking lot, he rejoined Ms. Branston and got her settled and ready to catch her flight, after they had taken care of her luggage and the ticket and boarding pass stuff."

Graham interrupted: "Did your men keep a watch on the Bentley, when the chauffeur left it in the parking area?"

Jenner looked sheepish and shook his head.

"I'm afraid not, Chief. They stayed with the woman and the chauffeur, one man with him, the other inside the terminal with her. We were short-handed."

Graham nodded, not laboring the obvious. Blanchard took care of that.

"Right then was when Marauder could have left the Bentley," he pointed out.

Reluctantly, Jenner nodded, keeping his eyes fixed on the map displayed on the large screen.

"If that was the way he worked it," Graham said.

Blanchard conceded the point with a grunt, but kept going: "All Marauder had to do was stroll inside, just another new arrival going into the terminal to catch a flight, but instead, he rents a car at one of the car rental counters, as if he had just come in on an arriving flight. Before the Branston woman's plane took off, he could have been well clear of Denver, headed east."

"Did you check the car renters at the airport?" Graham asked Jenner, to get the discussion away from Blanchard.

Jenner glanced at him, nodding, glad to be able to take his eyes off the map.

"Yes," he said. "Once we knew Marauder had gotten clear of Central Colorado and probably reached Denver hidden inside the Bentley, I had the crew already there check the auto rental agencies. One of the men who'd been on the night shift at Avis the previous evening identified Marauder's picture. Our Denver office forwarded the car's plate and description eastward to the regional offices in Kansas City, Minneapolis, Saint Louis, Chicago, Nashville, and Atlanta."

"Okay," Graham said. "Unfortunately, all this was sixteen or seventeen hours after our man could have started driving eastward, around midnight."

"Right," Blanchard agreed. "In a good car, Marauder might have gotten well past K. C. before noon yesterday. By the time we caught on that he had blown the cage, he might even have been past St. Louis…"

"No word yet?" Graham interrupted.

"Not at last report," Jenner replied. "But we expect something positive anytime."

"Yes," Graham concurred. "They've got the make of the car and its plate numbers. I'm surprised they haven't picked up on him already."

"What if none of this really happened?" Adams asked, out of a momentary silence.

Graham began to laugh. One by one, starting with Jenner, then Blanchard, then Reynolds, and finally Adams himself, they all joined in the roaring laughter. When it subsided, Graham glanced with appreciation at Adams.

"An excellent point, George," he said. "Perhaps it will turn out that the car renter's identification of the photo was mistaken, and Marauder will come staggering exhausted down out of the mountains behind the Branston estate."

The phone rang. Jenner grabbed it, telling Graham with a glance that he'd been expecting the call.

He listened, and when he hung up, Jenner's face no longer had the drawn look it had worn so far.

"They've picked up Marauder headed northeast from Atlanta." He checked the time. "If he maintains the pace he's set so far, he could be up here in Washington by dark."

Graham nodded and rose. "Good. At least we're no longer dealing with a basketful of maybes. Thank you, gentlemen. We have enjoyed our little laugh, and it broke the tension. Now let us get to work and try to see that no one at all has to be hurt. Including Marauder."

"If we can manage it," Blanchard said.

Graham looked at him steadily.

"Right. If we can manage it. Do your best, all of you."

CHAPTER NINETY TWO

Roper wasn't kept in the dark by Marge about Sam Mason's progress across country, not after the Bentley reached the Denver airport. Every time he called her she gave him another of a steady stream of reports, from the moment the man was picked up by her private detectives in the parking lot at the Denver terminal.

Like the Company's men, the detective agency Marge had farmed the job out to in central Colorado stayed with the Bentley, but in a simpler way: they passed the license plate and the make of the car along to a Denver detective agency, whose local people spotted it well west of the Divide and reported it on into the airport parking area.

But unlike the Company's men, they stayed with the Bentley, too, not just with the two people visible, the woman and her chauffeur. They had more manpower available than the two-man crew Jenner had assigned to the car and its occupants.

So when a figure on foot appeared near where the Bentley had been parked, after the chauffeur had gone back inside the terminal building to help Elyse Branston, the agency's watchers were there to note it and to remain within eyeshot of the man as he strolled inside the terminal, eventually ending up at one of the rent-a-car counters.

From there on, they simply stayed with him and his Chevy Impala in a remote way, as it headed eastward. Every east-west road for two hundred miles from north to south was covered, and every time an alerted local resident spotted the car with the make and license plate he'd been told to watch for, if it passed through his town or village or crossroad hamlet, he would phone the information and the time ahead, along with the route being travelled. That permitted the agency route tracker in Kansas City to alert watchers farther east along that and two or three paralleling roads north and south of it to remain on watch, so they, too, could report when the subject vehicle passed wherever they were located. It also permitted him to pass the word back to the volunteer watchers on paralleling roads, the ones who had been left behind, telling them they could go back to bed and get on with their lives.

Roper got back from Tucson just in time to pick up on this latest development. He was glad he had. He wasn't sure the Tucson trip had been worth the time or the risk.

His entry into the office of Roger Brent's attorney, Merritt, had gone smoothly enough, and he had gotten a look at the list of bequests Brent had left various heirs, including the Malacca walking stick he'd instructed the lawyer to leave to Sam Mason, long before Brent's unexpected murder . . . or had it been unexpected? Wasn't sending something to a man like Mason ahead of time a sort of signal that the sender had forebodings of one kind or another?

All right, Roper had gotten a look at the list, and in spite of a snoopy night watchman who kept worrying away at everything around the building while Roper was inside it, there had been no alarm, and he had gotten clear and away with what he'd come for. Now he simply had to write it off as something he had acquired which might not have been worth the trouble he'd gone to in getting it.

Still, down the road, you never know what might turn out to be worth getting, and what might not.

At any rate, he was in time to be in on the coverage of Sam Mason's unexpected bolt from his cushy retirement position on the Branston estate, out in central Colorado, and that was worthwhile.

He kept putting in quick calls to Marge, staying on top of Mason's journey eastward to St. Louis, then southeastward down through Tennessee and northwest Georgia . . . wondering if Mason was trying to get out of the country and was headed for a southern port, maybe down in Florida? That idea was scrapped when the travel route swung suddenly northeastward from Atlanta up into North Carolina. From Durham on, it became obvious that Sam Mason was headed for Washington.

Roper wondered if the people Reynolds and Adams worked for were going to let Mason reach the Capitol.

Which was why he decided it was time to put in a call to his two musketeers and find out if they needed their favorite Dispatcher.

Neither Reynolds nor Adams were at the Watkins office when Roper called, but the moment he said the name Dispatcher to whoever answered the phone, the voice told him: "They've been waiting for your call, Dispatcher. An assignment is ready for you. From now on, call back every hour."

CHAPTER NINETY THREE

"I don't care what Tollman wants," Blanchard growled into the phone. "You're running that operation, Reynolds, not Tollman."

"He claims he's put in for a transfer to Operations Planning," Reynolds said. "How do I answer that?"

"Tell him when his transfer comes through, if it comes through, then he can beg off working in the field. Until then, we need every man we can get. You heard Graham . . ."

"Okay, Chief."

Reynolds switched off his speaker-phone and stared across his desk at Tollman.

"You heard the man."

Tollman looked grim. "I thought I was out of the killing business," he complained.

"It's an emergency," Adams said, coming around from behind his desk and standing near the corner of Reynolds's. "They're bringing everyone in on this."

"Sure they are," Tollman said sarcastically. "But guess who's gonna be the one up front putting bullets into people." He pointed a finger at his own chest. "This boy. It happens every time."

"Oh, hell, Tollman," said Reynolds soothingly. "If it makes you feel any better, I'll put you on the detail guarding the Congressman's missus, out in Georgetown. A milk run."

"This Marauder must be pretty formidable to get Graham all worked up this way," Tollman observed, somewhat mollified by Reynolds' promise.

Adams nodded.

"Marauder was good enough to give them the slip and make it all the way across the damn country in a rented car."

Tollman grinned.

"Where's he at now?"

Reynolds checked the time.

"Should be closing in on this area right soon." Flipping a switch on his intercom, he asked the outer office: "Caldwell, what's the latest on that Marauder situation?"

After a moment, Caldwell's voice said from the intercom speaker: "He just passed Quantico on I-95. Should be here in an hour."

"Thanks," Reynolds said, switching off. "There you go."

"If they've got him bracketed that close," Tollman asked, "why don't they take him? What's holding things up?"

"Probable cause?" Adams ventured.

Reynolds agreed.

"He's given us no reason. All Mason's done is rent a car, after taking a leave of absence from his job as a groundskeeper out in Colorado."

"Hardly a reason to whack the guy," Adams pointed out.

"Is that the only way the Company has of dealing with agents who've been retired?" Tollman demanded. "Sometimes I think I'm working with a bunch of homicidal maniacs. Got a problem? Kill it."

"That's why we're being so circumspect," Reynolds explained patiently. "The Company can't take someone like Mason to court. We'd have to reveal all kinds of classified stuff just to book him."

"So we're trying to hedge the guy in," Adams said. "That's why all the available personnel are needed for this."

"We've got to guard anyone we think may be Marauder's . . . Mason's objective," Reynolds said.

"Who do you think he's after?" Tollman asked.

Reynolds and Adams looked at one another. Neither replied.

"Look," Tollman snapped, "if I'm gonna be part of this detail, the least you two can do is let me in on the most likely hot spot."

Reynolds shrugged elaborately. With obvious reluctance, he said: "They think he may be after Blanchard. I don't think he is. I think he's gonna try to blow away Congressman Melford . . ."

Tollman laughed and jumped to his feet. He held both hands palm upward.

"So you put me on Melford's house in Georgetown. Thanks a lot, Reynolds. That's a terrific way of giving me a milk run"

"I said that's what *I* think," Reynolds pointed out. "What the higher-ups think is another matter entirely."

"They also think he might be after Graham," Adams put in.

"Why Graham?"

Adams shrugged, but didn't reply.

Reynolds speculated: "Graham was the man in charge of . . . what went wrong . . . out there. Maybe that's it."

"Went wrong how?" Tollman persisted.

"On the Marauder Operation," Adams said.

"God help the poor bastard," Tollman sighed, pacing the floor back and forth, then stopping by the door. "Let's hope he makes it through the night, huh?" He watched the two of them with a sardonic gleam in his eyes. "But we won't bet any farms on it, eh?"

Reynolds shrugged elaborately.

"Part of the job," he said laconically. "Get whatever details you need from Caldwell, about the Melford place."

As Tollman nodded and opened the door to leave, Reynolds added: "Call in if anything comes up."

Tollman almost sneered, standing there looking back at Reynolds, his shoulders almost filling the doorway.

"A milk run," he murmured.

"Not that we expect anything to develop out there," Reynolds added hastily. "Just keep in touch. Mason could move in any direction, even out Georgetown way. Nobody knows who he blames for . . . that mess Operation Marauder turned into."

"Well, I'm sure we'll find out soon, won't we?" was Tollman's parting shot, before he pulled the door closed behind him and was gone.

CHAPTER NINETY FOUR

"We should run it, Walter," Tansy urged him.

Walter Noble hesitated.

"I'm not sure about this, Tansy," he told her and Bill.

Outside the open doorway of his office, Jerry and that new personal assistant of Tansy's just stood there, taking it all in.

"The graphics are ready," Bill put in.

"We've forwarded copies to the Arlington police," Tansy added carefully.

"But it's old news," Walter cried irritably. "How long ago did that damn shooting happen, anyway?"

"Walter," she said persuasively, leaning over his desk, "you owe it to Bill and Jerry. They nearly took some bullets in that station truck of yours."

"Now the truck is mine, is it?" Walter snapped sarcastically. His mouth tightened, but Tansy sensed that he was wavering.

"It'll just take five seconds, no more than ten," she said. "I promise. I'll read off the words, the pictures of those two men will be still shots as graphics, like criminal mug shots, and underneath them onscreen, the phone number to call, if anyone recognizes either of them."

Glancing at Bill, the editor asked: "You're certain that's one of the men you saw, the night of the shootout?"

Bill nodded decisively.

"That's him, all right. The square-jawed one. Walter, I'm good at faces. It's my job."

Walter returned his attention to the pictures of the two men Bill had caught with his camera in the Denver airport terminal. After staring at them another long moment, he nodded, and Tansy straightened in front of his desk.

"Okay, do it," he told her. "But keep it short, okay?"

"Short it is, Walter," she assured him.

Turning with a grin on her face, she hurried out to get made-up for the show.

"Now maybe we'll find out what's going on with those two bastards," Bill muttered, as he followed her out. All four of them hurried toward the studio.

*   *   *

Roper caught Tansy's show on TV, when he returned to where he was staying to shower and clean up, after all the running around he'd been doing all day, phoning Marge for her progress reports on Mason from a slew of street phones, all over the Capitol District. And it was getting harder and harder to even *find* street phones.

Sometimes, caution could get to be a pain in the ass, but Roper tried to stick with it. When you began getting slack about little things like phone conversations that went on too long, that's when you gave them an opportunity to close in on you.

Squatting in front of the TV screen, he examined the faces of the two men Tansy Burns was claiming were the alleged perpetrators who had shot up her camera crew's van, the week before.

Neither man was recognizable to Roper, but if they were mixed up in this Sam Mason thing, or with the rest of it, he wanted to know who to look out for.

When he was ready to go out again, he checked and oiled the weapons he carried, before stowing them in their clips and belt-holsters, and in the ankle harness. He also wore long body-armor, just in case.

At the first public pay phone he used, Reynolds came on.

"Dispatcher? Glad you called. Your assignment is ready. Subject is holed up in a motel on 16th Street Northwest, just off New Hampshire Avenue."

Roper jotted down the name of the motel and the room number, twenty four.

"His name's Mason. Supposed to be a skillful man in a tight spot," Reynolds cautioned him. "So watch yourself."

"Just move in, do the job, and clear out?"

"No, no," Reynolds cried. "Call me first, to clear it with me. When I give you the word, then you go in and do it."

"Okay," Roper agreed.

Although his time on the phone was getting close to the forty-second point, Roper read the info back, to be sure he had it right, and then hung up.

A couple of miles away, along the Beltway, Roper used another roadside payphone, asking Marge where the quarry was at that moment.

"He's still on the move," she told him, after a pause.

Roper's face stiffened.

"He hasn't holed up anywhere?"

"Not according to my latest reports. He's working his way across the city. Oh, here's another report on him. Subject just ducked into the subway. They almost lost him, but I've got a good inner-city team on Mr. Mason, so they stuck with him."

"Good. I'll be calling back, Marge. Thanks."

"You're very welcome, Mr. Dickson," she said sweetly. "Oh, and there are those other people trying to stay with Mason, too. My people are hanging back a bit, to keep from being spotted by them."

"The Feds."

"I didn't quite hear you say that," Marge said quickly. "What was that you said?"

"I didn't say a thing."

She laughed.

"Anyway, they lost him, when he ducked underground. But there's a lot of them. I'm sure they'll pick up his trail, wherever he exits the Metro."

Roper hung up and got back into his car, shaking his head at Reynolds and the business about the motel Mason was supposedly holed up in.

The sons of bitches are trying to shaft me again, he thought, just the way they tried when they took out Jeff Lasalle, up in New York. They just can't quit trying to double-cross people.

It made him all the more determined to get that final hundred thousand out of them. Now he had the name of his hit, Sam Mason . . . and, more to the point, he had it on tape.

He patted the little recorder he had taped the Reynolds phone conversation with, just now. That was his contract. Now all Roper had to do was deliver the corpse, and then make them pay the rest of what they owed him.

Swinging his renter into the stream of traffic, he thought grimly that it would be a pleasure to squeeze that final hundred G out of those government creeps. And with all the dough he'd been spending on Marge, keeping her minions employed, he needed it.

CHAPTER NINETY FIVE

"It will only be for a little while," Tim Melford assured his wife once more. "This man Tollman seems to be quite efficient. He'll see that you're safe here."

Norma nodded listlessly. She sat at the computer in the glass-enclosed balcony, staring off at the last rosy glow of sunset in the western sky.

"It never seems to end, does it?" she murmured.

"They think tonight may bring it to a close," said, bending over her, holding her hand and watching her face, concerned for her. This quiet passivity was not like her. It was as if she had given up on all of it, or as if something deep inside her had quit caring.

Recognizing the anxious tone in his voice, Norma tried to rouse herself and pretend to more interest in the proceedings.

"You'll be all right, won't you, my dear?" she asked, giving his hand a squeeze.

"I'll be safe as houses," he grinned. "There are two Secret Servicemen assigned to me on an emergency basis. Besides, I'll be in the House, most of the night. There are several key votes, if we can ever cut off some of those speechifying machines over there."

Norma laughed.

"All right, then." Rising, she slipped her arm inside his. "Come, let me see you out."

Strolling inside, they passed the library and went on along the wide upstairs corridor and down the carpeted stairway. She noticed the carpeting on one or two of the steps was approaching threadbare. She would have to get new carpeting put in.

The tall wide-shouldered man assigned to protect her rose from a chair, off to one side, where he could see both the front door and into the living room without turning his head.

"Take good care of her, will you?" Melford said to him with a smile.

Tollman nodded.

"I will, sir. They don't expect trouble here, but I'll be ready if any happens."

"Splendid!" Melford said, squeezing Tollman's upper arm. "I appreciate everything you men are doing."

Tollman hovered nearby while the front door remained open. Melford went out and the two Secret Service Agents waiting on the narrow front stoop went down the steps with him, one on each side of him.

Norma watched as her husband slid into the car's back seat, followed by one of the men, while the other got in front behind the wheel. Melford waved a hand to her, just before the door closed him in.

Norma lifted her own hand and watched the limousine pull smoothly away. Then she turned and went back inside.

"Well, Mr. Tollman," she said brightly, "now all we can do is wait."

"He'll be fine, Mrs. Melford," the agent replied. "Most of this is just precautions."

"Yes, I'm sure it is."

She passed him and went back upstairs. At the top, she could see him settled once again in his strategically placed seat, back in an alcove.

She was surprised to realize that if she hadn't known he was there, she would not have noticed him. He really was good at what he did.

Then she shivered.

Starting back toward the library, with the intention of returning to her contemplation of the fall of night on the balcony, she hesitated.

No, she felt too chilled to sit out there any longer. Instead, she turned and went into their bedroom, near the head of the stairs. Perhaps if she lay down awhile, the evening would pass quicker, and all this sudden upset would be over and resolved that much sooner.

CHAPTER NINETY SIX

Reynolds and Adams were using Watkins Construction as an impromptu command post for the time being. The communications men in the outer office were keeping lines open with Langley, able at any time to reach either Graham or Blanchard.

"No contact on this with Farris and that Gordon guy?" Adams called across from where he was working the phones at his desk.

"Are you kidding?" Reynolds laughed. "They're the last people we want in on this."

"Just checking," Adams grinned. "With Graham staying in his office, no special guards are needed for him. Just the ones out at his house. And even there . . ."

Reynolds chuckled in agreement.

"With all the electronic equipment out there, Marauder would have to be a ghost just to get near the place."

Adams listened to his phone, then hung up.

"Melford's reached the Capitol Building. Our guys are maintaining liaison with the Secrete Servicemen stuck to him."

"So he's all right," Reynolds said with satisfaction. "How many men are staying with Blanchard? He says he's gonna be moving back and forth between here and Langley, so . . ."

"Two should be enough," Adams said, making the statement a half-question. "Hell, Blanchard's no rookie himself."

"Okay, two should do it. That leaves the team waiting for Dispatcher at that motel."

"Caldwell's handling that," Adams said. "He's got seven men with him."

Reynolds nodded, but he didn't look happy.

"They're kinda spread out," Adams explained. "Two cars, two men in each car, one in the motel office, and two inside room twenty four. With that Dispatcher of ours, it's better to be ready . . . in case."

"Sure, seven's not too many." Reynolds checked his watch. "I wish the bastard would check in with me. I don't like our focus divided this way: part of the team trying to nab Dispatcher, and the rest on the lookout for Marauder. He still hasn't exited the Metro?"

"No," Adams said. "And by now, he isn't likely to."

"Helluva waste of manpower, if he got out of that underground without being spotted."

"You want me to order some of them off?" Adams asked. "We could add a couple of men to guard Melford's wife with Tollman, and bring the rest back here so they could be ready, in case trouble breaks out somewhere else."

"Give it another half hour," Reynolds decided. "Tell them to check every Metro station. Rush hour's finally over, so it shouldn't be too big a job. At least then we'll be sure Mason isn't hiding down there, waiting to break out . . ."

"Good idea," Adams said. He reached for his phone. "Another half hour should be plenty."

"Maybe by then, there'll be some kind of break in all this running around we've been doing." Reynolds grimaced in disgust. "All that manpower just to bottle up two men."

Adams finished speaking in low tones on his phone, hung up, and thought over Reynolds' last words.

"Well, with Dispatcher, we're dealing with an unknown quantity, so it's best to be careful. With Mason, we know what he's good at, so all the manpower seems justified. If it wasn't, an old fox like Graham wouldn't have authorized it."

Reynolds grunted. Grudgingly, he nodded in agreement.

"Yeah," he said, staring out the window at the night sky. "I guess."

CHAPTER NINETY SEVEN

Between payphone calls to Marge, Roper huddled in the back of the converted station wagon with the periscope antenna.

Panels had replaced the windows, so he had a dark area where he could put on a facial disguise. It wasn't as complete a job as Jeff Lasalle could have done, but Roper didn't expect anyone to see his face, either. If they did, they'd get an elderly man with a hooked nose, walrus moustache, and a fat chin with a double-chin underneath. It all came in one plastic piece you pulled on overhead, which left only his eyes, nostrils, and mouth clear and able to function. A lined forehead and thick bushy eyebrows beneath his hat-brim took care of the upper part of his face.

When he was ready, Roper turned off the light in the rear section and opened the door connecting it with the driver's seat.

Leaving the parking lot adjacent to a busy supermarket, he used the first street payphone he came across to call Marge one more time.

"Dickson, you're just in time," Marge told him. "Your friend eased out of the Metro, and he seems to have lost those other people in a flea market."

"But your guys still have him in sight?"

"Oh, yes, no problem there," she assured him. "Near as I can tell, he seems to be headed for Georgetown . . ."

*　*　*

Adams slammed the phone down.

"They've lost the bastard."

"Mason? Where?"

"Center City, somewhere. In one of those outdoor markets."

Adams snatched up his phone and began tapping in a number.

"I'm gonna tell them to spread out around that entire area . . ."

"Easy, George," Reynolds advised. "Let it ride. They'll pick him up again."

Adams frowned.

"But now we haven't a clue to where he's headed."

"He'll show, he'll show," Reynolds said soothingly. "Wherever he's going, we've already got covered."

"Okay." Reluctantly, Adams replaced the phone. "Damn, what a time to lose the sumbitch."

"Just have the men in that area spread out and keep their eyes peeled . . . and tell them to be ready to move fast, wherever he does show up. That way, they might make contact with him again, and they'll all be prepared to reinforce wherever he shows up in just a few minutes. It isn't that big a city."

Adams nodded, picked up his phone again, and began tapping numbers in, muttering: "Thank God rush hour's over!"

CHAPTER NINETY EIGHT

Roper didn't get his usual parking spot in the side street next to the Melford corner house, but when he sent the antenna up into the tree-foliage above, he could hear some sounds inside the house from the various bugs he had installed in there.

Patiently, he settled down to listen.

For awhile, nothing came through except the humdrum sound of a TV newscast turned so low that Roper couldn't make out anything being said. Eventually that was switched off, followed by the sound of footsteps, and woman's voice calling: "Mr. Tollman, have you had supper yet?"

Roper couldn't hear Tollman's reply, only his deep voice in the distance, presumably nowhere near any of Roper's bugs. But the important thing to learn was that Tollman was in there.

He must be one of the troops they had brought in to watch for and deal with their maverick, Mason the Marauder. Wondering how the name Marauder had gotten into the proceedings, Roper got out of the panel truck with the aluminum alloy extendable ladder he had used earlier, getting up to the receiver he had tucked into a nook, near the top of the brick wall enclosing part of the Melfords' side and back yards.

Checking in both directions, he saw no one walking a dog, so he climbed the narrow ladder, and switched the receiver's tapes, replacing the old one with a fresh one. When he was back inside the panel truck once again, he listened with one ear to the lack of sound coming from inside the Melford house, and with the other he took in whatever information the old tape had collected since he had last retrieved it, which wasn't much.

After putting it away, he sat there and went on listening.

* * *

In spite of all the care they had taken, when Norma Melford heard the soft thudding sound in the upstairs corridor outside the library, she knew it signalled the arrival of Sam Mason.

Tollman had carefully checked all the windows, downstairs and up. He had made certain the back door leading into the garden was locked and bolted. Everything had been seen to. The entire building was secure, and if entry was somehow effected, it would have to be done noisily enough so it was sure to be heard by Tollman.

But Sam Mason had dropped down from above.

He had come along the roofs, she realized. He must have gotten into one of the other buildings, farther along the block.

The soft under-belly! she thought.

She opened her mouth to call for the man they had assigned to guard her, but before she could, the library door opened, and Sam Mason stood there, looking at her.

Any words she might have called out froze on her lips. In silence, she watched as he moved inside swiftly, and quietly closed the door behind him.

Gliding across the room, he stood facing her across the desk, observing her closely. When he spoke, he kept his voice low so no one outside the room could hear him. "Don't make a sound," he cautioned her.

She nodded, unsure whether she should remain seated behind the desk, or get up and face him. She was reluctant to move, feeling inexplicably weary. Never in her life could she remember feeling so tired . . .

"You're Norma Melford?"

"Of course."

"I'm . . ."

"You're Sam Mason. The cause of all these precautions. And all the trouble recently."

Taking an envelope from an inside pocket of his jacket, he withdrew two letter-sized pieces of paper from it, and placed them on the desktop, side by side in front of her.

"Read the last sentence from both of them," he told her.

Glancing down at them, her breath caught.

Mason nodded at the sharp intake of breath.

"They look familiar, don't they?"

"I don't . . . I've never seen them before."

"Read the last sentence," he ordered her again, his voice low, his eyes boring relentlessly in on hers.

Unable to keep her mouth from quivering, Norma read the last sentence of the page on the left: " 'Air support will be provided as originally planned.'"

"Now read the other one."

Taking a deep shuddering breath, she read from the second sheet: " 'Air support will not be provided as originally planned.' But why are you making me read . . ."

"Just one word," Mason hissed viciously. "The word *not*. But that single word, missing from the first of those messages I received, cost thousands of lives . . ."

"And somehow you've decided to blame me . . ."

"Blame is such a silly little word for what was done here," Mason murmured. He was leaning forward, his arms extended straight downward, his knuckles resting on the top of the desk.

For an endless moment, he went on staring at her, then he grinned bitterly and shook his head.

"All those deep-thinkers in the Company's planning section!" he jeered softly, forcing himself to keep his voice subdued, but not having an easy time of it. "And the best they could come up with for a fall guy was Roger Brent. He had to be the one who sent that first fake message to my Marauder station. Not your Congressman husband, and of course not you! What reason could you possibly have to do a thing like that, either of you? Why would you or Tim Melford want to send me a doctored message? You hardly knew me. How many times did you and I meet, out there in college? Once? Twice?"

Shrugging, she averted her glance from the hatred in his eyes.

"You hardly knew me. So the Company's geniuses figured it had to be Brent who used your computer here to send the message. He was always in and out of this place, wasn't he? Who else could it be?"

He waited. When she didn't reply, he shook his head, baffled.

"Why? Why did you do it? To get revenge on me for Linda?"

Still she didn't respond.

Shrugging, he straightened.

"That's how far they had to reach to come up with any reason at all for why that message might have been sent by Roger Brent. They must have been pretty desperate!"

"But why are you so sure I sent it?" she cried.

"Keep your voice down," he growled, his fists bunching.

Norma felt a wave of dizziness sweep over her. She sank back in the chair, gripping the edge of the desk in front of her tightly with both hands, trying desperately to keep from fainting.

Breathe! She told herself. Breathe deeply! Don't pass out. Go on! Breathe . . . breathe . . .

"Brent sent me a Malacca walking stick," Mason went on, his voice low, even, controlled. "A man I never met or knew sent me a valuable walking stick. Recently a stalking horse from the Department of Information dropped in on me for a visit, out where they've got me stashed, till they can figure out what to do with me.

"That visit was what got me started thinking. I remembered the walking stick. When I took it apart, I found a microfilm." He flicked a finger toward the two sheets of paper in front of her. "That's what it contained, both those letters."

He stared down at her, waiting. Still she said nothing.

"Look at the time on the earlier one. Five AM Greenwich. Later the same day, the other one was sent to me, when I asked for confirmation of the earlier message. Look at the time on that one: ten-forty AM Greenwich. The second one contained the crucial word: there would not be any air protection sent to cover us that day in the retreat into the mountains. Which meant that those people were at the mercy of the Monster's tanks, and two-thirds of the day had been wasted. Why wasted? Because that one word *not* was taken out of the early-morning message that was sent to me. The message you sent."

"No, no," she screamed. "I didn't. I mean . . . Please, I didn't mean to cause any . . . I meant no harm!"

"Didn't mean to do anything but needle me, slip me a zinger for what you think I might've done to your friend Linda Stevens, all those years ago?"

Her eyes hardened, and she sat straighter in the chair.

"I'm sorry about whatever happened to those people," she murmured, "but I'm not one bit sorry about what it's done to you and your damned career. You had to go off and serve your country!" She almost spat out the last words.

"They called up my outfit," he snarled. "What was I supposed to do, say fuck you, Uncle Sam, hurray for Linda? Mrs. Melford, Linda and I had a few good months together. Then certain . . . differences began cropping up between us. If my R. O. T. C. outfit hadn't been dragooned, maybe she and I could have eased away from one another slowly, the way a lot of couples break up. Imperceptibly. With us, it wasn't allowed to play out that way. We weren't given enough time. It ended too abruptly. I admit that."

"So good of you to admit something," Norma sneered. "Sam, I blame you for Linda's death, as surely as if you were at the wheel of that car when it crashed, instead of poor Roger."

"So poor Roger had to take the fall for your little message of death," he snapped.

"How could I know all those lives were at risk?" she cried in desperation. "I just . . ." She shook her head, looking around wildly, trying to find some way of making him understand. "I simply wanted to get back at you, somehow, after all those years. I wanted to throw a monkey wrench into that onward-and-upward career of yours, to make you pay, just a little, for causing that beautiful, spirited, wonderful girl to practically throw her life away . . ."

"So thousands of people had to die in the shell-fire of the latest Monster the world keeps throwing up into positions of power. And the ones who weren't hit by the tank artillery got starvation, or they froze to death in the mountains, later that winter. Those were the lucky ones. Some luck!"

Staring down at the nearly identical messages on the desk before her, Norma muttered: "Anyway, I doubt the message I sent even got through. All the codes and keys and passwords they need to get those things past your CIA experts!"

He shrugged.

"It got through, all right. The one out of a thousand that managed to slip past all those codes and electronic roadblocks, the one message that shouldn't have gotten through, that's the one that reached me at mid-morning, out there in the middle of nowhere . . ."

"And now what?" she asked. "What do you expect to do about it?"

"Now I've come here to kill you," Mason said simply.

Norma sucked in her breath and stared at him. Her lips felt stiff, numb.

"I owe it to them," he went on. "To Yussuf and his women and children, and their children. To all the others who died there . . ."

Norma's eyes filled with tears.

"The government of the United States and its butcher-boy Armies and Navies and Marines and CIAs may not have a shred of decency or the slightest sense of loyalty to promises they make so casually to any people they need to use along the march to their nice-guy world conquest, but somebody has to pay the piper. Someone's got to . . ."

Behind him, the corridor door burst open. Tollman's shoulders filled the doorway. He had a handgun aimed at Mason's back.

"Freeze, Mason! Don't move. I don't want to have to shoot."

Sam Mason threw himself forward across the desk, his hands stretched out, reaching for Norma's throat.

Frantically, she shoved her chair backward, away from the desk, trying to stay out of reach of his hands.

Two shots cracked in the silent house.

Mason's face twisted with pain above her, then his body wrenched away, writhing across the flat surface until it fell off the side of the desk onto the floor.

Both Norma and Tallman stared down at him. And both were astonished to see his eyes flicker and open. He was still alive. But his eyes weren't seeing them. They were only trying to deal with the surge of pain one of the bullets had caused, when it shattered his spine.

CHAPTER NINETY NINE

When Roper heard Tollman's first words to Mason and then the two shots, he surged out of the panel truck and headed for the corner. Slowing from a sprint to make the turn, he strolled unhurriedly up onto the small entry porch, where he quickly went to work picking the lock of the front door. He wanted to get in there before Tollman came back downstairs.

The lock was familiar to Roper, because he had used this front way to get in when he placed the various bugs inside the house. Now his previous knowledge paid off: within seconds, the door swung open.

Closing it carefully and silently behind him, he relocked it from inside, then glided toward the rear of the ground floor. He was just barely concealed in a clothes closet back there when they started down the grand staircase from above.

Tollman was mumbling something to Mrs. Melford.

". . . can't stay up there with him, Ma'am. Wait down here with me, why don't you? I'll have help here within minutes . . ."

"Will they be able to save him?" she asked, as they reached the foot of the stairs and crossed to the living room and out of Roper's line of sight.

"Dunno," Tollman's voice drifted back. "He looked in pretty bad shape, up there. If only he hadn't jumped for you!"

Roper gave them a few beats; then he eased along the main hall to the foot of the wide staircase and started up. On the floor above, he didn't have to search for the room he wanted: light streamed through an open doorway, across from the head of the stairs.

Inside the room, he found Sam Mason lying on his back, his face rigid, his jaws clenched, just as another wave of pain struck.

Roper could see how hard the man was trying to suppress the agony he was going through, but a soft moan escaped Mason's tightly shut mouth, in spite of his effort.

Mason felt the pain recede for a moment. He already knew it would be back, within seconds. But for this brief moment, his vision cleared and he was staring up at the ceiling again.

The shot had taken him in the center of the back. Below his chest bone he could feel nothing. Paralyzed. Did that mean his lungs would no longer work? Would they have to keep him on one of those iron lungs . . . assuming he survived at all? Helluva way to spend the rest of your life!

A face hovered above him, blocking out the ceiling. His vision clouded momentarily. Squinting, he tried to see who it was.

Wrinkled forehead, bristly mustache, hooked nose . . .

"Yussuf?" he whispered.

The tribal chief stared down at him, out of the sun.

"Are the planes coming, Marauder?"

Mason tried to answer, but he couldn't speak. He didn't know what to say. What was there to say?

"What did the second message tell you?" Yussuf demanded, his voice suddenly harsh. "Will the planes protect us from the Monster's tanks, as the message this morning said . . . ?"

"The planes are not coming, Yussuf," he finally managed to say.

Yussuf stepped back, staring at him from outside the all-purpose vehicle that carried the radio, the decoder, all his equipment.

Mason held out the piece of paper.

"The message I received at dawn did not contain one word, a crucial word. 'Air support will *not* be provided as originally planned.' This message I just received does contain that word . . ."

Yussuf shook his head angrily, staring off into the distance, where the Monster's tanks were already beginning to raise narrow clouds of dust as they came slowly nearer.

"Marauder, do not speak to me of one word," the chief muttered. "If we had started for the high country at dawn, my people would be out of his reach by now . . ."

"Yussuf," Mason said quickly, "I'll go now. If I drive fast enough, I can still reach the pass through the first range of the western hills, before his tanks can stop me . . ."

Yussuf swung his head and glared down at him. His face was set furiously, and his eyes seemed to blaze with an inner fire. Then the anger was gone, and he almost smiled.

"Yes," he murmured softly, "you are right, Marauder. Now you will go, truly." His voice almost purred.

Turning, he squinted into the afternoon sun toward the still unseen tanks.

"If I can find out what went wrong," Mason sputtered, trying to convince Yussuf, knowing he couldn't possibly. "Maybe I can get them to send the planes if I explain what will happen if they don't . . ."

The old man's quiet voice broke in on him.

"We know what went wrong, Marauder. Your Central Intelligence Agency made a promise to us, and now that message in your hand tells me they will not keep that promise. The all-powerful United States has lied again, and today we are the ones who will have to pay with our lives for that lie."

Mason stared furiously at the message he held.

"I can't understand. Why would they say one thing in the morning, and the complete opposite in the afternoon?" He turned the ignition key and started the motor. "Let me go, now, Yussuf. If I drive fast enough, I might be able to find out who is responsible for this . . ."

Yussuf reached in, turned the ignition key and took it out.

"No, Marauder," he said gently. "Now you will go, that is true, but you will go with us. You will be our witness. You will see what happens when your Company fails to keep a promise it has made. You will testify to the mighty Congress of your Government what it really means to break a promise to send planes to protect us from someone like the Monster and his tanks."

Turning his head, Yussuf looked off to the northeast, toward the high country, and he chuckled bitterly.

"Who knows, Marauder, perhaps we will stumble upon an oil field in the mountains. Then the United States will surely be our friend again, and keep promises it makes to us . . ."

"Can you feel your legs?" a voice asked.

Mason blinked. He could see clearly again

It wasn't Yussuf. The face was old-looking, but the voice had the sound of a younger man's, not Yussuf's.

"Not a thing . . . below . . . chest," Mason gasped.

"Nothing below here?" The man prodded him below where he could feel.

"Nothing."

"You want that? From now on, I mean?"

Mason grimaced.

"Not much choice, is there?"

"There's one choice."

The man against the ceiling held up a handgun.

"Not the cheeriest choice," Mason grinned, feeling the approach of the pain again. "But it'll have to do . . . till another . . . comes along."

"You know any prayers, Mason?"

Mason sighed.

"Sure. An all-purpose prayer. Thank God, Amen! One life's as good as ten."

"That sounds as good as any," Roper told him quietly. "Adios, man."

He put two bullets into Mason where they counted. Then he turned in a hurry, to get out of there before Big-Shoulder Tollman heard the sound-suppressed shots and came charging upstairs.

This time, Roper didn't bother with the stairway. Turning the other way, he went out one of the balcony's windows and was over the perimeter wall within seconds of hitting the garden turf beneath the window he'd had to leave open behind him.

He left the lights of the panel truck off and was away, around the nearest corner, almost half a minute before he heard the first siren approaching in the distance.

The one good thing was that he'd worn gloves through all of it.

The bad thing was that he would have to chop up his boots. The law would be able to get prints of the shoe-soles in the dirt where he had landed, back there in the garden below the second-floor terrace.

Too bad! The boots were a good fit.

CHAPTER ONE HUNDRED

The police forensic teams worked quickly. So did the medical examiner. The body indicated the probable cause of death to be two bullets that had penetrated the heart, although, of course, a later autopsy would determine the exact cause of death.

The statement Tollman gave indicated that a third party had done the shooting, and had used a silenced weapon. Tollman had heard it, and gone back upstairs, moving slowly and carefully. He had found the victim dead precisely where he and Mrs. Melford had left him, only a few minutes earlier . . . except now there were two more bullets in him, which hadn't been there before.

Shortly, the body was taken away, and the library cleaned up as best they could, at such a late hour. Congressman Melford spoke with his wife on the phone, asking if he should come home, but Norma assured him it was all over. Sam Mason was dead.

The doctor had given her a sedative, to help calm her down enough to get to sleep.

"You're sure, now?" Tim Melford asked her.

"Yes, my dear, I'm sure. Has it come to a vote yet?"

"It might, later tonight. Tomorrow at the latest."

"Then stay there and see it through," she told him. "You've worked too long and hard on that INS Reform Bill to risk not passing it because you weren't there to push it."

"As always, my darling, you're absolutely correct," he agreed. "We do have a few extra votes, but with these things, you never know."

Tollman received a phone call from Reynolds, telling him he could go home. Norma saw him to the door, and thanked him once again for all he had done.

With all the coming and going taken care of, she was astonished to realize that she was going to bed just a few minutes after eleven. With all the horror and tumult which had filled her home for the past several hours, it had felt as if several days had passed . . . or even several weeks.

Dutifully, she took the pills the M. E. had left for her. The last thing she remembered was lying in bed, waiting to unwind, just beginning to doze off, listening to her own deep breathing.

Through the windows to her left, she could see the glass-enclosed balcony overlooking the back garden. Moonlight was shining out there tonight.

Just after midnight, one of the closet doors on the ground floor opened slowly and soundlessly. A stocky man emerged, looked cautiously both ways along the central hallway, and silently went up the stairs. His right hand held a knife, a long slender blade, almost a foot long.

On the upper level, he checked each room by listening outside the closed doors. When he heard the sound of breathing inside one of the rooms, he carefully opened the door and slipped inside.

Yes, there was the woman, asleep in her wide bed.

As he crossed the room, a touch of moonlight fell upon his face through the window. He was the man Bill had seen and taken pictures of in the Denver air terminal, one of the attempted hi-jack shooters.

When he reached the bed, he paused only a moment to look closely at the sleeping woman's face. When he was certain she was the one he wanted, the knife flashed, again, again.

The woman grunted only once. Then there was no sound but a drawn-out gurgle. Then, nothing.

Instead of wiping the knife, he took out a plastic bag and put the bloody weapon inside it, stowing the bag with the knife in it inside his baggy sweatshirt.

Washing his hands clear of blood in the bathroom, next door to the master bedroom, he left as silently and as unnoticed as he had come. Outside, he trotted off into the darkness, just another jogger in the night.

The Immigration Reform Bill went to a vote in the House and passed with a comfortable margin.

When Tim Melford arrived home at around two in the morning, he took the stairs two at a time, he was so anxious to tell his wife the good news. Even if she was half asleep from the sedative when he told her, he knew she would be able to grasp what he was telling her, and she would be happy for him.

Then he opened his bedroom door . . .

The shock to Tim Melford's nervous system was so great that all he could manage to say to the Medical examiner later was to repeat: "I was just talking to her on the phone . . . an hour or so ago . . ."

The doctor sympathized. He was the same one who had been there earlier, so it was perfectly understandable that this second murder on the same night in the Congressman's house should have a devastating effect on the poor man. So the doctor kept at it, repeating again and again that Norma Melford had almost certainly felt no pain from the knife attack which had killed her and spilled so much of her blood all over the bed.

Presently the doctor's words of comfort began to take effect, until a moment arrived when Melford stopped mumbling "I was just talking to her on the phone . . ." and began to look around.

Once that point was reached, it was only a matter of time before he was nodding in agreement each time the doctor reassured him once more that the pills his wife had taken before going to bed for the night had almost certainly deadened the pain of the repeated stabbings.

The Congressman recovered sufficiently so that, when the doctor asked if he wanted to spend the remainder of the night in a hotel, Melford shook his head, opting for the guest-bedroom.

Both men knew there was no possibility of him sleeping in the bed his wife had been murdered in, not that night. And perhaps not ever again.

CHAPTER ONE HUNDRED ONE

The three of them sat and stood around Farris's desk, taking in the newspaper headlines.

"Looks like the thing ended without any input from us at all," Earl Gordon muttered.

Farris shook his head.

"Wow!" he growled. "Two in one night! That Melford fellow must be around the bend from all of it. I know I'd be."

Then Farris seemed to catch the meaning of Gordon's words.

"Ended? Not likely. For you two, this thing has just begun."

Laurie and Earl looked at one another, then back to Farris.

"Sure," Farris elaborated, "Graham and his spooks over at Langley finally have a fair idea who sent a misleading message through their system to one of their men in the field, but our job now is to make certain it doesn't happen again."

Earl slid into the visitor's chair facing his superior's desk.

"Does that mean we'll be getting some cooperation from Graham's people?"

"It damn well better."

"I mean real cooperation," Earl insisted. "Not just one of those meetings on a park bench with a hammerhead like Blanchard."

"No," Laurie assured him. "They'll have to deal straight-up with us, from now on."

"After all this?" Farris jerked a thumb at the news stories spread all over his desk, in the two Washington papers. "For Graham, we're the best thing that could possibly happen to him and his Company, right about now."

"To give some legitimacy to their effort to clean up their communications system?" Earl asked.

"You got it." Farris grinned. "Now get started, both of you. I'm pulling you off anything else you're working on, since you've both got a head-start on this. You might as well follow through with the rest of it. Preliminary report in two weeks."

Rising, Earl turned to follow Laurie out, but in the doorway he turned and asked in a low voice: "Just between us three, why did they really off Roger Brent?"

Farris hesitated, then waved them back in.

"Close the door," he told Laurie, when she rejoined them.

She shut the door and leaned against it beside Earl.

"Nothing in so many words," Farris told them quietly, "but I gathered from a little something here and there from Graham that it was a down-the-road thing. Meaning Brent was some kind of compulsive snoop. He had to know what was going on. And not just what, but precisely how. He needed to know the exact process of everything. That's how he found out how to send Company messages into the field: he kept digging, worming information out of this source, and that person. With a guy like that, working for an up-and-comer like Melford, where would it end?"

He paused. Neither of the others said anything, waiting until he continued.

"Their theory was that, if Melford got into the senate in the next five or ten years, then maybe - who knows? - got the top job a few years later, he'd still have this loose cannon standing a half-step behind him, still an obsessive seeker after knowledge someone like him shouldn't be allowed access to."

Farris shrugged.

"Who knows why he was that way? Maybe if he'd had a wife and a couple of kids to worry about, he wouldn't have had all that extra time on his hands to go digging into all sorts of forbidden territory."

He spread his hands helplessly.

"Whatever Brent's reasons were, that's the way he was. Which left the possibility down the road of him causing . . . what? Was too much knowledge about missile capabilities the next area he meddled in? Or maybe even nuclear devices? With a man like that, where did it end?"

Farris looked from one to the other, before going on.

"I guess they just decided Roger Brent was too great a luxury for our society to afford. So, for him it turned out to be 'Goodbye, Old Paint, you're a'leavin' Cheyenne!' . . .whether you want to leave or not."

After a few moments of silence, Laurie nodded.

"Sounds close enough for me."

"This is just between us," Farris reminded them. "Nobody's ever going on trial for any of it, anyway."

"Gotcha!" Earl assured him, turning to follow Laurie on out.

CHAPTER ONE HUNDRED TWO

Tansy took Bill and Jerry along when she covered the Norma Melford funeral ceremony, out in the Congressman's Midwest state, but she left Hal Walker out of it. He was busy U-hauling his furniture down from New York and moving into the apartment they had found for him, partway between where Tansy and her family lived in Arlington and her Central City workplace in Washington.

Not that anything was permanent, for either of them. The way one of the Networks was waving big money in front of Tansy, she wasn't really sure how long she was going to continue at Amalgamated Cable News. The thought of leaving saddened her. She liked the closeness of working with Walter Noble, in spite of his occasional stubbornness, and her relaxed rapport with her crew, Bill and Jerry.

She didn't try for a personal interview with the grieving Congressman. It was neither the time nor the place. Tim Melford and his daughter Jessy had enough to deal with right now without anyone sticking a microphone in front of them, asking how did they feel about Norma Melford's brutal murder at the hands of a knife attacker?

While the graveside ceremony was in progress, Tansy discreetly drifted off a little distance. Bill pointed his camera at her while she spoke softly into Jerry's extended mike about the somber activity in sight behind her . . . just to have something on tape and video, for the finished piece that evening on the local affiliate. When that was out of the way, she rejoined the people gathered around the grave, while the local pastor was still speaking.

Tansy could see how hard the deceased's daughter was struggling not to break into tears. Once in awhile, Tim Melford slipped an arm around Jessy's shoulder for a comforting moment.

It seemed to be an end to the story, as nearly as Tansy could tell from the usual CIA run-around she and the other news media had been given. One of their agents had run amuck as the result of an unauthorized leak he had blamed on Roger Brent. When the agent later realized . . . rightly or wrongly . . . that the leak had not been Brent but the wife of the Congressman for whom Brent had worked, the agent had tried to take revenge on Norma Melford, perhaps even bringing in foreign agents of the tribe that had been decimated as a result of the leak. When the revenge-seeker had been stopped by the CIA agent assigned to guard Mrs. Melford, one of the terrorists had later managed to sneak into the Melford home in Georgetown and completed the execution.

At least, that was the story Tansy assumed was going to be the accepted one. Dealing with the spooks at the CIA, however, one could never be even half-certain about what was true and what was only partly true, because they used their National Security mantra throughout any story they gave you. Somehow, you ended up more confused by their responses than you had been before you asked your question.

One thing she had to admire, however, was the way Tim Melford seemed to be holding up under this catastrophe which had overtaken his family. Tansy reminded herself to make a mention of that on her evening program . . . nothing ham-handed, but just a touch, to show her admiration for the man.

Congressman Melford stood patiently by the graveside. It should be winding up pretty soon, now. However, the pastor of Norma's old church did tend to draw things out just a tad.

Glancing down at Jessy by his side, Tim Melford was proud of her. She was holding her tears in admirably. She had her mother's remote quality, and being able to detach herself a bit from situations like the present ones stood her in good stead.

He gazed down at the wooden coffin containing his wife. He would miss Norma, no doubt of that. She had been a good part of the brain-trust he'd had going for him in his political career. Roger Brent had been the rest.

Ironic, that two of the three people he loved most in life should have died as a result of the transmission of that computer message Norma had tried to forward that fateful night, presumably hours before he had gotten home from the House. She must have returned the flimsy carelessly to the file he had brought home the day before, with the intention of going over it to make sure his decisions on the Oversight Committee would be based on real knowledge, not mere guesswork.

Curious, he had sat at the computer, out there on the balcony, and retrieved the message she had attempted unsuccessfully to transmit. He almost failed to notice the single change she had made, the removal of the word not, which, of course, had completely altered the meaning of the message.

Melford had sat there, amused, wondering why she would try to send it to Marauder, way off in yet another of the back-of-beyonds of the world, which the United States had to keep trying to deal with, in recent years. He recalled mentioning Sam Mason's name as the field agent assigned to Operation Marauder, but it was only after going over the conversation in his mind that he recalled how closely Norma had questioned him about all the ramifications of the operation.

At the time, Tim hadn't thought anything of it. His wife was always intensely interested in the details of any problem he faced in his work in Congress. That instance had been little different from scores of others she had questioned him closely about.

Now they were lowering the casket into the ground. The machine that was doing it hummed softly.

Beside him, Jessy sobbed. He took her hand in his and squeezed it gently, as they both watched the wooden box go deeper into the neat rectangular hole in the ground.

Curious, how alike Norma and Roger had been. Both were like pit-bulls when they wanted to know about anything special. That was the only way Roger could have ferreted out exactly how to send a message off to one of those Operations the CIA was forever setting up *out there*. And of course, having discovered the hidden details of something that secret, Roger had to tell someone, and who safer and handier than the man he worked for, Congressman Tim Melford?

Which was how the Congressman knew how to take the changed message his wife had tried and failed to send into infinity, earlier that night, and sent it through the computer network himself, complete with all the necessary keys and codes and passwords the adolescents who had developed the computer world had come up with while they were doing it. If his loving wife wanted to zing Sam Mason after all these years, how could a dutiful husband refrain from helping her do it?

As the ceremony began to break up, and while he was still busy shaking hands with Norma's relatives and the local political types, Tim remembered the stealthy thought that had come to him, while he was entering the message into the computer, the uneasy suspicion that he might be doing this because of a nagging curiosity he had felt all through the years of their marriage, about just how close Norma had been to that Linda Stevens girl, during the months the two had been room-mates in the dorm at Margarita College.

One of the things that had most fascinated Melford about Norma Tyler had been that cool remoteness of hers. To this day, he was compelled by it. But as time had passed, and the remoteness in her remained unchanged, he had sometimes found himself wondering what other married men felt like, when they were alone with their wives, men who felt close to the woman they were married to, who felt a special bond with her, something they felt with no one else, a closeness Tim Melford had never experienced with Norma. Always, there had been that subtle wall between them.

Was that the reason he had sent off that message through the night, with the one word missing, because he was jealous of a woman who had been dead almost a quarter of a century?

The Congressman shook himself. He felt uneasy, contemplating such deep-down possibilities in the human psyche. There were more than enough real problems in the world out there without any man wasting a moment of his life digging for hidden motives as to *why did I do that?* He had done it, disaster had resulted from it, and now both Roger Brent and his beloved Norma had paid with their lives for it, as well as Sam Mason. He would just have to live with the responsibility for a long time, but he could only hope that none of those people at the Company, or at the FBI, ever got around to suspecting that he, Congressman Tim Melford, had been the one who had actually sent that doctored message on through to Marauder.

On his way to the airport, the Congressman pondered the possibilities before him. It should be interesting, playing the role of the grieving widower, and even more interesting trying some of the women in the Capitol who would be delighted to attempt taking Norma Melford's place in his live.

Except this time, it would be wise of him to select a woman who had a few millions to bring to the marriage, enough millions to make it a real possibility for him to try for one of the Senate seats from his state.

CHAPTER ONE HUNDRED THREE

The shop-owner had his fax machine warmed up and ready, he had the fax number Roper wanted to send to, and he had the single sheet of paper ready to slip into the machine. The stopwatch was only up to the tenth second, and Roper was wearing driving gloves.

Everything was right on schedule and going well, except the phone conversation itself. That wasn't playing anything like the way Roper wanted it to.

"Look, Dispatcher," the voice of Reynolds was saying firmly at the other end, "we don't owe you a thing."

"You owe me a hundred thousand dollars," Roper told him evenly. "I want it wired to the numbered offshore account I just gave you, and I want it before four o'clock this afternoon."

Reynolds laughed harshly.

"Our man put down Mason, not you," he said. "Once that happened, all bets with you were off."

"The gun I sent you will prove to be the one that put the two bullets into Mason, the two that killed him. All your man did was cripple him. Your ballistics people will confirm that."

"No way," Reynolds said with finality. "You aren't getting a dime more than the fifty thousand you already got. That's more than enough to . . ."

"The tape copy I sent you along with the gun contains our agreement," Roper interrupted, aware that the call had passed the thirty-five second mark.

"Tapes can be spliced," Reynolds jeered, but his voice didn't sound quite so cocksure anymore.

"I'm sending you a fax to lock it up," Roper said. "Four this afternoon."

"How can you send me a fax?" Reynolds crowed. "If you think I'm gonna give you our fax number here, you're . . ."

Roper ignored his words, nodding to the shopkeeper and pointing a finger at the sheet of paper the man held. Smiling, he tapped in the fax number Roper had given him, and slid the page in.

For a long moment, Reynolds was silent, until he realized what he'd been told.

"You son of a bitch!" he growled. "How'd you get our fax number? Have you been . . ."

Roper just laughed at him.

"Four o'clock," he said, hanging up and checking the stopwatch. Fifty five seconds. Way over the forty-second limit.

Thanking the storekeeper, he dropped the money he owed on the counter, retrieved the original copy of the fax he had sent, and got out of there. He didn't want Reynolds and his Company men nabbing him at this stage of the proceedings, just when he was trying to wrap the whole thing up.

Roper was out of the store and around the corner in a moment. Inside his renter, he used side streets to reach the Beltway, a few blocks off. Once he had tooled along that for a mile or so, he ducked off it and in among neighborhood streets again, parking so he could watch where he had exited the Beltway. During the two minutes he watched, no other car came down the exit ramp he had used.

So despite going well over the forty seconds on the fax store's phone, Reynolds' technical people still hadn't gotten a fix on the call's location.

Relaxing, Roper went on his way, checking the time.

Over three hours until he found out if they were going to pay him the money they owed him. If they didn't, he would have to take steps to make them wish they had. In this kind of work, you can't let anyone stiff you on payments for a job you've completed, however clumsily you managed to complete it, not even the Feds.

* * *

Furious, Reynolds slammed the phone down, then picked it up again, and began punching in a number out at Langley.

From behind his desk across the room, Adams watched him.

Stoddard appeared in the doorway to the outer office.

"Fax just arrived," he said, handing it to Adams.

"Did you make copies of it?" Adams asked.

Stoddard nodded and left.

Adams studied the fax. It took a few moments, but he got the full message when he read the last line, below the list that covered most of the page.

"I don't care if this isn't the usual day," Reynolds was snarling into the phone. "I want this place swept within an hour."

Slamming the phone down, he glared across at Adams and noticed what he was holding.

"Is that a fax?"

"Sure is. It just came in . . ."

"That goddamn Dispatcher sent it. He has our fax number, which means he's been in this office."

Adams nodded.

"Only way he could've gotten it."

"I'm having this place swept."

"I know. I heard."

"If the bastard can get in here and get our fax number, he can leave some bugs behind, too."

Adams didn't say anything."

After awhile, Reynolds simmered down.

"What's the damn fax say?" he asked, almost reluctantly.

Adams crossed the room and handed the flimsy copy to him. On his way back to his desk, he stopped in the open doorway and called out: "Stoddard, you better make some more copies of that fax. Half a dozen or so."

Seated behind his desk again, he watched Reynolds until the message got through to him, too.

"Addresses," Reynolds was mumbling, as he scanned down the page. "Graham's. Blanchard's. Home phone numbers. Your address. Mine. Caldwell's. Stoddard's." He looked up, wide-eyed. "He's even got Tollman's!"

Both men stared at one another for a long time.

Softly, Reynolds whispered: "I don't believe that bastard!"

"Notice the last line?" Adams asked wryly.

Reynolds glanced down and began reading aloud: "Eenie, meenie, miney, moe, which of these will be first to . . ."

He looked up.

"That's all it says."

"He left out the last word," Adams said. "I guess."

"But why?" Reynolds complained. "It's pretty obvious this is a threat of some kind . . ."

Adams shrugged.

"Maybe for legal reasons? If he includes that one word to make it read 'which of these will be first to *go*,' maybe we can sic the Attorney General on him. Using the mails to threaten government officials? Lots of trouble for our Mr. Dispatcher. But this way . . . maybe all it means is a variation on an old nursery rhyme that he doesn't quite finish. He's in the clear."

By now, Reynolds had quieted down completely. He stared at the list of names, addresses, and phone numbers awhile, then glanced inquiringly across at Adams.

"Think we ought to send a copy of this along to Blanchard?"

Adams nodded.

"And tell him Dispatcher wants the hundred grand by four this afternoon," Adams advised.

Reynolds nodded and picked up the phone. While he was tapping in Blanchard's number across the river, he said stubbornly: "But I'm damned if I'm gonna recommend they pay that bastard. I don't want that sort of endorsement in my jacket . . ."

Blanchard listened to what Reynolds had to say and told him he'd check with the higher-ups and get back to him.

They settled in to wait.

The electronic crew arrived and thoroughly checked both the inner and outer offices. They found no bugs, no phone taps, nothing.

"There were a couple of minute scratches on the outer door lock," the man in charge reported to Reynolds.

"From a break-in of some kind?"

"Could be," the man admitted. "Nothing provable, you understand . . ."

"Good enough," Reynolds said. "I've got reason to think someone's been into this place."

"I'll have that lock changed," the man said, turning and following his crew on out.

Adams spent the time doodling with a sheet of paper on his desk. Reynolds paced restlessly.

At three-thirty, the phone rang. Reynolds picked up, listened, nodded, and said, "Okay, Chief. Thanks." He listened some more, nodding again. "Yeah, I think so, too."

Hanging up, he looked across at Adams.

"Which way?" Adams asked.

"They're paying him," Reynolds said in a subdued voice. "The money's on the way."

Adams let his breath out, put down his pen and rolled up into a ball the sheet of paper he'd been writing on, throwing it into his wastebasket.

Curious, Reynolds asked: "What's that?"

"I was just calculating how much it would cost me, how many I'd need . . ."

"How much what would cost? How many what you'd need?"

"Sandbags. How many I'd need to pile around my house, and how high. Ten feet enough? Or maybe twelve feet high would be better . . ."

The agents in the outer office heard the two of them start laughing. Stoddard and Caldwell and a couple of others glanced toward the open doorway to the inner office, exchanged glances, chuckled, and went back to whatever they'd been doing.

Presently, the laughter in the inner office subsided, and everything went on as usual.

THE END